Tales of the Anointed Skeletons and Love

Lahari Mahalanabish

Ukiyoto Publishing

All global publishing rights are held by

Ukiyoto Publishing

Published in 2022

Content Copyright © Lahari Mahalanabish

ISBN 9789361727030

All rights reserved.
No part of this publication may be reproduced, transmitted, or stored in a retrieval system, in any form by any means, electronic, mechanical, photocopying, recording or otherwise, without the prior permission of the publisher.

The moral rights of the author have been asserted.

This is a work of fiction. Names, characters, businesses, places, events, locales, and incidents are either the products of the author's imagination or used in a fictitious manner. Any resemblance to actual persons, living or dead, or actual events is purely coincidental.

This book is sold subject to the condition that it shall not by way of trade or otherwise, be lent, resold, hired out or otherwise circulated, without the publisher's prior consent, in any form of binding or cover other than that in which it is published.

www.ukiyoto.com

Forword

Lahari Mahalanabish's collection of short stories, "Tales of the Anointed Skeletons and Love" is a set of thought provoking, thoughtful narratives which are certain to resonate with readers everywhere. They are based on everyday situations, and take place in settings that are readily recognizable. Yet, through the quiet flow of the narrative, they show up sudden, strong truths that gleam and glisten in the surrounding murk, a revelation of an aspect of character, perhaps, or a set of events that seems everyday on the surface, but is transformative, in the end.

The stories all move forward through the actions of the characters, who can be, sometimes, minor, though sometimes they are the protagonists as well. "Towards the Gates" is a story of despair, humiliation and hopelessness, but also of grit and determination. The protagonist, Lakshmi, ekes out a precarious living for herself and her four children by selling sprouted gram at the gates of the zoo. Her husband has abandoned her and his children, though he does visit the hut at times, completely drunk, taking from her what she earns, and also whatever belongings she may possess, to sell. In the one room hovel which Lakshmi and her children share, he rapes her on his visits, sometimes, to her shame, in full view of the children. There are feeble rays of hope sometimes in her life...news of a job as a household help, for instance. But every time, the doors to what would have been an easier life for her and the children are slammed in her face. And yet she finds solace in the smallest things. A hibiscus flower that blooms in a tiny patch of land in the ugliness of the slum gives her happiness, and the hope she has for a better future sustains her as she educates her children.

"The Gift" is about appearances, about how not everything is as it seems. Characters can present a facade, and the balance of circumstances can change in unforeseen ways. It is a story of old loves living new lives, and the masks that urban living sometimes demands of people. This story, in a middle class setting, shows how the weight of relentless aspirations can break people. How the need to keep up appearances can have huge, unforeseen consequences, how livelihood itself can be precarious. In the end, though, it is a story of unexpected kindness, of humanity coming from a completely unanticipated source. For if there is cruelty in the city, there is also compassion.

"Higher than the Hills," on the other hand, is a gentle story of young love, innocent in spite of the poverty in which they live. And yet there is no squalor here. Unexpectedly and delightfully, the protagonist is a magician who performs tricks for tourists who come to the hills for trekking or to the lake for boating. With the flow of tourists coming to a stop during the pandemic, his income, too, takes a plunge. Yet love, as always, finds a way.

In "Dilemma", the protagonist, burdened by the weight of housework and the responsibilities of children, finds escape in the daily bus ride she takes to drop her children off at school. The little things are minutely described, as are her feelings, her small joys and the accompanying feeling of guilt.

These are realistic stories, sometimes stark, but mostly ending on a small note of hope, to which her protagonists cling. Human nature, the struggles of people across various spectrums of society, are described in a clear and almost matter of fact way. But it is this very matter of factness that gives the stories their power, and ultimately, their strength. The characters are minutely observed, the settings painted with brush strokes of realism. And yet, inspite of the rootedness of the characters in their settings, there is a universality in them which will appeal to all. The narratives flow smoothly, leaving the reader with little nuggets of truth, which show an aspect of life as it is lived.

Mitra Phukan,
Guwahati, Assam
5th June, 2022.

Dedication

I dedicate this book to my beloved daughter Nirjhorini, my husband and parents. I am grateful to Eyelands Book Awards for shortlisting the collection in 2019. I am indebted to the following literary magazines for publishing some of the short stories that also appear in this collection: The Bombay Review, The Bangalore Review, Soft Cartel, Indian Review, The Criterion, Ashvamegh, and The Quiver Review (renamed as The Kolkata Arts). Special thanks to Jayanto Ghosh, Sati Chatterjee, Rajita Chowdhuri, my father Devananda Chatterji and my husband Subhadip Mahalanabish for being the first readers of these stories and providing their valuable suggestions.

Contents

The Gift	1
The Christmas Eve	14
The City of Gold	28
The Attraction	41
Towards the Gates	46
The Trapped Spirits	57
Nowhere Else on Earth	73
The New Law	87
Barricaded	107
The Single Bed	115
Half as Good	133
Unconfined	146
Higher than the Hills	159
Dilemma	173
The Scimitar	178
The Ventures in a Locked Study	200
Silver Jubilee	212
The Dawning	229
About the Author	*238*

The Gift

The lane in front of the school was a nightmare with its worn-out tarmac, non-existent pavement and with the huge buses, mud flecked cars, rickety vans, hooded rickshaws and over-packed autos weaving in and out. Sandeep reached the dark blue, wrought-iron gates twenty minutes late, thankful that the security guard allowed each child to leave only with the person carrying the identification card. He did not have to flash his card though. The man at the gate still recognized him as the honest policeman in a prime-time serial aired on a popular regional channel five years ago.

The salt and pepper moustachioed guard was keeping an eye on a group of little girls bouncing to the pool car when he noticed the actor and beamed at him. Sandeep smiled back. His son Neel, who was ambling towards the gate, spotted him and broke into a run. Before the guard could warn him about the water that had spilled from another child's bottle, Neel stepped upon the wet patch, and for a speck of a second, the protracted school building, the high boundary walls and the pruned shrubs whirled around him. Sandeep lunged forward to prevent a fall but a hand, encircled by a silver bracelet, had already gripped the boy's wrist. A cascade of brownish hair blocked Sandeep's vision as the lady clung to the five-year-old until he had steadied himself.

"I hope you are not hurt." Sandeep heard a familiar, mellifluous voice ask his son and sensed the thrust of a wave within him.

"Neha?" he asked in a tone tinged with hesitation, still wondering whether his ears were playing tricks.

Dispelling Sandeep's doubts, the woman flipped her hair and turned to face him. For a moment, he lost the ability to speak and his lips hung somewhere between a smile and a gape.

The glimmer of recognition lit up her eyes too. "Sandeep!" she squealed and laughed, clenching her fists in the way people do when something unbelievably exciting happens.

There were dark circles shadowing her hazel eyes, discoloured patches flecking her fair cheeks, a pair of parallel creases grooving her forehead and even a hint of facial hair above her upper lip — something which was not there or Sandeep had not noticed earlier. It was obvious that she was not ageing gracefully. Once he had finished scrutinising her appearance, he could not help feeling vindicated that his wife was not only much younger but also far prettier than her.

"Your son?" she asked, affectionately ruffling Neel's tiny curls. The boy tilted his face slightly upwards to take in her face and hair, his deeply set eyes streaked with curiosity as he wondered who she was.

"Yes."

"I'm sorry that I couldn't attend his rice eating ceremony nor your wedding," she apologised. "My husband has been posted in New Jersey."

"No problem," Sandeep replied. He recalled inviting her to the two happy events in his life just to spite her.

"Does your child study here too?" he asked.

"I have no children," she responded with a shrug.

"Excuse me," said a young teacher, clad in a yellow *salwar-kurta*, hurrying out with a pile of answer sheets. Sandeep, Neha and Neel trooped to the shade of a mango tree that grew out of an unpaved corner of the school grounds.

"Then?" Sandeep asked.

"I'm trying my hand at catering. I had a discussion with the headmistress about the food packets we will distribute on Foundation Day."

"That's great! With your brains and hard work, I'm sure you'll succeed in whatever you do," Sandeep remarked with an encouraging grin, although her choice of vocation astonished him. He had always considered her to be academically inclined rather than business oriented. But he reminded himself at once it was only a tiny surprise compared to the mountainous shock she had imparted to him before.

Both overwhelmed and discomfited by the praise, Neha beamed with her eyes cast downwards. Neel, who was getting impatient, began to recite a rhyme at breakneck speed.

"I think we need to go," said Sandeep and pursed his lips in an apologetic smile.

"Bye," said Neha, her eyes lingering on his face before resting on the child.

Sandeep turned on his heels, but there was something hauling him back — an inexplicable force that compelled him to take another look at Neha's blemished countenance. He halted to say, "Please come to my house when you can find the time. My wife would love to meet you."

"Your house means..."

"The one you used to frequent." Sandeep's gaze drifted to the long queue of students wending their way through the grilled verandas, past charts and maps pinned within glass covered boards.

"Sure, I will," Neha replied.

"Please bring your husband along...if he's in town," Sandeep added to maintain propriety.

"No, he isn't. He's in Sydney."

"Well, at least *you* come..."

"I'll love to," she said, gently squeezing Neel's cheeks, before exchanging numbers with his father.

As Sandeep navigated through the choc-a-block lane, clutching his son's hand, he wondered whether inviting Neha had been a wise thing to do. Or had he inadvertently fanned his subtle desire to meet her again? He tried to quell the nagging disquiet by telling himself that it was just a polite gesture, and before he could ruminate any further on the chance encounter, he sensed a continual vibration deep down in his trouser pocket. He realised with a jolt that he had been dying to hear from his wife. She had been a bundle of nerves since last night. Awash with momentary relief, he glimpsed her name on the throbbing screen.

"The news is bad," she almost wailed into the phone.

Sandeep tightened his grip around Neel's wrist as they reached the main road.

"Did they call?" he asked calmly, suppressing his own tension. A grey Swift bearing the physician's symbol of entwined serpents was honking behind a blue Indica with a learner's sign.

"Yes, everywhere it's the same answer. They don't want someone who has not been working for seven years," his wife sighed. "I wish I had not left the call-centre job soon after our marriage," she lamented.

"What do you mean? Work under a boss who molested you?" he objected, aghast at her regret about quitting the organisation that had paid no heed to her complaints.

"I should have taken up another job before resigning from that one," she rued.

The Swift ceased to beep as the Indica picked up speed and Sandeep craned his neck to read the number stuck in front of the bus looming behind them.

"Don't worry. I've many auditions lined up next month," Sandeep assured while waving to the bus to stop.

The whistling noise of her father's snores reached Neha in the next room. Cross-legged upon her single bed and propped up against a cotton pillow, she logged into her mailbox. No apologies from her husband. Not that she had expected any. Her eyes fell on the bruises exposed by the rolled-up sleeves of her oversized nightdress — the one her mother always kept washed and ready for her visits. She imagined the shock clouding her parents' faces when she would tell them about her decision. They were as clueless about her marital life as they had been about her relationship with Sandeep when they fixed her marriage with Ranvijay. Not that she could blame her parents for the course her life took the day they introduced her to the man of their choice.

Tall, well-built, with sparkling eyes, an aquiline nose and shapely lips, Ranvijay was no less handsome than Sandeep. Moreover, the fun of being a rich man's wife was too much to resist. She pictured herself flitting across Ranvijay's palatial house, donning silk gowns like the ones she had seen only in movies, sipping red wine, tapping her feet in the concerts of her favourite musicians, cheering her preferred team from the best stands or just lazing around in a fancy yacht. Her conscience pricked as the days knocked on each other, urging her to arrive at a decision, but she found a way to deal with it. She dragged in forgotten arguments with Sandeep, and unearthed and re-opened sealed and buried points of disagreements. Then she went on to blow up like a balloon his slightly annoying habits and clubbed all his minor failures together so she could revisit them again and again whenever in doubt, just the way she would revise her lessons before the exams.

Neha heard her mother's footsteps in the corridor, the heaving of a jar and the tinkle of a glass. She wished not to cut into her parents' pension. Though relieved at bagging the contract of supplying food packets to the school where her cousin taught, she knew she would have to seize bigger assignments to carve out a living. Ranvijay might utilise her absence to realise all his fantasies concerning Mrs Khambatta, his long-time obsession, but if Neha knew anything about him, it was unlikely he would grant her a quick divorce. Even if he did, she was unwilling to accept alimony or any form of help for her survival from him.

After downloading the attachments mailed by her graphics designer friend, Neha clicked them open one by one, pondered over their respective appeal and finally selected the motif of her business card. She would get it printed before she went to meet an acquaintance whose daughter's wedding was being planned.

Turning off the lights, Neha removed her slippers and climbed onto her bed, but sleep refused to creep upon her eyelids. She recalled sitting on a long, narrow park bench with Sandeep, gazing at the fountain water that branched and twisted to the music. He drew her so close she could smell his deodorant and listen to the throb of his racing heart. She turned to look into his desirously burning eyes and he lowered his face on hers until their lips met, brushed lightly against each other, and then locked with all the vigour and yearning of their youth.

Barged into Neha's mind, a vision of Sandeep's wife — whose photo she had seen on Facebook — wrapped around him, sleeping contentedly after a bout of lovemaking, shadowed by his large, laminated photograph of dancing peacocks. In the next room, their child inhaled the scent of new toys and hardbound story books as a realm populated by the most amazing cartoon characters opened before his shuttered eyes.

*

Reena was lying like a corpse under the action of two tablespoons of cough syrup. She had been called in the evening for an interview. The air-conditioning in the lobby where she was asked to wait had worsened the cold pursuing her for weeks. She was unaware that her son had run away from his room to cuddle beside her for safety. Awakened by the brush of his soft silky curls, Sandeep cradled his head, coaxed him out of his drenched shirt and patted his palpitating chest. Neel shivered all of a sudden, scared by the recollection of the nightmare. Sandeep whispered to his son that he could tell him what had haunted him. He assured he would not laugh or scold or call him a sissy, but the child did not speak.

Nightmare was what Sandeep's life had become when Neha met him one evening after his rehearsals and announced her decision to split. He, too, could not express what he was trudging through - the pain spiking his heart; the heaviness weighing down on his scalp; the fond memories and never to be fulfilled dreams criss-crossing into barb-wire fences that barred any gaiety from riding in or the gloom from escaping. He expected no consolation from his parents, who never liked Neha for reasons unfathomable to him. His friends would try to brush off his sense of emptiness by remarking that he would soon find many more desirable women. Attempts at diversion crashed against the walls; his yell for help fruitlessly echoed with her name. He fumbled and stumbled in the dark, tripping upon all her broken promises and abraded by the coarse arguments that tried to justify her decision.

*

The flaming sun scorched Neha as she stepped out of the bank after cashing her cheque. It was 11:30 AM. The young Neha, a class topper and an aspiring economist, would have never believed, if someone had told her then that she would earn her first income a decade after graduation. Only one condition Ranvijay had laid down before their marriage: since his profession involved a lot of travel his wife could not have a career of her own. What was the point of marriage if the wife would not accompany him on his tours? His reasoning had made perfect sense to her. Her BA part two results were also nowhere near her expectations: Ranvijay had breezed into her life two months before the tests, slashing her concentration and cramming her mind with all sorts of sights, sounds and touch.

No 379 whizzed towards her followed by bus numbered VH19. In a flicker of a second, Neha opted for the second bus instead of the first which could have taken her home. Inside the bus, she swayed from side to side, gripping a vertical rod. Luck favoured as a woman near her soon left her seat and tottered towards the door. She quickly slipped into the vacated seat, took out her phone and clicked the number hurriedly saved the day before. Sandeep's wife, who picked up the call, sounded genuinely happy that she was coming to visit them. Neha was unsure why she decided to go. Was she feeling nostalgic for the house she used to frequent or eager to meet once more the man whom she had loved but yet not loved enough to choose him over the prospects of a good life? Was she curious to meet the woman who replaced her in his life or did she want to play with his child whose existence ebbed her guilt?

The bus screeched to a stop in front of Narayan Mandir. Neha stepped on the pavement and stared at the temple: the walls bore a fresh coat of white paint and the blue, yellow and pink flags flying from its spires glazed against the sunlight. Through the grille gates, she noticed that the plants had been trimmed and a pool had been dug and populated with blooming pink lotuses. A bunch of volunteers bustled about, ensuring that the devotees queued in a single file. It was a far cry from the time Neha had been scared to approach the main shrine with Sandeep's kid sister, fearing a stampede.

The beggar sat hunched over his bowl near the temple gate. His shrivelled face had caught her notice the last time she had passed by him: now he was ancient — with a few wisps of white hair on his bald pate, a toothless mouth and the sun-burnt skin split up by innumerable lines like a land with too many inheritors. Neha heard her coin clink against the bottom of his round steel bowl as she moved on to take a halt at the pet shop from where she had once bought a pair of goldfish. In an aquarium near the door, there was a tiny fort castle. Black mollies, swordfishes, tiger sharks and discus swam in and out of its oval windows, slid between the broad leaves of the anubias, dug into the grey flecked white stones for delicacies and paired up behind the bubble blowing dolls. She passed by the familiar neem tree with its pointed leaves tapping on the tiled roof of a tea shop. Spotting a sweet shop, she stepped in to buy a box of silver foiled *barfi*. With a turn towards the left she sighted Sandeep's blue and white painted house, but its front door was blocked from her view by two burly men: one clad in jeans and a sleeveless denim shirt and the other wearing a brown checked shirt and khaki trousers. Neha narrowed her eyes, wondering what brought these strangers to his house at precisely the time of her visit. She trotted past a new apartment complex and the revamped coaching centre, her eyes shielded by a pair of green tinted sunglasses and her fingers, reluctant to be unoccupied, clutching the straps of her handbag. With a few more steps, she could see Sandeep standing at the doorway, facing the men who began to yell. Before he could glimpse her, she slipped into a narrow lane between two houses, her heart thumping in apprehension.

"There's still fifty thousand left," bellowed the man in jeans, who was taller among the two.

"I'll pay it by next month," Sandeep insisted.

"Haven't we heard that already a million times?" sneered the man in khaki.

There was a stifling silence, then an incoherent noise, which Neha guessed, to her horror, had escaped from Sandeep's lips. The windows of the neighbouring houses slid open and shut noiselessly as she peeped to find the taller man drag her friend away from his door. Though Sandeep had picked up a few karate chops during the shooting of a film, he could recall no moves and only flailed his arms in self-defence. The man in the brown-checked shirt grabbed him by the collar of his beige, cotton *kurta* and banged his head against the shutter of a cigarette shop. His companion joined in with a massive shove that sent Sandeep tumbling towards a parked cab. His cranium missed the vehicle by inches and he fell on the tufts of grass that had sprouted near a foul-smelling drain following a recent spate of rain.

Reena rushed out of the house, her eyes dilated in shock and her *pallu* slipping off her left shoulder. Hurling abuses on Sandeep's attackers, she aimed a punch at the one nearer to her, but he promptly clasped her hands and broke into a mirthless laughter. Her bangles clattered and her face furrowed as she frantically shook her hands to free them from his grasp. Suddenly he let go of his grip causing her to hurtle backwards. She managed to regain her balance by embracing a lamppost and hastily rearranged her *pallu*.

"One more chance. If I don't get the money by next week, she'll be raped," threatened the man in khaki, stroking the sleeve of Reena's blouse with a grubby finger. She shuddered, but instead of retreating inside the house, she stayed rooted to the spot, her eyes blazing through her smudged kohl. Sandeep wobbled to her side and quelled his dizziness with a clench of his jaws.

"And also, your sister whom you married off with our boss's money," barked the denim clad man. He lurched towards Sandeep, raised a hairy arm and pointed at his face. "We'll make you watch." He smirked, curling his betel-stained lips in an oddly twisting manner.

"Your boss's money? Where would the money be if my father had not helped him reclaim his property? And have I not returned most of it?" Sandeep's nostrils flared as he spoke. With his hands drawn into fists and his teeth gritting in a spell of ferocity that was provoked not only by the current humiliation and also by the blows in his past, he stomped towards his assailant.

"Leave them. They are not worth it," his wife whispered, grabbing his right arm.

"We are not here to answer your questions," drawled the shorter man, kicking away a dusty stone that plopped into the putrid waters of the open drain. He leered at Reena and then brushed past her to stand right in front of her husband such that their faces were just inches apart. "We want the money by next week," he said and spat between Sandeep's feet before turning and swaggering to his bike. Straddling the two-wheeler, he shot another menacing glance at the couple while his companion swung his leg high to mount the other bike.

Neha removed her hands from her gaping mouth. Her lips had gone dry from wordless screams. She took out a bottle from her handbag and gulped down all the water. Fingering her hair, she found it wet with sweat and unfolded a napkin to towel it as much as she could. She would not embarrass Sandeep and his wife further by letting them guess she had witnessed the ugly scuffle.

Twenty minutes elapsed before she rang the bell. Sandeep opened the door, gave a warm smile and looked into her eyes for more than a few seconds before ushering her into his house. Reena introduced herself although there was no need and led Neha to the living room she was well-acquainted with. The couple had changed their outfits, sprinkled a sweet-smelling powder and touched up their hair: Sandeep had neatly parted his mop of curls, Reena had braided her long, straight locks. Neha tried to avert her eyes from his bruises lest he felt the need to cook up an explanation.

"Neel," Sandeep called. "Say hello to Neha Auntie." The little boy came darting out of his room, a smile of recognition playing on his lips. Neha bent down to hug him and gifted him with a toy ship and a fluorescent green T-Rex she had bought on the way. He tucked the dinosaur under an arm and intently inspected the ship: as soon as he spotted a lid on its deck, he got busy trying to slide it open with his thumb.

The furniture was the same as before: a couple of strategically placed cushions hid the holes in the sofa but scratches were discernible on the round central table, even across the floral carvings along its circumference. Reena flopped next to her on the double sofa to chat, unaware that every gesture and word from her was being subjected to scrutiny.

It was during one of the ordinary turns in the conversation that Neha let go of the comparison and eased into Reena's spontaneous company. She picked up their family album from a shelf and flipped through its pages, pausing at the photos of baby Neel and close-ups of Sandeep's sister in bridal wear. After regaling Neha with some interesting incidents on the sets of the serials he had acted in, Sandeep asked her about the countries she visited and she satisfied his curiosity with precise descriptions.

As Neha was led to the dining table, she felt a ravenous appetite stir up within her: it seemed a blessing to experience a craving as uncomplicated as that of hunger. She broke into the mound of steaming rice on her plate to let the coriander sprinkled *dal* pool in the gap. Wolfing down mouthfuls of the *dal* soused rice, she occasionally bit into crispy cauliflower *pakoras* and munched on the crinkled *papad*. She took more helpings of rice to douse it with the spicy gravy of tomato chicken, which was served to her in a boat shaped blue china bowl.

Once lunch was over and the table cleared, Reena excused herself to read out a story to Neel. Sandeep and Neha slumped on the living room sofas and got drawn into a debate over a movie he loved but she loathed. A pall of silence fell over them when the spirited discussion ended with both remaining glued to their own opinions. Unable to think of anything interesting to say, Sandeep was about to compliment her on her outfit — a black *chikan salwar kurta* dotted with silver, star-shaped sequins, but restrained himself as he deemed it inappropriate, for reasons not quite clear to him. Neha fiddled with her handbag for a while, scratching on the zip and stroking the shoulder strap. Suddenly she said, "Please accept a small gift from me for your wedding and your son's rice eating ceremony. I would have loved to attend them but unfortunately could not."

Sandeep's eyes popped out of his sockets as he watched her write a cheque of fifty-thousand. "Why the need for this formality?" he exclaimed in embarrassment, his mind set into turmoil by the opposing currents of relief and shame.

"What do you mean by formality?" Neha, who had expected such a reaction, rolled her eyes. "It's out of affection."

To shake off his discomfort, Sandeep reasoned with himself that fifty-thousand was not a large amount, coming from a rich man's wife. If he got his big break, he would not hesitate to gift her generously on any occasion in her life she would invite him to; perhaps on one of her lavishly celebrated wedding anniversaries. It was another matter that she told him about the champagne, but not the chilled waters under which Ranvijay had thrust her head, in a fit of rage, when she chanced upon his messages for Mrs Khambatta. She narrated the first ride in his BMW, skipping the fact that after running down a mongrel he had shoved her out of the car, when she failed to plug in her tears or steady her voice. She vividly described the descent of the snowflakes at night, outside their log cabin in Japan, but omitted mention of the snow balls he had stuffed in her mouth, when her pregnancy test results turned out to be negative.

Reena, who had entered the room and seated herself, squinted in disbelief at the digits on the cheque. Sandeep remained stuck in his chair, staring at nothing in particular, the respite from his immediate crisis intercut with the stinging knowledge that the money from his ex-girlfriend — the gift from a woman who had left him for another man — would bail him out. After the guest left Reena minced to the next room, unlocked the cupboard and tucked Neha's first and only earning safely within the folds of a sari. At last they could free themselves from the debt.

*

Neha collected the change from the ticket counter, let it slip inside the external pocket of her handbag, zipped it and sprinted down the stairs to the underground platform. She saw the time of her train flashed across the board and glimpsed at her watch. There were eight minutes to go. She located a half empty bench and dropped next to an elderly gentleman. With a long whistle a train whooshed onto the track behind her and the doors opened with a loud swish. As she turned her head, her eyes fell on a young couple who were holding hands while stepping inside the train that would travel in the direction opposite to hers. After crossing the penultimate station, the track would slowly slope upwards along its subterranean tunnel to emerge under the sky and glint in the streaming sunlight. Hearing the rattling of the train, people would turn to see it snake past the boundary walls; grit against the bridge that hung over an algae infested canal; send tremors through the soil clutched by the dense, extensive roots of towering, age-defying trees; sever the hum of monotonous routines and deaden the echoes of clashes: those unfamiliar with that part of the city would mistake it for just another train, unaware of its long journey underground. Such was the course of some emotions, too, she reflected and sighed.

The Christmas Eve

The bus Tushar had alighted from went on to cross a series of bumps before disappearing into another rugged lane. He had sat in that crammed vehicle for three hours, with a sack of vegetables encroaching on his feet. Many a time the passenger standing next to his seat had toppled over him, pushed by other jostling men.

Tushar looked around, hoping to spot one of the van rickshaws plying between Membagicha and Nimpur. The roads were muddy after a brief spell of rain and he was glad that he wore a pair of rubber soled, leather *chappals* instead of shoes. A warm sense of satisfaction oozed out of him as his eyes fell on the lush greenery on either side of the road. Few people of his age group could afford a second home and even fewer were lucky enough to own one in the countryside.

Again, it began to pour; this time heavily, accompanied by such strong winds that Tushar's umbrella tilted and attempted to fly out of his hands, baring him to the rain's battering. He scanned the rows of peepul, neem, arjun, amla and jujube trees for shelter, but their flexing branches and vigorously shaking leaves promised little to protect him from the downpour. The breeze gained in strength and with a cyclonic force it swept aside a couple of papaya trees, providing a glimpse of a man-made stone structure.

Tushar crossed the street cautiously so as not to trip on its wet surface. He made his way into the clump, avoiding the jutting branches and the twisting creepers that sought to entangle his feet. Two pillars, about seven feet high, stood supporting a patch of roof that was wide enough to shelter two humans at least. He stepped under it and turned his gaze to the carvings on the pillars; his eyes wandered to similar engravings on the ceiling. In many places, the forces of nature had flattened the carvings. Yet he could make out the tip of a petal, the mid-vein dividing a heart shaped leaf and the raised trunk of an elephant. As he looked more closely, he discerned the angle made by the elbow of a dancing maiden. Time had scraped her face and a film of moss provided an additional fold to the cloth wrapped around her spindle-shaped abdomen.

Wiping his hands with a black-bordered handkerchief, Tushar slipped his fingers inside a transparent waterproof folder and patted the documents. The folder was a good one as the papers were as dry as they had been within his steel cupboard. He glanced at his watch repeatedly, wishing he had brought his own car instead of opting for public transport.

Left with no choice, Tushar gazed at the incessant rain, often stamping his feet to ward off mosquitoes. He wondered how old the structure was and whether there were any more ruins hidden among the trees. The bristling grasses that encircled the pillars were missing from the patch of ground between their feet. From here, a narrow path of brown earth went deep inside the clump. He overcame the itch to follow the track: it would be unwise to get drenched any further at the time of seasonal change, especially with a toddler and an infant back home. Once the downpour reduced to a drizzle, Tushar spotted a van rickshaw approaching the main road from a lane on its right. He unfolded his umbrella, stepped out of the shelter of the ruin and elbowed his way through the intruding branches. Nearing the road, he waved his hands frantically and called out to the driver till he took notice of him and pedalled the vehicle to a stop.

The subsequent years saw Tushar and his family spend several weekends in their countryside cottage. It stood next to a bungalow built by his wife's ancestor Samuel Silkenson. Instead of building a new house they had wished to buy the bungalow, which had already changed hands several times in the last century. But despite their persuasion, its current owner — a writer, famous for his spine-tingling fiction — had refused to part with it. The rumours circulating around Samuel's mysterious death probably drew the novelist, who had earned the epithet 'King of Horror' to the house.

*

It was the first week of December. The mild sunlight trickled in through the grilled window, drawing scales on the chequered dining table. Grace was shelling peas, picking up bunches of pods from a water-filled bowl. Seven-year-old James bit into a toast splattered with butter. Swarnali, aged ten, sliced off a piece of golden-brown bacon and chewed it with relish. Tushar, who was brewing coffee in the kitchen, reached for the porcelain mugs upturned on a high, glass rack.

"Christmas is on a Friday. So your father and I are getting an extended weekend. Let's spend it in Nimpur," Grace suggested.

"Mom, you know we love spending Christmas with Grandpa and Grandma," Swarnali whined, looking up from her plate. "How nicely they deck up the Christmas tree!"

"Not Nimpur again," James grunted through a mouthful of toast and bacon.

"They can stay at my parents' place while we go to Nimpur," Grace turned to Tushar, who had just arrived at the table with two mugs of coffee.

"That's fine with me," he replied, pulling a chair. Both of them believed in giving their children the freedom of choice in such matters; they also looked forward to luxuriating in each other's company for three days after an uninterrupted schedule of meeting professional deadlines, steering the household and raising their children.

*

Tushar and Grace got into their car from the same office on Thursday evening. Tushar had to manoeuvre through a multitude of vehicles that headed towards the packed restaurants, reverberating discotheques and clubs. They curbed their boredom during the innumerable halts at traffic signals by gaping at the lights strung across the shop facades. Dazzling orbs winked from glass walled bars and little bulbs drew glittering perimeters around the colourful hoardings. Clad in Santa Claus coats and caps, youngsters huddled around the festoon draped Christmas trees, their faces patchily lit by the 'stars' twinkling between the needle-like leaves.

Even through the shortest route, the car took two hours to leave the precincts of the city.

"Aren't you missing the Christmas Eve get-together?" Tushar asked his wife, racing down a desolate road that connected a few isolated huts. Their inhabitants seemed to have crept onto their beds already after turning off the kerosene lamps.

Every year, Grace would wrap up her work early on Christmas Eve, pick up her kids and rush to her parents' house in Swancross Street. Her husband would turn up later, armed with a bouquet of seasonal flowers and a bottle of wine. While the children ran about in the spacious three-bedroom flat, the adults would park themselves in the cosy living room with colour coordinated furniture and curtains, sipping their wine slowly and tapping their feet to the festive music. The dining table would be laden with purple tinted crystal bowls and plates, brought out of an old, mahogany closet. The merry group would gorge on roasted turkey and mashed potatoes with generous helpings of cakes and puddings. It was also the rare occasion when Grace would abandon all her worries about gaining unsightly bulges in her otherwise shapely figure.

"We have spent so many Christmas Eves with my parents, Aunty Martha and Uncle Derek. I adore them, but this time I needed a change," Grace confessed, raising her hands to twist her long hair into a bun.

"We have been to the cottage so many times as well," pointed out Tushar, flicking the indicator as they approached a turn. "And it won't be any different on Christmas. I don't think the Nimpur villagers have even heard of it, at least going by the dilapidated condition of the church built by your ancestors."

"True, a time comes when life stops throwing surprises at you." Grace sighed, stroking a tiny teddy hung from a string that swung wildly as the car leapt over a bump.

"What about celebrating the next Christmas in London?" Tushar's eyes glinted as he proposed the idea.

"That will be awesome! If there isn't another bout of recession, both of us should get our promotions by the coming June. That will stop me from feeling guilty about such splurges."

"You'll get to meet your Uncle Daniel."

"And Tom and Rebecca," she squealed in delight.

Grace, born in a struggling Anglo-Indian family thirty-five years after India's independence, had never been to the country of her great-grandfather. But she carried faint memories of a visit by an uncle from England. From those few reminiscences and several photographs, she had built an entire world around him and his children like a palaeontologist relying on unearthed bones to decipher the habits of a species of dinosaur.

"But one year is too long to wait for a surprise," Grace remarked, playfully resting her head on her husband's left shoulder.

"You want one now?"

Grace nodded and smiled, her eyes twinkling with anticipation.

"You will get one on the way, a few minutes before reaching our cottage."

"Really?"

"Really. But a small one…"

"That doesn't matter."

Tushar now felt like kicking himself. It could be the pleasure of driving through the uncongested road or the general hilarity of a holiday after three weeks of late-night office work or both that had relaxed his habitual cautiousness. How risky would it be to alight from the car with his wife at such a desolate spot? But Grace was a stubborn lady, and sure enough, when they were only half an hour away from reaching Nimpur, she reminded Tushar to reveal the surprise.

"It's too late now. I'll show it on our way back."

"That won't do, Tushar. We will hit the roads late on Sunday as well. You have promised to take Rakhal's sister to the hospital for her checkups, remember?"

"We will come here tomorrow. Or on Saturday."

"If we can't even spend two whole days in our cottage after such a long time, what's the point in shelling out thousands of rupees for its maintenance? Besides, don't you think it will do us good to reserve those couple of days for complete rest?" Grace argued, turning to her husband to catch his expression.

Tushar's impassive face suddenly softened. "Can't risk your safety. Love you too much," he professed, resting his left hand on his wife's thigh before grabbing the gear handle to negotiate a turn.

"Why do you think I carry a gun?" she retorted. Her gun was as dear to her as the car was to Tushar. Daughter of a policeman, Grace remembered fiddling with a pistol even when she was a kid; on attaining adulthood, she had been determined to possess one, despite the hassles of acquiring a licence.

"I...can't remember the exact place."

"Don't lie. I'll never speak to you again," Grace threatened in mock anger and turned her head away with a sudden jerk that reminded Tushar of their courtship period. Those were the times when he would secretly spend an hour each day reading aloud English poems to improve his diction in the language. The reminiscence ushered in him an urge to impress her once again. He called to mind his training in Muay Thai and how he had practised it rigorously for years. Besides, his wife not only possessed a gun, but also the skills to put it to use in case they were confronted by armed miscreants.

With the decision firmly pegged in his mind, Tushar parked the car opposite to the second right lane after Membagicha Crossing. Locating the clump, he held his wife's hand and slid himself through the gap between a papaya tree and a honeysuckle shrub. His elbow got scraped against the coarse bark of a babul and she dodged in time to avoid being blinded by a pointed branch. Their fingers unclasped as they navigated through the close-knit undergrowth, dived under the low branches and found themselves squeezed by the increasingly straggling vegetation.

"Look," Tushar said, pointing at the ruins and watched, with satisfaction, the flash of delight brightening up her eyes.

"You didn't tell me about them all these years," Grace complained while admiring the carvings on the pillars. "There may be many more." Grace brought out her mobile phone from the pocket of her tweed jacket, switched on the torch and focused the light on the trees ahead. The woods were silent except for the incessant drone of insects. Darkness layered the ground under their feet; shadows morphed into varied shapes between the contours of creepers. Grace halted next to a cluster of jujube trees, her eyes following the dots of light flitting between the ovate leaves. Beyond the swarm of fireflies, the uninterrupted darkness swallowed their footprints, sucked in the little trickle of their torchlight and almost crushed every trace of their presence under its overpowering sweep. A pack of jackals began to bark, their whistling cries carried across the woods through the covert paths beneath the arching stems of the undergrowth. Between the towering trunks of densely growing trees, threads of sky descended like strings tied to baits lowered into the den of beasts.

"Thank God, the phone has at least one utility even when the network does not work. Since there's a path, there must be something..." Grace said.

"Listen darling, we can't leave our car parked on an empty road for such a long time. The keys are secure in my pocket but car thieves find enterprising ways to pinch," Tushar cautioned.

"You don't think it's a happy hunting ground for enterprising thieves! How many people park their cars in the middle of nowhere?" Grace turned to him, her smooth unwrinkled face thrust forward and her hands deep within her pockets.

"We can't leave things to chance," Tushar argued, his face puckering into a scowl as his feet sank in a patch of mud.

"Well, then please be in your car while I explore this place." Grace's firm tone meant that she was determined to resist his cajoling.

"Are you mad? I'll leave you inside this forest alone!"

Without exchanging another word, Grace trotted along the path and Tushar reluctantly followed her deeper into the woods. So vast appeared the area now that Tushar realised he had been right in calling it a "forest" rather than a mere "clump of trees." With a shudder, he came to an abrupt halt on glimpsing something long and narrow a few inches away from his toes. He stepped across it after ascertaining it was a winding branch and not a snake as he had feared, although a sense of dread continued to tingle his calf muscles. Glared at by a pair of blazing yellow eyes, he gave a start; Grace too had stopped in her tracks. The wild cat bared its fangs to let out a raspy cry and leapt onto a knotted branch.

"There it is." Grace pointed at a dilapidated pillar overlooking a lemon tree.

"There's another one," said Tushar. A pair of gnarled trunks with crooked, bare branches flanked the column he had spotted. There were many more pillars, screened from each other by dense, prickly bushes and separated by the moss coated fragments chipped off from them by the vagaries of nature. They were reduced to different sizes, depending upon their degrees of vulnerability before the wind, rain and sun. Climbers with thick stems and spiny leaves wreathed around them and lengthening roots from the neighbouring trees inched towards their precarious bases. There was not a scrap of roof on them unlike the first couple of pillars they had encountered.

"That must have been some kind of a hall." Tushar remarked since these pillars were arranged across a huge rectangular space.

Staring upwards, Grace nudged her husband.

Tushar looked up to see a ball of fire shoot into the sky and burst into a hundred golden streaks.

"It's like the rockets we release during Diwali!" he exclaimed, an amazed expression animating his face.

A trail of light snaked its way through the sky with a loud hiss followed by a white blaze that went zigzagging, sputtering out rings of violet flames. Soon the forest sky erupted with many more fireworks but the couple's joy was short lived. An unending bout of cough seized Grace, who was allergic to the smell of crackers. In a matter of minutes, the escalating acrid smell defeated the smell that pervades the air during the festival of lights. Her pupils moved upwards, her head spun, and she slumped against a crumbling, termite ridden pillar. Before Tushar could hold her in his arms, she slipped further, grazed by the uneven surface of the ruin and whipped by the hair from her loosening bun. Her head thrashed against a hard tree-stump as she fell with her eyes closing shut, and then she rolled over a carpet of crackling, dried leaves. Gripped by a surge of panic, Tushar shook her vigorously, calling out her name again and again; she lay spread-eagled, still as a corpse, though he could feel her heartbeat when he pressed his sweaty palm a little below the round collars of her buttoned-up blouse. No allergic reactions before had affected his wife to this extent. With trembling fingers, he clutched the loose strands of her hair and threw them to one side of her face; he inspected, with an urgency he had never sensed before, her head and neck for signs of injury, but luckily there were none.

Seeped into Tushar a little bit of hope as he noticed Grace cross her left foot with her right. Then she brought her arms down to her sides. But before he could conclude that the scare was over and that she was back to normal again, scarlet-red eruptions burst out on every patch of her exposed skin. They inundated her stock-still face, ridged her slender neck and swelled her recently manicured fingers. Her dry lips parted, but only to express a feeble-voiced defiance against the malaise invading her diligently maintained body. While lying at the same spot she floundered like a trapped fish, the devilish pain doggedly challenging her endurance. Determined not to waste another minute, he proceeded to lift her and carry her upon his broad shoulders. There was a bottle of drinking water in the car and also a small, white container full of anti-allergic medicines.

To Tushar's utter astonishment and despair, he failed to raise his wife by as much as an inch. How did she suddenly become so heavy? He gasped for breath and realised that he was perspiring heavily on a December night.

"My mistress will have a cure for her," a female voice whispered in his ear, causing him to jump out of his woollens. He swerved to find a young girl, no more than fourteen, observing him with limpid eyes. Her assuring smile, like a lamp, burnt away his fears in an instant and he recoiled a bit with shame for being so visibly startled by her.

"Who are you, dear?" Tushar spoke in the manner he often adopted to speak to his children's friends.

"I am Kamini, the princess's maid," she replied.

"Which princess?" he asked, gaping at her in further astonishment.

"Princess Kumudini of Pakshipur."

"But I haven't heard of any place called Pakshipur." His eyes crinkled as he tried to recall the names of all the nearby towns and sub-districts.

The teenager laughed, displaying her pearly white teeth. "This forest and the adjoining villages were all part of the kingdom of Pakshipur. The ruins you see are the remnants of splendid palaces. My mistress is the daughter of the last king."

"What are these fireworks for?" Tushar inquired, as another shower of light sprayed down in huge arcs behind a distant eucalyptus.

"It's the first week in the month of Nauri. The people of Pakshipur celebrated it with a lot of grandeur. They worshipped Goddess Bhulakshmi, the reigning deity, with all the flowers that grew in the gardens. Even though my mistress's noble ancestors had left this world, she keeps alive the tradition of lighting fireworks and taking a dip in the pool before midnight," Kamini explained.

Grace let out another groan, threshed towards a flowerless shrub and fell silent, the gap between her lips altering to release the surfacing cries that got aborted before they could be strengthened with sound.

"But where does she stay?"

"Oh, the kingdom ceased to exist before she could inherit it, but there's still a lot of wealth in her name. She has many houses, and she inhabits them as and when she pleases."

"You are saying she will know a cure for my wife's condition?" He scrutinised her face, wondering whether he could rely on her words, and her smooth, calm visage conveyed only a picture of compassion and innocence.

"Of course." The path forked and Kamini pointed to the left. "If you walk straight for about half-an-hour in this direction, you will find a clearing marked by two mango trees. Their trunks are creased with age and one of them has a hole. The princess's great-great-grandparents had planted the trees. She is there, preparing herself for the Goddess's worship."

"But I'm not able to lift my wife…"

"Don't worry about that. I'll look after her while you meet the princess. You are lucky in fact. She stopped interacting with men after her husband's demise. She makes an exception to her rule only during the first night of the festival, which is tonight."

Tushar hesitated, but he had no options. He needed the princess's help to cure his wife of the painful symptoms, at least to make her fit enough to accompany him to their car. Curiosity chipped in: he wanted to see the woman, who had stepped into the forest at night, accompanied by a teenage maid, to preserve the tradition of her defunct kingdom.

A sudden question cropped up in Tushar's mind. "Why are you here while your mistress is all alone deep inside the forest?"

"She has sent me to look for injured animals. Whenever I find a wounded bird or a rabbit, I take it to her. She has learned the healing powers of a thousand herbs from her father's late guru and she never misses a chance to make use of her knowledge for the benefit of others." Kamini paused to watch the flicker of hope in Tushar's eyes spread to his face, shrinking the creases that had grown prominent in the last few minutes following the allergy attack on Grace. Then she continued, "But I must say, in this forest, it's the first time I am coming across a human in need of her help. We rarely see anyone in these woods and that too at such a late hour."

Tushar sighed, wondering whether Kamini had ever met anyone as obstinate as Grace. He stuck to the path, carefully choosing his steps to avoid trampling on the creepers lest there were snakes intertwined with them. The fireworks stopped and his mobile phone ran out of charge, hurling him into the darkness of the moonless night. His cell phone's behaviour bewildered him as he had taken care to charge it while driving. Tushar trudged along, beating the ground with a picked-up branch to ward off poisonous creatures, his fear of the forest overpowered by his anxiety about his wife's condition. Ardently hoping that the princess would know how to heal his wife, he wanted to believe the girl, though whatever she said sounded incredulous to some extent. The strike of the branch added a strange beat to the quiet night. In a short while, a woman's melodious vocals came flowing to accompany his unintentional, random percussion. He took a step back, caught unawares by the latest surprise, though he had to admit that it was an exceptionally pleasant one. He stared as far ahead as his sight could carry him and then drew back his gaze to a thorny thicket intruding his path. Skirting it with quick steps, he resumed his gait, but after a while, he paused from time to time to turn here and there and pry through the leaves for a glimpse of the singer.

Soon Tushar realised the sonorous voice was wafting exactly from the direction of his destination: it impishly tickled his senses, implored him to pick up speed, to leap onto the clearing and blend into the source of the magical song. Pulping tender flowers with the tread of his feet, he kicked through the rows of tall slender grasses, often finding himself hopping over fallen, many-branched offshoots. He frisked about the knobby tree trunks lying in his way and skidded across the wet patches of earth, somehow preventing a nosedive into the treacherous soil. The distance separating him and the singer seemed to have burned out like the fuse of a firecracker by the flame dancing within him. He neared the tree with the hollow at a pace that far surpassed his own expectations.

Tushar's heart sank as he saw no one. He scratched his clean-shaven chin, shifted his now weary feet, turned about, and attempted to pierce the darkness with his eyes, which still shone in anticipation, like polished metal. An entire minute passed before a splash of water scattered away his doubts as if they were teensy seashells on a sandy shore: he realised, with a sigh of relief, that he would not return disappointed. A female figure waded out of a pool so small it could be mistaken for a bathtub. Tushar's heart stopped beating as she approached him, slowly, one step at a time, her jewellery tinkling from different parts of her wet body. He blinked in disbelief when she stood before him, a drenched sari loosely coiled around her. A diamond ring sparkled on her long, sharp nose and a pair peeped like enchanted lotuses from her dark, wavy tresses. Tushar regretted that he had never ventured into these forests before and silently lamented that he had brought along his wife when he did finally come. What if Grace was now in the city, running around the Christmas tree with their kids, or in the cottage, tucked under the blanket with an engaging book? Alas, even the unparalleled beauty of the woman, swathing him in her layers of unrevealed surprises, failed to obliterate the marring stains of reality.

"My wife is in great pain. Please help," Tushar spoke at last, trying hard to cling on to the role of a dutiful husband.

"Of course, I will. But I left my bath abruptly on hearing your footsteps. It is inauspicious not to rinse oneself before the start of the festival. Please bring my soap from that vault in the tree bark and join me in my bath," she requested. Tushar's eyes fell on the dainty pimple above her bow-shaped upper lip as the words cascaded out of her delicate mouth.

Tushar stood transfixed, unable to utter a single word. He could no longer hear the drone of insects, nor whiff the fuming ashes of burnt fireworks, nor discern the tapering leaves dangling from a branch that almost brushed his cheeks. She syphoned his gaze into her large, piscine eyes with her steady, contemplative stare.

"I'll perish in a fever if I have to remain wet for so long. But I promise to help you once I have bathed and dried myself. I am hungry and thirsty but even those needs can wait."

Unable to bear the thought of her illness and death, Tushar skipped across the grass to reach the scarred tree trunks. Without thinking twice, he thrust his right hand into the hollow. When he glanced at his open palm, there was a round soap, dotted with bubbles, pervading the forest with the fragrance of sandalwood.

"Now follow me to the pool," beckoned the woman, displaying her long fingers, tipped by painted nails.

There was a loud scream and a frenzied rush among the leaves as Grace appeared out of the dense vegetation, closely chased by Kamini, and threw herself at Tushar. Without pausing for breath, she directed the light from her mobile phone's torch towards the pool. The liquid brimming in it was not water but dark, viscous blood.

It was Tushar's turn to collapse on the forest floor, striking against a mound of earth near the princess's feet and crushing a tangle of frilly herbs. Grace aimed her pistol at the woman's forehead and pressed the trigger.

The City of Gold

"A *school ma'am* came yesterday," informed Gita, dragging aside the steel trunk to mop the patch of floor it had occupied.

Arati, who was dusting the wooden pedestal where the idol of Lord Krishna stood, turned to say, "She is not a school ma'am. She is a social worker from an organisation called Rang."

Gita, for whom every working woman was a "school ma'am," asked, "Remember the boy who had spilt my tea last year? Will they bring him again?"

"That was a different NGO… I mean a different organisation involved in doing something for the society. This year they will take us to a picnic near the Ganges."

"Picnic?" Gita was carried back to the memories of the only picnic she had participated in; the one organised by the strongmen of her locality. To her surprise, she discovered that she could still recall the film songs the young men had danced away to, their shirts knotted up, arms raised skywards and wrists swivelling.

*

Arati had just climbed out of her bed after her afternoon nap when the caretaker knocked and announced that a lady had come to meet them. Smoothening their crumpled bed sheets, she and the other women rearranged the pleats of their saris and clumped to the room for receiving visitors, some bursting with curiosity and the others still struggling to suppress their yawns.

It was the lady from Rang again. "Picnic. Picnic," Gita whispered to Binati who blinked and rubbed her sleepy eyes.

"We are not planning a picnic, but a week-long stay at Sonpur," the lady who had overheard Gita corrected her with a smile.

The revelation sent out a wave of excitement across the room: the name Sonpur was something that got embedded in their minds like a seed when they were younger. As the years went by, it had grown into a tree and spread out branches with its many associations; sprouting leaves where myths were scribed and nourishment prepared from the mingling of crystal-clear water with sunlight dripping down the temples, palaces and shops. Even after the commotion died down, Gita and Arati's conversation continued, a word for every word, like the long braid trailing down the back of the social worker, the only woman with hair, in the room full of shaven headed widows.

After she left, many of the women found themselves daydreaming while singing devotional songs in the temple adjoining the *ashram*, even as the rickshaws honked, autos screeched, and garrulous men queued at the ration shop or crowded around the tea stalls outside the gates. Would they get to see the five-headed elephant? Would they get to take a boat ride across the Purple River? Such questions fanned their innate curiosity that had lain hidden somewhere under the trappings of their routine and they could barely suppress their restlessness as the day of departure approached.

The women had little to pack. It hardly took them any time to bundle up the one or two saris they owned, a few currency notes and palm sized pictures of Gods and Goddesses. Meena could not do without her betel box while the representative from Rang strongly dissuaded Shanti from carrying her pillow, assuring it would be provided.

The night before the trip, Sunaina whispered to Binati, "Don't take your jewellery there. There is a thick network of anti-socials beneath all the glitter."

"Are you mad?" Binati hissed, "Do you expect a widow like me to possess jewellery?"

"Don't fool me. I'm not saying you wear them, but I've seen you bring them out of their cases and admire them when you think we are asleep."

"Only in your dreams will you see me in jewellery," Binati snapped and went off in a huff to the next room.

*

The twenty women from the shelter for widows reached Sonpur after two days of train journey. From the tall gates dazzling them with their decorations of light the word Sonpur flashed with the 'S' styled like a bird. They were escorted to a resort with a small pond, surrounded by pruned shrubs of yellow and orange marigold.

As per the itinerary the widows were driven to the Mahakali temple on the first day of their stay at Sonpur. Though daunted at first by the long queue of devotees outside the entrance, they sighed with relief when Dipti, the representative from Rang, flourished a blue card which allowed them to enter through a side gate. The women had to strain their necks to spot the third eye of Mother Kali as she was the tallest deity they had ever seen. The Goddess' gold crown almost grazed the ceiling: a boy stood on a ladder garlanding her with the hibiscus wreaths brought by the worshippers. According to rumours, between two of the Goddess's toes there was a trap door leading to a secret chamber, where the family, who had owned the temple several centuries ago, had stored their immense wealth. Visitors to the temple would not have noticed such a door even if it existed as layers of flowers covered the deity's feet, formed a mini hillock and spread out to carpet a considerable portion of the cold stone floor.

A tour of the palace was scheduled the next day. The women strolled around its stately pillars, climbed up the winding staircases, minced in and out of the unending corridors, and ambled in the huge hall lit up by the strands of sunlight pouring in through a row of arched windows.

Occupying a large part of the royal bedroom was a canopied bed with legs shaped like nymphs. The table on its left, with the emblem of the erstwhile kingdom carved at its four corners, was paired with a similarly designed chair. On the right was a dressing table, its mirror alive with the reflections of the widows who passed it on their way to the other furniture. The antique glass finally got a moment to replicate Aditi's face: her large eyes curved slightly downwards towards a straight nose that ascended to a sharp point overlooking the thick, naturally pink lips.

She was drawing her forefinger over a cheek that appeared spotted and felt rough, when she discovered, through the mirror, Uma's eyes narrowed on her. Instantly, she turned and busied herself in tracing the butterflies patterning the silk curtains.

In the evening, the women were driven around the newly developed localities of Sonpur, dotted with offices designed in modern architectural styles. They could barely control their gasps on spotting a seventeen-storied hotel with the water shooting up from an infinity pool on its roof, descending all the way down the height of the building, to collect in a sparkling water body in the adjoining garden.

A cruise along the Purple River awaited them the next day. The name of the river originated from the purplish stones scattered across its bed. An emerald encrusted statue of a five headed elephant arched its trunk over a flight of marble steps that led down to the water. The boat ferried them through a tiger sanctuary, where they caught glimpses of deer and wild boars, and further downstream, a large gharial sunning itself.

"There's a tiger!" Arati exclaimed, pointing to the rows of teak striating the hushing darkness.

"You are fooling us," Meena replied, without shifting her gaze from the bow of the boat.

"No, I really saw one," Arati swore.

"Impossible. Only trees are there," Uma dismissed.

Emerging from the forest, the boat trailed the river through the villages and nestled up against a fairground. The women stepped down to savour hot *jalebis* and spicy *chaats,* and bargain over jute mats.

The shops formed a rough circle. While walking past the bangle shop, all the widows happened to maintain the same distance from it, as if bound by a silent agreement. This shop, which Uma had crossed thrice on her way to the adjacent earthenware store, displayed glass bangles of all colours that one could think of, glittering under strategically placed bulb lights. Bangles of the same colour were arranged one after another to form long tunnels; the red tunnel nudged the yellow one, the yellow tunnel contrasted with the dark blue, the blue sparkled beside the pink but it was a shade of violet that caught Uma's attention: it would have perfectly matched the sari she had worn to rendezvous with a man for the first time in her life.

On Thursday, Dipti led the group to a multiplex and joined the queue for movie tickets.

"We don't watch films," Aditi protested, mustering all her resolve.

"But its story is similar to the Ramayana," insisted the volunteer.

"This is not Ramayana," Mrinalini frowned, scrutinising the posters depicting a couple locked in an embrace, with cars and gunmen in the background.

"Like Lord Ram rescuing Sita from the clutches of Ravan, the hero defeats the villain not only to save his beloved, but also the planet earth from utter destruction. It's about good triumphing over evil," Dipti explained.

"I don't think it will be a sin to watch this movie," Naina whispered to Aditi and Mrinalini, who were only too willing to take their seats in the plush chairs of the multiplex.

*

"The scenes are so beautiful," Shanti remarked as the end credits rolled, awed by the cinematography and the special effects.

"Difficult to believe these are just characters in a story and not real people," Arati raved.

"What lovely songs! The first one is still ringing in my ears," Mrinalini gushed as the audience cleared out of the hall.

The only one among them to remain silent was Sunita, who had shut her eyes at every flash of a weapon, the clenching of a fist and the spark of a fire.

The women were given three hours to spend in the sprawling mall; to shop and lunch in any of the four restaurants.

"How can we roam about in a place like this?" Uma uttered in shock, staring at the shoppers - a woman wearing an off-shoulder top, two teenagers in ripped jeans, a middle-aged lady who had paired her sari with a backless blouse and a young mother in a skirt with a hemline as high as that of her little daughter's frock.

"People come here to buy things. Just like those who flock to the shops near the Lord Shiva temple close to your *ashram*. It's just that some people here have a different taste in clothes. They will not bother you, ma'am," Dipti quickly put her at ease.

Instead of accompanying the other widows to a restaurant to have *puri* and *aloo-dum*, Binati complained about feeling bloated and sat down on a bench overlooking the children's play area. She was waiting for the queasiness to abate, she explained. She stepped in the food zone only after the other women had finished their meals and set their sights on the shops.

As Binati joined the others in front of a bedding store, the excited chatter between Mrinalini and Sunita abruptly died down. Aditi looked past her while drawing Uma's attention to the ceramic vase she had bought.

"From where did you buy these herbal medicines?" Binati asked Sunaina, pointing at the bottles peeping from her bag, but the latter pretended to be captivated by a pair of goldfish that swam in a glass bowl atop a shop counter.

Binati hurried to a vacant window seat. Shanti glanced around for a seat near Naina and the nearest one was beside Binati.

"I'm glad we saw the movie," Naina turned back to speak to Shanti as she settled down beside Binati.

"The parachute sequence was so thrilling. I've seen nothing like it," Shanti said, her eyes widening as she recalled the scene where the hero had leaped from a whizzing aeroplane, popped open his parachute and clutched the hand of the falling heroine.

"The island where the hero met the heroine was so beautiful!" Binati remarked, turning to Shanti.

Avoiding eye contact with Binati, Shanti leaned sideways to look through the front window of the bus.

Naina chortled at Arati's joke. When Binati cracked one, it was met with silence. They had covered half the distance to the lodge when Meena, four rows in front of Binati, turned back and hollered, "How could you eat non-vegetarian food?"

"I would never eat such a thing! How could you accuse me of it?" Binati retorted,

"Arati had left her purse in the restaurant by mistake. You were so engrossed that you didn't even notice her when she went to fetch it," Meena fumed.

"She was mistaken. I ate vegetable cutlets," Binati insisted, although her heart pounded at the premonition of a nasty altercation.

"Binati, I was not a widow since birth. Being born in a non-vegetarian family, I can easily recognize a chicken item," Arati countered, her eyes flashing as she spewed out the words.

Binati's face shrank as she realised she had been caught. She fumbled for words to carry forward the argument, but found none and finally gave up. Failing to push aside the suffocating curtains drawn around her, she kept to herself for the rest of the bus journey. Every moment spent in Sonpur burdened her with a sense of despair, till at one point, she sincerely hoped that the clock hands would sweep immediately to the day of departure. Then a cold fear crept into her: back in the *ashram*, in the absence of any new distractions, it would be even more unbearable to cope with the torrent of snubs. She wondered how long the wall of isolation, intentionally crafted by the only companions she had known for years, would imprison her like an accused without trial, who remains in the dark about her sentence.

*

Alone at the washbasin after dinner, a quiet nudge made Binati turn around and face Gita.

"How did it taste?"

Flabbergasted, Binati stared blankly.

"I wish I, too, had eaten some chicken preparations. Men can eat all these even after their wives die. Why not us? Are we not humans?" Gita wondered.

Speechless with relief on finding a confidante, Binati felt a great weight lifted off her chest, allowing her emotions to flow unconstrained. The eagerness to discover what was in store for them on the last day of the trip crept back, prodding her on to cross the bridge of sleep to a new sun-soaked morning. She rested her head on the pillow with a renewed surge of peace slowly claiming its lost place.

Like most nights, sleep did not come easily to Gita. She stood on the balcony overlooking the pond, reminiscing over her life with her husband. Deprivation had corroded her days like insects boring into the page of an old book, but her husband had been there, also drilled with poverty, as if he were the facing page of the same book. Once he was gone, his absence had been the central pit in her life. Like the shifting of soil, those around her, including her grown up children, had removed whatever small privileges she had enjoyed and in such a manner that her existence sloped towards the pit, draining all colours in its unfathomable depths.

*

The twittering of sparrows greeted Binati as she hastened to the windows to bolt them. The birds had assembled at the garden path to peck at the grains strewn by the staff. Cramming an umbrella, a folding fan and a small packet of puffed rice inside her bag, she nipped to the balcony to collect the handkerchief she had left there to dry. The roses were sprinkles of red and pink in the reigning green. The jujube fruits had matured to a shade of brown and green dots speckled the shimmery waters of the pond.

"Where are we going today?" Uma asked as she climbed into the bus waiting outside the lodge.

"That's a surprise," Dipti replied with a mysterious smile.

The conversation revolved around the movie and the mall as the bus navigating through the Friday morning traffic settled into its own rhythm. Binati took her seat beside Arati, who suddenly found interest in the billboards outside, and turned back to spot Gita in the second last row, next to Sunaina. She suppressed a yawn and picked up her knitting needles to stay awake as she wished not to miss another glimpse of the hotel with the fountain.

The women's chattering came to a stop as the bus braked in front of a pair of nondescript grey gates. Putting on her sunglasses, Dipti hopped down from the bus, trotted to the security kiosk and flashed the blue card. The widows craned their necks for a glimpse of their surprise destination, but all they could see was the spiky crown of a date palm grazing the top of the high boundary wall. As the gates opened the bus breezed past a row of gulmohar trees, and stopped next to a small, square lawn with four red benches. It was only after the women had got down from the bus and taken a few steps towards the tap for drinking water that they sighted a roller coaster track — twisted like a crawling snake — in the distance.

"There!" Shanti exclaimed, pointing in another direction. The others followed her gaze to find a huge water chute.

"Have you brought us to...to...an amusement park?" Sunita asked Dipti, stuttering in shock.

"Yes, an amusement park." The representative from Rang beamed.

"No signboards at the gates. Why?" Uma asked sharply.

"We came through the back gates," replied the volunteer. Aware that the widows would not readily warm up to a park unabashedly declaring itself as a venue for amusement, Dipti chirped, "I'm sure you will not mind a toy train ride."

The widows scuffed behind Dipti, with their eyes downcast, overcome by a tussle between whether to stay or demand to be taken back immediately to their lodge. With long strides, the volunteer walked far ahead of them. Unwilling to draw attention to themselves the women refrained from calling out to her. Gita and Binati marched on without the slightest hesitation, almost keeping pace with Dipti, much to the others' resentment.

"Look at Binati. She has no repentance...after what she did yesterday," Meena sneered, her voice growing loud in indignation.

Uma tried to say something, but held her tongue on noticing a couple stare at Meena as if they were sizing her up.

Nearing the queue of tourists waiting for a ride, the *ashram* women looked ahead at the toy train slowing down next to a yellow flag that fluttered by the track. At the first glimpse, the train, with a different picture etched upon each carriage, resembled a drawing book in motion. The first carriage bore a sketch of a birthday party, the second of an elephant in a zoo and the last one depicted a little magician brandishing his wand. As the passengers hurried out of the vehicle and headed towards the other rides, the people in waiting jumped in and took their seats. Unshackled from their reservation by the sight of so many children, the squeals of laughter, the colourful train and the prevalent spirit of innocuous hilarity, the women made place for themselves in the vehicle for a peek into all the wondrous corners of the park.

"Which one do you want to try next?" asked Dipti after the ride.

The women huddled together and murmured among themselves. Since the moment Arati had read out the name of a ride called 'Hell to Heaven' from a board they had spotted during the train trip, the widows could barely contain their curiosity. But its so-called association with "hell" intimidated them.

"The perfect ride for Binati," sniggered Meena. "She has to go to hell anyway as she has eaten chicken."

"I'm curious," said Gita, ignoring Meena's comment.

"I'm not going to hell," Sunita said in alarm.

"No one's asking you to go to hell. It's just a ride," Gita assured, with a chuckle.

The ride 'Hell to Heaven' took the women down a narrow, cobweb-ridden staircase to a cold, dark artificial cave that echoed with the roars of hungry beasts. Under the flickering flames of lamps, they saw a pool of boiling water and a large bowl-shaped object, partly concealed by smoke, dangling over its edge. As Binati tiptoed towards the pool with bated breath, the bowl lowered itself, apparently on its own. She climbed into it and on finding it had two seats, she called Gita to join. As the bowl carrying the two women skimmed over the bubbles, more such vessels came whooshing along the invisible cables for the widows who had assembled at the pool's edge. The pool narrowed into a stream and flowed through a passage inhabited by grotesque demons, who either made a grab for them with their sharp claws, or snarled to display their serrated teeth, or let out a chilling laughter though the single orifice on their face. Shadowy ghosts hovered over them, their stretched limbs elongating till they were just lines. In the first few minutes, Binati had peered through her fingers, her heartbeat resounding through her ribs. Gradually attuned to the scares, she clutched the rim of the bowl and leaned forward, eager to encounter the next spectre sprung upon them. The fuming stream ended at the foot of a mound with bones embedded and arranged into letters that spelled out the sentence — "The river continues to flow underground."

Soon the passage widened and became illuminated by rays emanating from its walls. Gliding over the map of India, where each state was a garden in bloom, the cable car rose above the snow-capped peaks of Nepal and made its way through the soft, woolly clouds over the pristine plateaus of Tibet.

After crossing the icy cool waters of Mansarovar, it slowed down so that the sojourners could inhale the fragrance of petals showered upon them by the winged maidens, who were draped in twirling rainbows and bejewelled with strings of stars.

"Lord Shiva," Gita exclaimed.

With the snake coiled around his neck and a sliver of moon perched upon his knotted hair, Lord Mahadev sat on the summit of Mount Kailash. His consort Parvati tapped her anklet clad feet to the rhythm of the hymns sung by the devotees thronging at the foothills. Chubby Ganesha snuggled on his mother's lap; Saraswati strummed her *veena*; Lakshmi petted her owl and Kartik checked his stunning reflection in the waters of Mansarovar. Further away, on another mountain, Lord Brahma, with his eyes closed and his flowing white beard reaching down to his waist, was deep in meditation. Lord Vishnu reposed on a huge, black snake in a stretch of water that rolled and unrolled at the edge to resemble the waves of an ocean. All the statues were so lifelike that devotional tears rushed down Uma's cheeks and Sunita, shaken by the ride through "hell," at last stopped cursing the trip's organisers.

The next ride that caught the women's interest was captioned — 'The Best Ride You Will Ever Have in Your Life but only for the Bravest.' Crowding near the ticket counter with the money handed by Dipti, the widows exchanged glances and shuffled their feet. Their breaths fell heavily from the effort of speculating over their own limitations. Finally overcoming her trepidation, Binati opted for the ride irrespective of the others' decision.

"We will take the ride after you," Sunaina said, and the others nodded.

It was the first time that anyone other than Gita had spoken to her since the trip to the mall. Binati's spirits rose at once and she cantered to the red vehicle waiting at the start of the track. The vehicle chugged through a tunnel which was so dark she could barely make out what lay ahead. As it accelerated to a huge speed, she gripped the handles with all her strength. The vehicle darted straight for a while before it started to take unexpected detours like her handwriting, when she had signed her name for the first time at the age of forty, guided by a volunteer at the *ashram*. Though she wondered when she would be freed of the strange sensation in her stomach, she knew she would miss it when the ride would come to an end. She screamed in terror as it took a sharp ascent and whooped in glee when it plunged downwards. She would have got to her feet in feverish excitement, if not for the belt fastening her to the seat, as she went zigzagging through a series of cracker-fast turns and finally spiralled up to the gradually expanding hole of a sky.

When Binati appeared at the other end of the three-dimensional maze, her luminous eyes poured the wealth of her experience and her breaths felt like the gusts of a much-anticipated season. Her face shone with such radiance it seemed all the unhappiness in the world would bounce off her instead of seeping in. Obliging to the other widows' requests, she took the ride once more, this time along with them. On beholding the twenty widows, clad in white saris and ecstatically yelling their shaven heads off, as they emerged from the enclosure, their bright red vehicles cavorting towards the end of the track, some smiled, some muttered, and some others clicked their cameras.

The Attraction

As Priti stood in front of the full-length mirror, combing her hair that rippled down to her waist, the glass showed her what men gaped at whenever she stepped out on the streets. Lustrous locks. An hourglass figure. Glowing complexion. Bee-stung lips. She was contemplating on whether the sea-shell earrings would match her pineapple yellow top, when her phone came alive with the chime of bells. The chiselled face of a young man appeared on the screen. After a brief chat with her boyfriend, she clutched her purse and bade goodbye to her parents. Then striding out of the house, she mounted on her bike. Her hours were long, but her work was lauded and the pay enabled her to both splurge and save. What more could she want at twenty-three? Yet something nibbled at her happiness.

If she compared the human mind to a churning sea, some aspects of it would be analogous to icebergs — made of it, a part often unnoticed, but steady even in the swirl. In her world a tiny piece of ice was melting, adding to her already brimming life and inducing little spills here and there — ever since she found herself attracted to one of her colleagues.

Not that Priti was two-timing her boyfriend. Or harboured any intention of replacing him with this alluring colleague who probably had no inkling of her feelings. If she imagined courtship as two minds fitted into each other like two pieces of a jigsaw puzzle, due to their affinity towards forces of change the matching projections often underwent alteration in shape. Small spaces crept in at places where they had once perfectly interlocked. In Priti's relationship with her boyfriend, the differences becoming visible over the years were not of such magnitude that they would drift them apart. They remained attached to each other and had matured together to treat the small gaps as peeks into the future. Her relationship status being what it was and also because her crush was not single either, she refrained from pondering on ways to take the attraction to the next level. In case of any overtures from him, she was clear she would not succumb to the lure of a casual fling as she believed the consequences of such liaisons to be unpleasant. She did not even want him to feel a similar attraction for her, but she just could not stop thinking about him. The insignificant conversations they shared, the silly jokes they laughed over, and the few nuggets of office gossip they exchanged to amuse themselves and relax between work played on and on in her mind in a loop.

Priti's crush was not handsome in the conventional sense, but unknown to him, his piercing eyes followed her around — on her way home, in her bath, during her hasty meals and along the crumpled edges of her disrupted sleep. Whenever their eyes met while discussing work-related issues, she felt numbed for a few moments. As if the earth had paused its rotation to give time a break in its journey towards the night. As if all the things unrelated to the regular flow of life could happen during this brief repose. His eyes burned her, the heat baking her consciousness like a cake in the oven and spinning a distinct aroma amidst the dreary and often difficult office work. Long periods of embarrassment followed these few moments of ecstasy. At one point of time, it so happened that she could not look him in the eye lest he suspected something. She had never imagined herself in a situation where she would fail to make eye contact with someone. She forced herself to meet his gaze while speaking and in doing so sometimes she forgot to blink causing her eyes to water. Again, she prayed that he noticed nothing.

The sight of him caused Priti's memory to play tricks. If she was walking towards a teammate's workstation and her crush was in the way, she forgot about the destination and returned to her own cubicle. If she was discussing a delivery challenge with another colleague and he came forward to offer his suggestions, she found herself stupidly stopping in the middle of her sentence. She had the habit of retreating to the restroom and staring at herself in the mirror whenever she felt awkward. Assuming she was reeling under stomach-related ailments, her amiable supervisor would often enquire about her health.

Priti often asked herself why she was so mortified, especially since she had not crossed the boundary of propriety, she had set for herself. How did the initial rush of elation throw her into a trajectory of embarrassment? Did she always see herself as *the* centre of attraction and a subconscious sense of vanity prevented her from accepting her entirely one-sided feelings for someone else's boyfriend, leading her to experience a kind of discomfiture with herself.

Like the humiliation of a child scolded by her teacher in a class of fifty, overshadows the shame of a reprimand at home, the incident that would pale all the others came along one Friday evening. It was 6 PM when team lead Suman ushered Priti and her co-workers to the canteen. Ravi laid down a big cardboard box at the centre of a table. Deepa scratched out the Sellotape and pulled back the cover to reveal a cherry studded cake, layered with cream and chocolate. It was brought to celebrate a milestone. Priti fixed her gaze on the icing that spelled out the company moniker, aware that her crush was ambling behind them with his hands tucked in his pockets. In another ten minutes, their supervisor arrived and asked Priti, the youngest team member, to cut the cake and distribute the slices. After offering a cherry topped slice to her boss, she turned to the person on her right who was none other than her crush. She picked up another piece of cake and raised her hand towards his. Her fingers trembled. He touched the cake and was about to grip it, when it slipped from her hands. A prominent glob of cream stuck to his brand-new formals as the cake brushed against his shirt before dropping on the floor.

That moment of abashment refused to spare her during the client calls, the report making, the traffic jams she encountered on her way home, the after dinner conversation with her parents, and the nightly call to her boyfriend before bedtime, till such a point came she realised, with an urgency more palpable than ever before, the need to defeat her own demons. In the battle against her ongoing discomposure, the first step was to overcome the fear of making a fool of herself. Fear caused the mishap to happen many times — several instances in the mind before the actual one in reality. In her case, fear was a kind of wet clay that preserved the footprints of the apprehension running amok in her mind, leading her to follow them to their materialisation. Priti asked herself whether there was anything to fear. If her crush had not yet noticed her unblinking eyes, halting sentences or shaky hands, he never would. In either way, it did not matter what he thought of her as she expected nothing from him.

On the weekend Priti jaunted to a scenic spot by the river with her boyfriend. She pressed her eyes to a pair of binoculars to observe the birds perched upon the trees that grew along the banks, the river breeze loosening her from the grip of her routines. Her gaze followed a yellow-tailed bird as it disembarked from a swinging branch, flapped its way up and glided past the pearly white specks of cloud. A flock of birds with blue-green bellies burst into her view and she glimpsed many more as she scanned the sky, their wing tips gilded by the sun. Her boyfriend poured into the pages of *The Book of Indian Birds* by Salim Ali to look for the winged creatures they had sighted so far. At the designated hour, they queued up at separate counters, the young man being a vegetarian. Priti polished off her plate in a matter of minutes and licked her fingers, certain she would never forget the scrumptiousness of the tiger prawns. And the mushroom manchurian she had picked up from her companion's plate.

On the way back, watching the increasingly distant islands thinning into lines like the slits of sleepy eyes, she found it easy to stop worrying about things peripheral to the natural course of her love life. It also helped that her crush took a week's leave towards the end of the month to enjoy the serenity of Munnar. His absence was a change for Priti and she found herself in a better position to interact with him normally when he returned the following week.

*

A year had passed. Priti was in the mall to buy a parting gift for her crush on behalf of her team. There were only three days to go before he would collect his last salary from their firm and join the organisation of his dreams.

Priti let her fingers rest for a moment on the door handle of a gift shop as she contemplated the items on display beyond the glass walls. Then she stepped back and continued to stroll along the corridor. A group of youngsters strode out of an ethnic wear shop, carrying large, beige paper bags imprinted with the logo that also flashed above the store entrance. Couples stopped by the furniture shop to eye the cushioned sofas and double beds for their future homes. Bouncy children, accompanying their parents, slackened their pace near the chocolate kiosk.

Despite having a boyfriend, Priti found it difficult to buy a present for a man as many items in the world were out of bounds for the heterosexual male. Selecting a gift for a woman was comparatively easy with options in the form of jewellery, cosmetics, purses and soft toys. She could not gift him chocolates: he was on a diet following a drastic weight gain after marriage. Although the present was from the entire team, she wanted it wrapped in her own personal choice. So, she ruled out the usual gifts for colleagues like wallets, ties, mugs and pen stands.

What would be the perfect present? The clues about his likes and dislikes obviously lay among the words they had exchanged in their cubicles and the elevators, during the group lunches and the brief tea breaks, on the way to the bus stop and while switching off their computers. But Priti felt the need to rummage through her mind and reach beneath the piling memories to recall them.

Towards the Gates

Five men and women had chased Lakshmi away from the zoo gates. They said the zookeepers already provided the animals with adequate nourishment and they would fall sick if overfed. For a week they had been trying to persuade her and the other vendors on their pavement to stop selling gram to the zoo goers. She could not recall if it was the same group that had turned up with placards and banners on an excruciatingly hot day several months ago. The *paanwallah* near the petrol pump, the one who occasionally lent her money, had recognized the three of them. His sharp memory had inscribed their faces when they visited his alley half a decade ago to distribute saplings among the locals. He assured that the group was neither linked to the zoo nor the police.

But the enlarged photos of sick animals, carried by the volunteers, disturbed the chickpea seller. The voice of a frail, elderly lady still rang in her ears. She had put forward her request in a most gentle manner, but it carried the stupendous strength of a mother ensuring protection for her children. Lakshmi was reminded of her late parents in the village who used to feed stray dogs and cats even when they could hardly satisfy their own hunger. Did humans too fall sick from overeating? What about the fat boys from the tall flats who overpowered her children at the park? To mask her despair at their ordeal she would reprimand her younger son and elder daughter for going out to play instead of devoting that time to their studies.

Such thoughts criss-crossed her mind as she lay on the double bed she shared with three of her children. This piece of furniture was the only item from her dowry she had managed to retain. Raghu, her eldest, slept on a spare mattress stretched upon the floor, near the door. Above the single square shelf hammered to the wall, a stained and scratched mirror hung, flanked by outdated calendars depicting luridly coloured deities. Beside the meticulously washed utensils, a pitcher of water stood, its roundness contrasting with the thin strips of shadow cast on the floor by the window grilles. The smell of *dhania* from the neighbouring shanty intruded into the dark room and an old, melancholic Hindi film song, playing in someone's radio, included her among its many listeners before she sank into sleep.

As usual, Lakshmi woke up to the screeching of shop shutters. Such was the urgency of the chores lined up before her that she shook off her drowsiness in an instant and tiptoed to the other side of the room to nudge Raghu, who juggled his ninth standard studies with his job as the milkman's helper.

"It's morning," she whispered as he parted his eyelids. The younger children could enjoy a little more sleep.

After flattening the balls of dough into circles with the rolling pin Lakshmi puffed them on the *tawa* till they swelled like a balloon. She lowered the age-old steel kadai over the flame, and waited for the oil to sizzle before tossing in the spices and the uniformly sliced potatoes. Raghu, clad in a pair of grey shorts, a wet checked towel slung over his bare shoulder, stepped inside the room after a bath at the common tap. Wrapping the towel around his waist, he knotted it with the cautiousness of a mountaineer securing his rope and quickly slipped into a pair of baggy trousers. At the cue of the toothy comb placed back on the shelf, Lakshmi sat down on her haunches to serve him breakfast. Then she rose to her feet to wake up the other children — another son and two daughters.

Lakshmi had planted okra in the narrow strip of earth between her hut and the next. The plant was yet to yield, but she watered it during the dry spells, waiting eagerly for the yellow flower with the purple core to emerge among the five-pronged leaves. Next to the okra there was a hibiscus shrub. It might have sprung from the seeds dispersed by the birds. Whenever it flowered, Lakshmi would trot to the tiny box shaped temple at the centre of the settlement, a bunch of fresh hibiscuses held close to her chest.

The chickpea seller cupped the bright red flowers at the idol's feet, joined her palms and prayed fervently to get Raghu promoted to the next class. She was even more anxious as his studies had been disrupted several times in the months leading up to the annual examinations. First, there was an attack of dysentery; then water logging from the untimely rains when their bed resembled the island inhabited by a herd of barking deer — a sight she could still recall from her only venture beyond the zoo gates. Raghu had resumed his preparations as soon as the water receded. Lakshmi was grateful to the Gods for a son like Raghu, who, unlike many other teenagers in their slum, seldom frittered away his time by roaming the streets or indulging in vices.

The mother of four trudged in with a bucketful of water. She boiled some of it. When it cooled, she would store it in a pitcher for drinking. Then she peered under the bed, picked up a torn petticoat, dipped it in the water remaining in the bucket, and wrung it with a force more than necessary as if to ascertain she had enough strength for the rigours of the day and mopped the uneven floor. As Munmun's raspy voice reached her ears, she glanced up to find the squat and wheat complexioned woman standing at her door. Lakshmi envied Munmun, a part-time maid in a posh locality a kilometre away. She felt sorry for her too: she could never imagine a life without her children while Munmun was unmarried. After her mother's death, Munmun's father became so preoccupied with finding a new partner for himself that he forgot to search for one for her. There was a time when Lakshmi, unaware of Munmun's family members, had wondered why despite having all her earnings to herself, she shied away from the occasional feasts and the little jaunts to the seaside. Much later she came to know how Munmun would relinquish her claim over much of her salary to provide for the upbringing of her half-siblings in the village.

"My *bhabi's* friend is looking for a maid and I told her about you," Munmun declared the purpose of her visit, sparing no moment to exchange greetings or niceties. *Bhabi* was the lady she worked for. Lakshmi's eyes pooled with gratitude: she recalled almost pleading with her a week ago to find her a job as a domestic help. The maid's job would haul her out of uncertainty by ensuring a regular income and if she managed to gain a decent reputation, there would be several households vying for her services.

An hour later, Lakshmi stuffed a polythene packet with paper bags — folded out of the newspapers brought by Munmun from the household she served — and tucked it into the *pallu* encircling her waist. The paper bags were of two different sizes — the smaller ones for selling grams worth five rupees and the others for ten. With more than a little hope flickering in her mind she sped off towards the zoo, the lidded tin container of sprouted gram, strapped around her neck, swinging to her gait.

The path wriggled between the cramming huts and cut across the slime at sudden clearings. Young mothers, in attempts to pacify their babies, clinked their conch bangles, and pointed at the crows flying off with scraps of bread and the sparrows nibbling at the grains that had slipped with the water drained outside the doors. A little boy's eyes widened in alarm as his prized bicycle began to skid. Lakshmi loped to his side and drew it to a stop by grabbing the top tube and the seat post. She noticed for the first time that the hut she would walk past before stepping upon the main road had got its windows repaired and painted a dark shade of blue.

The queue at the ticket counter continued along the pavement, following the turns of the zoo boundary. Lakshmi and the other vendors traversed the entire length of the queue, eagerly running their eyes across the faces of the visitors while waving the wares under their noses. The lozenge sellers swooped down on children alighting from the cars; the balloon sellers eyed the toddlers chaperoned out of the exit gate. A skeleton-thin vendor with crooked teeth slipped a feathered hat on the head of a little girl in a flouncy frock, who, much to the man's dismay, returned it to him hastily and backed away in alarm. The man with the whistles gave a long blow to one, piercing through the cacophony and startling the decked-up teenagers engrossed in whispering secrets. Couples paused their love talk to munch on salted chips and a pensive youngster chewed his candyfloss, his eyes cast down, his ears shut to the blabber around. Most revellers shook their heads or glanced away when Lakshmi neared them with a paper bag full of chickpeas. She wondered whether the activists had influenced them. Or could it be that the zoo-goers no longer found amusement in tossing a handful of gram through the bars of the cage? She sighed and questioned the Almighty why a day did not spontaneously lead to the next. She had to scale towards each moment while clutching on to her needs, which had shrunk in the absence of alternatives to become narrow like the stems of creepers — paradoxically aiding the gradual climb.

On her way back from the zoo, Lakshmi would stare at the two-storied and three-storied buildings of brick and cement. Her gaze would rise to the parapet, hover under the ledges, stencil along the ornamental balcony railings, and bounce off the closed window panes beyond which all the answers to her curiosity lay. She imagined a dozen armed chandelier swaying gently above the carpeted floor, a table draped with a tasselled tablecloth, cushioned double sofas with backs spread like unfurled wings, a sculpture of a pitcher balancing maiden or a spear wielding soldier, richly embroidered tapestries hung beside oil painted portraits of the demised forefathers, and the lady of the house, clad in a maroon velvet robe over her pink satin nightie, strutting down the winding wooden staircase. The rich man's house she had gaped at in the potboilers remained indelibly etched in her memory.

Compared to the other days, Lakshmi took even more interest in those houses. She tried to imagine the sweep of the breeze coursing through the rooms on the terraces. A three-story building drew her: there was a staircase that spiralled all the way to the roof where potted oleanders towered over a swing and faced a shrine embossed with symbols.

The aspirant maid finally spotted the house she would visit tomorrow. Pairs of tiny shoes were set to dry in one of the cage-like enclosures built around the first-floor windows. The sun, peeping behind the new white building, imparted a golden glow to the upper edge of the parapet surrounding the terrace. It reminded Lakshmi of a white gift box with a golden strip along the top edges. Soon after being deserted by her husband she had stumbled on it while earning a living as a rag picker. Could the house gift her a less constrained existence? Her tenacious optimism and also her dispiriting doubts both intensified with each passing hour.

Lakshmi switched to selling chickpeas when her cousin — her paternal uncle's son, started cultivating it in his village. He gave her the flexibility of paying later: after selling off the current stock. But he expected her to settle the payment for every seed bought by the end of each quarter of the year. She knew her cousin, too, had to plough through the adversaries of fate, unable to extract a suitable price from the middleman for the rest of his stock.

The mother of four pinched her nose as she strode past the graffiti ridden, crumbling walls of a public urinal. The ebbing sunrays dropped behind a residue of thoughts. What if Raghu had failed his exams? A year repeat seemed catastrophic: for them, each day was a journey that might not culminate in reaching the destination but should avert the strangling tether of the starting point. Her neighbours often suggested that she pack him off to a faraway place to slog as a labourer like their sons. She had ignored them for so long.

A sudden guilt possessed Lakshmi for failing to provide Raghu either the nutrition or the environment he needed. Memories inundated her: first of a spindly toddler scratching the alphabets on the earthen floor with the stick of a palm-leaf fan; then his smooth ten-year-old face lit up by a broad grin at Munmun's gift of a green ballpoint pen; and finally the expectant glint under the teenager's bushy eyebrows, when a better off acquaintance promised to help him with his Maths. Her eyes drifted from her surroundings and she was just in time to step aside and prevent herself from being mowed down by a bike which had bolted, with no horn, from an adjacent lane.

Raghu, who had been trying to secure a job in an acquaintance's fishery, had set out for a village in the neighbouring district. He would return to the city the next morning by the seven o'clock train, and stepping out of the railway station, he would board a bus to his school. Since his mornings went by distributing milk, Lakshmi could not decide whether to wish for the new job as it would leave him with less time to study and exhaust him further.

"I'll study at night," he would say. "I won't stop, Ma, until I graduate from college," he would assure.

*

If anyone peeped into her hut at night, the mother and her three children would seem almost indistinguishable in that sole bed. The lack of space around them conspired with the darkness, giving the impression of a "mass", a term often used to refer to them by those in whose houses they sought employment. A loud knock woke up Diya and her mother, who lived in perpetual fear of that sound; a tremor shot through the deserted wife as she immediately recognized it. The toddler let out a little cry but Lakshmi, despite her body growing numb, shushed her and stroked her head till her eyes drew close once again.

Stepping down from the bed, Lakshmi tottered to the door and turned the key with trembling fingers. The last time, he had tried to burn down the hut when she had delayed. Before jerking the door open, she stood for a moment, clutching the ring-shaped door handles, and contemplated edging past him to run away into the night. She was compelled to discard such thoughts immediately out of fear for her children. What if she never saw them again?

"How are you Lakshmi?" Her husband grinned, staggering in. His irregular teeth were stained black by tobacco, his protuberant eyes bloodshot and breath heavy with the smell of cheap country liquor. Unaccustomed to his appearance of late, she recoiled as if she were seeing a hideous ghost. He flung out an arm to encircle her, but it felt more like a strangle than an embrace, and then he gave her a push. "Go get ready," he drawled, his face breaking into a scowl as he noticed his children sprawled on the bed. She resigned herself to fate and retreated to the bed, her head hung down. She knew none of her neighbours would come to her help: for them, a woman once married off to a man always remained bound to him.

"Go to Munmun's house. And take Diya along," Lakshmi urged, shaking her children. Kusum fidgeted in her sleep and Ravi peered through half-closed eyelids.

"Wake up, wake up," the mother called out desperately, tugging at the son's shirt. He blinked and gawked at her; his eyes ruled by incomprehension.

"Your father has come to meet me. You must not stay here now," she said quickly, hoping her words would register.

Lakshmi's husband had reached the middle of the room by the time Ravi sat up in bed, yawning and stretching his limbs. Something scraped at the inebriated man's feet as he lunged at his wife. Startled by a tide of swear words, Ravi flapped open his eyes and looked around in panic. His father, now freed of the habit of leaving his rubber *chappals* near the door, was trampling on his textbooks in a diabolic trance.

The sight wrenched the boy out of the last dregs of drowsiness. He leapt from the bed and darted to his books, which were lying scattered all over, their spines broken and the pages blotched with muddy footprints. Ravi's father continued to kick them, cursing and gesticulating wildly.

"No! No!" Ravi yelled, swept over by a sudden chill as he recalled his class tests were scheduled next week, and flung himself on the floor to snatch away the books from under his father's feet.

"Son of a b***h," Ravi's father slurred, his eyes glowing like chips of coal in the pits of his sockets and he kicked him aside, too, before pinning the screaming and convulsing Lakshmi to the bed.

"Ravi.... Ravi," yowled his mother, fearing that he had incurred an injury. Sick with worry over her second born, she thrashed about on the bed and struggled to disentangle herself from her husband, but no matter how much she tried, the jerks of her emaciated limbs were no match for his vice-like grip.

Kusum sat up with a jolt as the rickety bed creaked and gasped in horror at the scene unfolding next to her. Lakshmi, who had resolved not to shed tears even under the most trying circumstances, shut her eyes tightly in shame, gritted her teeth, and prayed to all the Gods and Goddesses she knew to let it be over soon.

*

As Lakshmi woke up to the horn of a scooter, her gaze fell on the tousled bed sheet but not on the man who had messed it up. She guessed that he had left for his mistress's pad. Ravi had escaped his brutality with only a single bruise on his leg as far as her inspection of the sleeping boy yielded. She thanked God for these mercies and stepped out of the door to brush her teeth with a neem twig, trying her best to unburden her mind of the resonations of last night.

After winding her chaotic curls around her hand and tucking them in a bun, the aspirant maid carefully pleated the sari she had swathed herself in for the appointment. Looking into the mirror, she consoled herself with the fact that her own husband was the only man who barged into her hut on random nights. Zarina, the hazel-eyed beauty, inhabiting the shack at the far end of the slum, was forced to tolerate many.

The mother of four rang the bell and waited, her heart thumping in anticipation. A lady appeared at the first-floor window; her forehead creased in questions.

"I am Lakshmi. Munmun, who works for your friend, has sent me," said the chickpea seller.

The lady unbolted the door. She looked thirtyish; her neatly trimmed eyebrows peeped over golden rimmed glasses, gold studs glinted on her earlobes and strands of shampooed hair curled around her shoulders. She neither asked Lakshmi to come in nor responded to her polite smile, but explained her duties while standing on the threshold. Lakshmi's face fell when she heard her wage at the end of the long list of chores.

"*Bhabi*, I can't work for such a little amount," the chickpea seller pleaded. "I have four children to feed."

"I can't pay more," she said with a shrug. "You can take a day to decide," she added with a cold finality to drill in the point that she was unwilling to negotiate.

Even after hearing the squeak of a bolt and the soft clapping of receding footsteps, Lakshmi remained rooted in front of the door, the familiar sense of despair cornering her with its inescapable jabs.

*

Lakshmi kneeled down on the floor, to separate the stones hiding among the rice. Diya was fiddling with a wheel that had rolled away from a toy car. Kusum and Ravi were at school. As their mother picked up yet another stone from the grains, she sensed her vigour was draining away. Her heart beat at an unusual pace. *Why hasn't Raghu returned? His results should have been out hours ago.* She decided to leave the stuffy room and sit for a while in front of the temple. As she rose to her feet, the plate flew out of her shaky hands. The room spun at a relentless pace and reverberated with the clang of the steel plate against the floor. Then the ground slid away. Diya's face paled with a sudden fright as her mother collapsed among the scattered rice. With her cheeks bulging with the onrush of a cry, she ran to Lakshmi and shook her with all the strength her little hands could muster. No faces peered through the window and nobody came bounding to the door, hearing the child's wails. Their neighbours were away at work.

*

Lakshmi's face twitched at the sprinkle of cold water. At first, all she saw were orange dots pricking a black veil. As more water struck her face and trickled down her ashen cheeks, she recollected what had happened and slowly parted her eyelids. With her blurred vision she saw someone waving something flat — something that resembled a piece of paper. In a few more seconds, her ears, too, started to function, picking up the sound waves all around.

"I have passed, Ma," she heard someone say. On hearing him repeat the words, she recognized the voice of her elder son. She lifted her head, and then pressed her palms to the floor for support to straighten her back. Raghu sprang forward to help, but she gestured that she was fine. He sighed and closed his eyes with relief, and muttering his gratitude to the Almighty, he observed her as she rearranged her limbs to settle into a more comfortable posture. Diya, who had been leaning against the wall with her hands encircled around her knees, finally got to her feet and scuttled to her mother's lap. Tears stained her face and a sense of confusion still flickered in her eyes. Raghu had spotted her in the lanes. After listening to whatever she could convey between stifling sobs he had carried her home, dashing through the lanes, heedless of the filth he was trampling on: the litter he kicked or the rot he squashed.

Lakshmi planted a soft kiss on Diya's nose tip, which was shiny and rounded just like her own. With a purr that only her mother would hear, the toddler buried her head in the hollow of Lakshmi's shoulder, twirling her coarse curls around her tiny fingers. After a while she raised her head. Her eyes trailed the sunlight that glided through the window, draped the pitcher, banded the floor and splintered into fragments among her siblings' stationery. These slivers of sunshine were such shaped that Diya could imagine each of them to be a different thing — the round spot a ripe fruit, the narrow fleck her playmate Mukti's luminous caterpillar, the triangular chip the dazzling pyramid she had glimpsed in Kusum's textbook and the one resembling a bell was nothing but the golden chime in the slum temple.

Shifting her gaze to her son, Lakshmi asked, "What took you so long?"

Then stopping her son's lengthy explanation in the middle with a restless shrug, she inhaled deeply and noisily as if relishing the power to breathe.

"So my boy is now in the tenth standard," she said slowly as if she was pondering over the years gone by and the years to come, her eyes sparkling above the dark patches and her chapped lips curling into a smile for the first time in many days like a drought threatened river curving from its course, to live…

The Trapped Spirits

Crouched behind the lion statue, Naresh peered out on hearing his sister's footsteps. He saw her run across the hall, her sequined green *ghagra* twirling around her ankles.

"I'll find you," she called out in a singsong voice, as she encircled every pillar to search for him, occasionally taking a peek at the river outside through the fissures in the walls.

Secure in his hideout, with a smug smile, Naresh observed the dusty cobwebs hanging down the cracked ceiling. Suddenly he felt something crawling on his shoes. Glancing down, he found a ten limbed insect inching towards the bare patch of his leg between the sock and shorts.

"Ewwwwww!" He jumped to his feet and frantically tried to brush off the insect with his other foot.

"Caught you." His sister came bouncing, and spotting the troublesome insect, she clapped her hands in glee.

The buzzing of another insect disrupted Naresh's reminiscences by compelling him to get on his feet and fetch the mosquito spray from the shelf. Despite the scare from its multi-limbed inhabitant, Naresh had tripped to the old fortress again the next day and on most of the days making up the month-long stay in his paternal aunt's home. It was in the ruin-dotted village that Naresh's love for old buildings had originated, but like many others, his family had brought him up to believe career and passion needed to be separated like cinder and match sticks. As expected, he had chosen a profession that did not concern buildings.

Naresh bent down, sprayed under the table and walked up to the cupboard to line its back with wet arcs of the repellent. He opened the window so that the mosquitoes could leave the room for good, and stared out, unmindfully clutching the black-and-white striped curtain.

Whenever Naresh's eyes wandered outside his chamber, he found himself drawn to a ravaged beauty — a deserted house, whose paint had peeled off revealing a skeleton of bricks. Its open, hinged windows pulled him with the gravitational force of a black hole and the broken grilles of the veranda stuck out as beckoning fingers. A stairway spiralled down from a balcony of the two-storied building to the backdoor near a well, like a snake approaching the opening of its burrow. Slithery creepers draped the three steps leading to the front door and a climber twisted its pointed leaves around its ornate knob. The ground-floor window grilles, shaped like long-necked birds, hid themselves behind a screen of dark green leaves. At the centre was a rectangular courtyard, with a derelict shrine rising amidst a tangle of plants, broken chunks of the roof and a few dislocated window bars. The ledges above the windows resembled dense forests, and Naresh was certain he had seen bats flying out of the room on the roof which, despite the missing window panes and the huge cracks on its walls, had survived, perhaps on the sling of shadows.

There was no rush of patients in Naresh's chamber, a situation faced by all new doctors. However, the dentist remained available for a fixed number of hours every evening, engrossed in the books by his favourite authors. He visualised whatever he read while crunching on chocolate crackers, which he replenished regularly in the jar on his table, and hoped for new patients to turn up.

*

The dentist was enjoying a particularly well written fiction of horror when he heard the click of sandals. He looked up to see his mother's friend walk in, accompanied by her teenage daughter. Among his few patients, most were relatives, friends or acquaintances selecting him over a more established dentist as a favour. After examining the girl's crooked teeth and recommending braces, he waited for her mother, Mrs Kolhapuri, to pay his fees. However, she kept on eyeing the dilapidated building while fiddling with the prescription instead of tucking it inside her bag. Her behaviour took Naresh by surprise as he had never expected her to have anything in common with him. But then he remembered.

"Was the house in this condition even before you got married and shifted to Gulabpur Road?"

"Oh, yes. It's been like this for ages! I used to stay in a nearby paying guest accommodation and pass this house on the way to my workplace," Mrs Kolhapuri replied in a dreamy tone as she cast her mind back to her early life.

"Any idea about the mansion....like who built it?"

"I wish I knew." She shrugged, before unzipping her black, leather purse to pay his fees.

Naresh, who could not wait to devour the last few pages of the story he had been reading, pounced on the book as the mother and daughter headed towards the lift. An hour passed before he slammed shut the book. He glanced at the wall clock which had just struck eight and mulled over the climax, while drumming his fingers on the table. The ending left him dissatisfied, especially after such a gripping build-up. Craving for more thrill, he decided to put into action the plan churning in his mind ever since he had glimpsed the ruined building.

A heavy, rusty, century-old lock hung from the gate of the compound. On surveying the chain of brightly illuminated stalls across the road, Naresh felt it would be unwise to climb the fence from the front as that might attract the attention of curious shoppers. Instead, he trotted to the back of the building: the adjoining street and the pavements were deserted, probably owing to the forbidding look of the trees that clasped each other, casting large, conglomerated shadows.

Just as Naresh was about to lift his leg to climb the back gate, someone whispered, "*Babu*, don't go there, you may never return."

Naresh turned back with a jerk of his head and saw an unshaven man, clad in a black full sleeved shirt and faded grey trousers; his wares — identically designed violet and golden eye masks that looked incongruous in such a forlorn lane — were displayed on a board tucked under his left arm. The man had yellowish eyes, but strikingly white teeth that appeared slightly sharper than usual.

"I have to find out why I may never return," Naresh quipped.

"Very well, *babu*," muttered the man and turned away, leaving a sense of chill that continued to linger on the young dentist's nape.

Naresh climbed the gate and carefully stepped on the other side, his feet sinking in the tall, tapering weeds. The ring of light thrown by his torch was like an eye mask, through which each illuminated blade of grass and every highlighted leaf glared back at him. What was the dense clump of trees, the scarred walls of the building and even the air circulating around them masking from him? The young man made his way towards the house, trudging through the scraggly bushes and trampling the enmeshed creepers. Sometimes, he halted to listen to the slither among the grass or crush the life out of blood swollen mosquitoes. He had been carrying mosquito repellents and carbolic acid ever since he had resolved to explore the crumbling mansion and its overgrown garden.

One by one, the dentist set out to inspect the rooms lined up along the corridor framing the courtyard. The first room he entered had a four-poster bed with a pink ladies gown stretched across it in such a way that its frilly hemline tickled the floor. He guessed someone had left the gown there recently as only a few grains of soot speckled it compared to the dust caking its surroundings. In another room, there was an empty dining table covered by an eerily clean cloth while cobwebs clung to the chairs and shards of broken china littered the floor. A slight sense of trepidation throbbed within him, but his fears, instead of accumulating into an avalanche, dispersed and latched on to random moments, further spicing up his exploration of the chambers.

In the next room, he found two small cots bare of all bedding and a locked wall cupboard with a black cat, about the size of a human head, engraved on it. The feline's green glass eyes shone with a strange life like gleam and Naresh blinked on noticing its whiskers twitch for the second time, but brushed it aside as an aberration of sight incited by his fanciful thoughts.

"A nursery!" Naresh said aloud as if to dent the disquieting desolation around him. However, his own voice, emphasising the absence of any other soul in sight, gave him the creeps. Not one to cower so easily, he busied himself in scrutinising his surroundings and found empty milk bottles lying and gathering dust under the cots. The eastern window offered a view of the apartment where he worked, and he experienced a new surge of thrill on recalling how he would sit there, musing about the mansion he was now exploring. He peered through the rusted grilles and then gazed up at his chamber with its dim lights on. The glossy pages of the calendar on the chamber wall fluttered, caught by a sudden gust of wind. The golden digits of the wall clock — an antique he had acquired after a lot of bargaining — glimmered even in the inadequate light.

Suddenly, something cold touched Naresh just below his neck. Instantly, he turned, his heart jiggling, but there was nobody around. Innervated by a fresh stream of excitement rather than fear, he dashed outside the room, but failed to spot anyone. Running back to the nursery, he swivelled his head to observe the ceiling, the fan with blackened blades and the walls criss-crossed with scratches and crayon marks. Finally, he rested his gaze on the floor, when he discovered something other than his own footprints — imprints of tiny toes in the dust. Not human footprints, but paw marks of a cat. It was difficult to believe a cat would leap to touch him below his neck and vanish into thin air. Naresh followed the feline spoors only to find them disappear among the tangle of wild bushes in the courtyard, which was devoid of any living creatures except for a house sparrow plucking out straw and fabric from the assembled junk. He gazed at the overgrowth, contemplating his next course of action, when a loud sound drilled into his ears. But this noise was bereft of any supernatural connections as it happened to be the ringtone of his mobile phone. His friend Raja, who had flown down from California, had called to say he would visit him in half an hour. Naresh had no option but to return home after rushing to his chamber to switch off the lights and pick up his attaché; he might never meet Raja again for years. He avoided glancing back while navigating through the thickets on his way to the gate, lest the allure of the place bound him and drew him back to the mysterious rooms. It was only while he was climbing down the gate with his face towards the building that he saw the lady's gown pacing the long veranda on the first floor. The gown only! No human in it!

The next evening, Naresh plunged into the mansion's premises like a man too intoxicated to realise the ill effects of more drinks. First, he darted to the room where he had experienced the unexpected touch and noticed something he had overlooked the day before. Carved into a wall was a niche, about the size of the cat inscribed on the cupboard. Fingering the sides of the empty niche, he found it to be a little damp. He looked around, hoping to stumble upon a more comprehensible clue, but much to his disappointment, there were none.

Since Naresh's foray into the other rooms on the ground floor proved to be futile once again, he climbed the staircase leading to the upper floor. He tried to be extra cautious as most of the railings had fallen off and the steps attempted to slide off from under his feet. He had almost reached the landing when he stopped in his tracks, his heart thumping loudly. It was a skeleton that greeted him, its bones yellowish with age and patterned with shadows cast by the walls.

It was disconcerting to look into the empty sockets: glance instead of being returned by a glance slipped through two holes and tumbled in the darkness of the skull. He gathered his wits and shone his torch all over the skeleton. It was the most inanimate object possible, just hung from the ceiling with a string. Even then, Naresh experienced an irrepressible shudder as he hurried past the dead man's framework.

As if making up for the skeleton's inability to utter a sound, the loud laughter of a woman reverberated through the first floor, rattling the windows and startling a furtively glancing house lizard. It seemed to poke at the cracks and shake up the loose door panels. Despite the fear creeping under his skin, he chased the unearthly laughter to arrive in front of a room on the right wing. The exuberant cackling abruptly stopped. The chamber was locked and all he could see through the keyhole was pitch darkness, yet undoubtedly, the shrill laughter had emanated from within. Naresh sprinted to the other rooms, but found nothing except some dusty paintings, fractured sculptures, threadbare tapestries and chipped flower vases. The ticking hour hand of his wristwatch reminded him of a dinner invitation. When realisation dawned that he could not stay here all night, waiting for the source of the strange laughter to emerge from the room and show herself, he grudgingly stepped down the stairs and made his way to the back entrance. This time, there was no inexplicable spectacle to puzzle him as he climbed down the gate.

*

Naresh hoped he had succeeded in convincing his young patient, who had just undergone a root canal surgery, to gargle with warm water several times a day. As he got up from his chair and passed by the window to check the stock of cotton wads in his white box, his gaze fell on the mansion. He did not get time to visit the house for several days. His reputation as a competent dentist, which had been growing, but too slowly like the revival of an endangered species, had reached a point where it was more easily noticeable. The young man decided to venture into the house that night, however late it might be. He intended to stay there till dawn, to make the most of whatever specimens of strangeness got hooked to the bait of his five senses.

The day before, Naresh had crossed the street and walked over to the grocery to buy coffee powder.

"Who lived in this house?" Pointing at the dilapidated building, the dentist asked the grocer, half expecting him to shake his head and say he has no clue.

"It belonged to a diamond merchant named Vasant Gour. He had also produced some films during the thirties," replied the man behind the counter.

"Isn't he the same person who owned another building in this locality?" Naresh asked, his curiosity spurred.

"Yes, he built these two mansions for his two sons. A well-known enterprise has bought the other one and made it into a hotel — the Redwood Hotel."

"Why is nobody buying this one?"

"It's said to be haunted," whispered the shopkeeper.

"Why?"

"Whenever Vasant Gour took an interest in any of his actresses, she would disappear, leaving no traces. People said the merchant cum filmmaker locked them in an underground chamber beneath the house. There are rumours that someone found his dead body lying in that hideout and his malevolent spirit still haunts the house." The grocer's eyeballs rolled and his voice changed its pitch innumerable times as he spoke: it seemed he, too, was blessed with the talent to make a mark in films.

*

By the time the last patient had left and Naresh had strided to the mansion with his usual ammunition of mosquito repellents, carbolic acid and a torch, the shops had shuttered down and the streets were deserted. The dentist seized this opportunity to climb the front gate for the first time and landed on the compound with a jump.

The story of unexplained occurrences in crumbling mansions, passed on in a chain from one person to the next, sometimes became a talisman protecting old buildings. Naresh wished he had conjured up some scary tales about Shankh Bhavan, which got demolished a year ago despite a leading architect's campaign to preserve it. Instead of circulating a humble petition to save it, a ghost story might have achieved the objective.

The skeleton hung from the same spot. The locked room that had generated the eerie laughter the other evening was silent, but filled with a sense of motion, like a closed mouth, wordless to gulp down water. Naresh marched to the next room: it was empty except for a cobweb entangled carpet rolled up and propped against a wall. He ambled out of its other door to enter a small balcony. The collapsed railings made way for the intruding neem branches that stretched, branched further and cast feathery shadows on the dry-leaves strewn floor. Like Naresh, the tree seemed to revel in exploring. It was from this balcony that the serpentine staircase twisted down. He trod cautiously on the first step, glanced down at the well and caught the gleam of water. He tiptoed down the steps, sometimes bending to dodge, sometimes raising his hands to shove away the rod like branches and indented leaves. At the last step, to his surprise, he found a cat sitting on its haunches, its sleek ears pricked up and emerald eyes focused on a dome-shaped bush, which was trembling from the presence of a bird or rodent. With its glistening black fur, it resembled the cat chiselled on the cupboard of the nursery. The feline stood up sensing his presence. It turned at him and snarled, providing a glimpse into its pink mouth. Was it the same cat whose paw marks dotted the room where he had experienced the mysterious touch?

Rummaging through his bag, Naresh discerned the contours of a biscuit packet. He pulled out a round biscuit, crumbled it by pressing it with his fingers and tossed the pieces gently towards the cat. The cat which he identified as a female, sniffed them suspiciously, twitching her whiskers. Once satisfied, with a few swift movements of her mouth, she took care of every speck of the biscuit dotting the grass that sprouted in the cracks of the step. Out of deep affection for all felines, Naresh's right hand shot out to stroke her furry back. Alarmed by the stranger, she swerved away and his fingers hit upon a steel handle, concealed by the greenery matting the stair. He stepped back on the second last step to bend over the last one, curled his slender fingers tightly around the handgrip and pulled with all his might. The upper surface of the step yanked out like the door of a cupboard to reveal a rectangular hole. He directed his torchlight into the dark void and sighted fragments of marble tiles laying a few feet below. Not the kind of man to hesitate or have cold feet before plunging into the unknown, he lowered himself into the opening, and jumped. As his sneakers hit the fractured surface of the marble floor, he looked around and found another flight of stairs that spiralled down to an underground corridor. So, the rumours had some basis!

Naresh climbed down the stairway, his pulse racing in anticipation, although he knew it would be impossible to make a quick escape from the subterranean passage in case of any danger. No matter what perils awaited him at the end of the flight, he felt his own curiosity would crush him if he retraced his steps.

It was only after landing on the floor of the corridor that Naresh could discern the arches of doorways on either side. He lifted his right leg to step forward but his feet froze. Instead, his arm swung in front of his face to shield his eyes from the sudden, unexpected light. Slowly he looked up to find the chandelier in perfect condition; not a single bulb cracked or missing. He realised with a jolt that the staircase he had just climbed down, had no gaping steps or splintered railings unlike the one snaking down from the balcony or the one inside the house leading to the first floor. Shifting his gaze to the walls, he blinked in astonishment, unable to believe he was within the premises of a building that had been unfit for human habitation for decades. In between the doorways, full-length mirrors dazzled within ornate frames and a velvet cushioned stool was arranged in front of the middlemost glass on either side. He stared ahead; his senses perked up to tap on anything unusual that might come his way. The corridor led to yet another doorway — this one veiled by mauve silk curtains. His head buzzed with questions: who switched on the lights and who prevented this passage from degenerating like the rest of the building?

A faint rustling noise seemed to emanate from beyond the curtains. Instinctively, Naresh curved his palm over an ear to improve his chances of catching the sound, but soon the noise grew loud enough to be heard without such manoeuvre. As he stood under the full glare of the chandelier, reflected by the mirrors on either side, all he could do was hurl guesses regarding what he was about to encounter. But his conjectures grew increasingly unpleasant as the seconds ticked by. Robbed of the capability to think any further, he counted each breath whooshing out of his chest, his gaze unwavering from the doorway at the end of the passage. A silhouette appeared behind the silk. The curtains parted.

The figure, whose head almost touched the ceiling, moved towards Naresh, three steps at a time — right, left, right, pause, then left, right, left, pause — probably thudding on as many dreadful moments as possible before the final strike. Its grey, high-necked coat reached down to the knees and the black trousers covered not only the legs but most of the feet, exposing only the freakishly long, thin, hairy, centipede-like toes. The dentist recoiled, the horror scouring his insides enhanced manifold by memories of childhood scares. Instead of hair, there was a dent in the middle of the creature's head from where blood trickled out and criss-crossed its scabby forehead. Its nose, lips and ears were distorted so much it seemed that a right hander had drawn its face with his left hand. Its complexion was ashen and its cheeks were spotted with as many skin eruptions as the holes in a net. It glowered at Naresh with eyes that appeared like two fire reflecting, jagged edged glass shards jutting out of round, dark sockets. The young man's eyes bulged out and his teeth got jammed such that not even a whimper could escape past them, let alone a scream. Blood frothed in his capillaries and his heart frenziedly bumped against his rib cage. Undaunted by the light, the spectre curled its gelatinous, blood-red lips into an ugly smile, revealing its sharp canines.

That was it. With his dental knowledge, Naresh immediately recognized them as fake teeth and made a dash for the creature. Sensing trouble, it flung off its false feet, turned on its bare heels and ran into a huge hall through the nearest arched doorway. They raced amidst bulging sacks and empty barrels, jumped across splintered portraits and dismembered sculptures, and skirted piles of Thermocol boxes and electronic wastes. With their feet often entangled by tattered rugs or hit against clattering utensils, they kicked the obtrusions aside and doubled their pace. When the disguised man, who was familiar with the underground hall, gained in speed, Naresh realised that mere running would not help. With his eyes on a sturdy cabinet, he stepped on the saddle of a luridly painted wooden horse. As it began to rock, he flung his arms around a huge roll of bedding and quickly clambered on to its top. From here the crest of a cabinet was not far. Without losing a second, he scaled the cupboard; then using the advantage of its height he dived to get a grip on the man, knowing he would be hurt badly if he missed his target.

The man fell with a yelp with Naresh upon his back. The dentist took out a piece of rope from his pocket and bound him to a leg of the cabinet. He wrenched away the man's mask which included the hideous head and clicked a snap of his real face with his mobile phone. The exposed "ghost" was still panting for breath when Naresh took a few steps back and surveyed the cluttered room. There were cans of paint for makeup and other grotesque masks similar to the one the man had worn. Nudged off a hook during the chase, the pink ladies gown was lying crumpled at the feet of a bronze statue. The man, reeling under the brunt of Naresh's attack, let out a long-drawn groan and tried to sit up but slumped on the floor.

Satisfied with the firmness of the rope, Naresh stepped further away from him to pick up the dress. Turning it inside out, he found cloth handles stitched to its inner lining. Now he understood how the trick had worked: the gown was put on a small person — probably a child or a dwarf who would reach only up to its middle. He would slide his arms through the handles and lift them upwards so it seemed the dress was worn by an invisible being. The feet would remain hidden as the dress was long enough to trail the ground. The tied-up man, writhing before him, was of normal height; he could not have worn the dress to scare him.

"Who else is there with you?" Naresh interrogated.

The man remained silent and stared at the spotted moths swirling around a light bulb.

"It won't help to hide anything. I've got your photo," thundered Naresh.

"That was my son," mumbled the man, rolling to his left and kneading his back muscles, though his gaze still lingered on the insects.

"And the laughing on the first floor? Was that your wife?" The dentist tossed out the most obvious guess.

"No, she's dead. That must have been my sister or her daughter," replied the man. His mouth twisted to let out another agonised cry.

"How many of your family members are here?" the dentist asked, his eyebrows raised in surprise.

"Other than my son, sister and niece, there are two more relatives and another family of four — neighbours from my old locality." The tied-up man shifted his gaze slightly to look at a new moth flying in to join the others.

"It must be painful for your son to stretch his arms up for so long, in that dress." Naresh recalled his grade one teacher had forced him to lift his arms and remain in that posture for half an hour as punishment.

"Not more painful than living on the streets when they are flooded." The man sighed. The unexpected words pierced Naresh more deeply than those fake canines could ever have. In the speck of a second vaporised the feeling of smugness swelling in him after he cornered the "ghost." The stranger's eyes were lost in their sockets. He had a longish nose and cracked lips. Though covered with an unkempt beard, the hollows in his cheeks were prominent like the pits dug in the ground to bury wastes.

"You better tell me your story," Naresh growled, coercing himself to sound harsh to extract the reason behind his disguise.

"We were pavement dwellers, who lived opposite the Raj Lakshmi cinema hall. We had landed in this deserted house during one monsoon when the entire locality was waterlogged. Soon, we came to know the house had other inhabitants. We could stay and have food for free, but on one condition: we would have to disguise ourselves as ghosts and scare people away."

The man continued to pant loudly even after he had finished speaking. Naresh regretted gulping down even the last drop of water from the bottle in his bag. Spotting a wooden chair lying on its side, beside a bundle of ink spattered rags, he hopped over the junk and carried it to the former pavement dweller. Its back was missing. He slid his arms under the man's armpits, pulled him up and made him sit by leaning against the legs of the chair.

"What is your name?" the dentist asked.

"Rahim," replied the man, adjusting his legs to sit a bit more comfortably.

"On whose orders do you turn up as ghosts?"

"Men with ill-gotten money frequent these chambers. Sometimes they bring women against their will."

So, Vasant Gour's vile tradition had resumed. Naresh let out a deep breath, mulling over the fact that though years passed and dates changed, the nature of human depravity remained the same.

"I've also come across a bundle of fake notes and once found a trunk full of tiger skins," Rahim continued.

Naresh bit his lips, thinking about the variety of heinous acts the house had witnessed. He regretted that flesh and blood humans like the one before him were being subjected to the same fate as the inert building.

"But nobody has seen anyone enter or leave this mansion," wondered the dentist.

"Some of these rooms have secret passages," the former pavement dweller revealed.

"Where do they lead?" Naresh asked, hit by a fresh wave of excitement.

"One opens into the garage of the Redwood Hotel."

The information startled the dentist. But as the fact sunk in, he realised it made perfect sense that the diamond merchant would connect his two properties.

"And the rest?" Naresh could barely suppress his curiosity.

"I don't know about all of them. But there's one we frequently use. The room with curtained doors."

"The one from which you came out to scare me?" Naresh interrupted.

"Yes," Rahim said, glancing at the floor. "It has a flight of stairs that will take you inside a cupboard in a room on the ground floor.

"I felt someone touch me when I was standing in that room and looking through the window," Naresh exclaimed. "Was it you?" he asked.

"No, must have been one of my relatives," Rahim replied, yawning.

"How did he or she open and close the cupboard door so quickly making no noises?" Naresh grabbed the chance to put into words the question that had been nagging him for days.

"My relative did not open the cupboard door," Rahim said.

"Then?" Naresh clasped and unclasped his hands, impatient to find out the answer.

"Have you noticed the cat engraved on the cupboard door?"

"You don't mean…" The dentist tried to guess what had happened.

"Yes. It's movable and covers a peephole." Rahim gave a faint smile, his dejection slightly diluted by the satisfaction of quenching the dentist's curiosity.

"So, your relative poked me with something like a stick through the peephole?" It was now as clear as water to Naresh.

"Exactly," confirmed Rahim with a nod.

The two men remained silent for a while. Naresh ruminated over the revelations and Rahim wrapped his hands around himself in pain.

"Sorry for this," Naresh apologised, pointing to the rope, and hastened to untie him.

"I should be the one to show remorse," Rahim remarked with a sad smile.

"It's not your fault. You had no options, but to obey," Naresh condoled.

"You must leave this place at once. My masters might arrive any moment. They always come on Fridays," Rahim cautioned the dentist. Then clutching one of his knees with one hand and massaging his back with the other, he slowly stood up.

Naresh shuffled his feet, alternately glancing at the walls and at the bearded man, who was brushing off the dust from his clothes.

"Please don't delay. Run." Rahim pushed him with his palms to stress the urgency.

"Will you come with me? You and your son can stay at my flat tonight. Then I'll see whether I can arrange a home and a job for you," Naresh said, stirred by Rahim's concern for him, although he had no idea how he would find employment and lodging for a man who flashed his false fangs for survival.

"That's kind of you to say, but I can't go." Rahim shook his head. "They will torture my relatives."

"Okay, I'll come back when I can take all of you away from this hellhole," Naresh promised before turning towards the staircase.

Naresh roared through the desolate streets on his bike, traversing the shadows of noiseless apartments and vacated malls, fragrant white *chhatim* flowers showered on him. He sorted out his options. The most obvious step would be to approach the police. If the law keepers failed to intervene, he would rally his friends, their friends and as many people as he could reach through word of mouth, blogs and social networks to build pressure on the authorities, to put a stop on the nefarious activities being carried out in the ruined mansion, and free Rahim and his clan from what was nothing short of modern day slavery.

Nowhere Else on Earth

Digging into the watered clods of earth, Trishulpani listened to the majestic voice of Mr Tamang. Another kind of tilling was being carried out on the slope below. After the school anthem and other inspirational songs, Mr Tamang explained the protocols of the institution to a fresh batch of students, who occasionally nodded their tiny heads as proof of their attentiveness.

"How time flies! Just the other day he was welcoming the previous batch," Trishulpani said to himself as there was nobody else around.

The farmer noticed Rumi perked up in her chair, next to the other teachers, her hands on her lap, head slightly tilted back and eyes fixed on the podium where Mr Tamang stood speaking into a mic. He wished his wife was alive to see the residential school come into existence. How wholeheartedly she looked after the needs of Rumi when her mother went out to work in the tea gardens! He recalled his wife boiling the rice till it was soft as cream and then rolling it into small balls that could effortlessly slip into the toddler's tiny mouth. How she would find the girl hiding in the bamboo shed and cajole her into taking a bath by pouting like a fish! A twinge of regret struck him as he remembered that her days, too, were numbered in this village: her family had fixed her marriage with a doctor in Dehradun.

An hour ago, having slipped into absent-mindedness while cooking a meal of assorted vegetables, Trishulpani had scalded his fingers. His hand seared while holding the plough, but he found it impossible to restrain himself from cultivating his land even for a day. He glanced up from the furrowed patch of ground to map out an outline around the land he would till before squatting down for a break.

The hamlet, tucked away in the Himalayas and overlooking the Moonpoong Lake, had not been completely unexposed to visitors before the school came up. Crowned as the most beautiful place on earth by an international magazine, Roopar Village attracted photographers from all over the world. They pitched tents to stay during their assignments since the settlement was yet to develop into a tourist spot. But the magnificence of the mountains failed to root Trishulpani's son to the village. He was struggling to set up a furniture business in Haridwar.

Trishulpani, who owned three cows, was one of the milk suppliers to the boarding school. Instead of asking the farmer to plod to the school kitchen to deliver it, the mess- supervisor had instructed Ramlal, the cook, to collect it from his home. However, Trishulpani chose to carry the milk to the school: the early morning trip gave him an opportunity to chat with the gardener who tended the gladioli, carnations and roses.

As Trishulpani cycled along the long-pebbled path snaking through the vast school compound, the Nanda Devi peak slipped behind the swelling clouds and soon the murky sky began to pour. He felt sorry for the photographer he had befriended a while ago: he could not click the famed sunrise, when light blends with snow; pink at dawn morphing to gold in the morning — delicate prettiness of early romance to ripened beauty of mature togetherness. His new friend's eagerness to capture the first glimpse of the sun reminded him of a poet-painter, who had backpacked to their village a year ago and written a poem entitled, "Nowhere Else on Earth."

Hastening to the shade of the poplars, Trishulpani heard someone sobbing. The crying stopped as he came closer. The person had realised his presence. A boy wiped off his tears furiously as the farmer alighted from his bicycle. Suddenly, the rain stopped, leaving the isolated drops clinging to the blue poppy petals or dripping from the sharp pine needles.

"Who are you?" the boy asked sharply.

"I'm Trishulpani, a farmer. I live nearby and supply milk to this school," he replied as softly as possible.

The boy was probably ten years of age — old enough to be ingrained with the prevalent views on manhood. His tone of speaking made it clear it was best not to ask him the reason behind his secret outburst of emotion. The farmer was wondering what he should say instead when something appeared bridging their silences.

"Look son, over there," he gestured towards the northern sky.

There was a rainbow — a multicoloured sash across the distant snow-specked mountain. Rainbows were not rare in the firmament of Roopar, but Trishulpani could not help brimming with a child-like joy every time his eyes rested on one. It seemed that the boy had sighted a rainbow after a long time and he stood rooted by the pebbled path, keenly tracing its colours with his gaze.

As the two hurried towards the hostel, Trishulpani remarked to the boy, "You must be fond of painting."

"How do you know?"

"Just guessed."

The farmer's son, too, was fond of painting and he noticed in this boy's eyes the same eagerness while watching the rainbow. Before bidding goodbye to the child, Trishulpani learned that his name was Ankur.

With the purpose of endowing its students with money management skills, the school asked them to buy their own stationery out of a fixed sum of money, collected from their guardians at the beginning of the year. Sometimes, in the afternoon, while visiting the shops owned by his friends, Trishulpani would run into Ankur. The schoolboy and the farmer would strike up a conversation and the latter got to know that the child's parents, who had separated a year ago, used to teach in a college in Chennai. While his father had shifted to Delhi, his mother continued to reside in the southern capital.

Soon, Ankur began to wait for Trishulpani, near the kitchen, when he came to deliver milk. The farmer would stroll around the compound with the boy, marvelling at the uniformity of the grass in the tennis courts. They would steal a glimpse inside the roofed apiary before halting at the security guard's table near the front gates. Ankur would sift through the envelopes piled on an adjacent table to see if there were any bearing his name. Sometimes, he would start reading the letters addressed to him, then and there, flanked by Trishulpani and the table, impatient to soak in the familiar ink.

"These are all lies!" Ankur yelled out one day, crumbling a letter and trashing it in the bin. He had been taught not to criticise his family members, but the piece of paper had inflamed him beyond such boundaries of imposed conduct. He blurted out to Trishulpani how his paternal grandparents had accused his mother of misbehaving with them, driving his father to despair and having unmentionable relationships with her colleagues.

Back in his house, the farmer trotted to his sparse kitchen to emerge with an empty tin can. Peering into the tank, used for collecting rainwater, he could count the scratches on its craggy bottom. If the clouds hanging over the peaks glided away that night, he would rush to the river the next morning to fill up the buckets and cans. As he retreated to the kitchen with the filled can, Ankur's face flashed, creased with pain and indignation; the child's anguished words echoed against the stone walls of his empty house.

*

Trishulpani was stowing fresh straw in the mangers when Ankur bounced into his cowshed. The farmer, who had studied till the tenth standard, was reminded of his own exuberance before the vacations.

"Amma has agreed to stay here for a week." Ankur's delight was palpable as he waved a postcard in front of Trishulpani's face.

Initially, Ankur's mother had planned to visit Roopar village only to escort him back to Chennai for the summer holidays; they were supposed to leave by the next train. Yielding to her son's ardent wish, she postponed their return journey by seven days. So long, she had been the one introducing him to new places, acquainting him with uncommon sounds and ushering him through the array of amazing sights. The chance of a role reversal prompted his spirits to leap across the abyss of the impending month-long absence of his friends, who had steered him far ahead of the day he had wept behind the cover of poplars.

There were no mobile towers in Roopar village. The children's parents could call the landline in the residential school in case of any emergencies. At other times, as per the rules, the children would communicate with their families only through letters. It was through Ankur's letters that his mother Selvi got familiarised with Trishulpani much before her arrival.

The sky was as clear as a pair of regularly used field glasses. Sleep still glued Selvi's eyes when the train chugged into the quiet station. A hired SUV dropped her in front of the high boundary walls of the boarding school. She signed her name in the security register and walked through the gates.

Selvi was ambling towards a pool of tepid sunlight that immersed the hedges around the rose beds, when Ankur spotted her from the balcony and skipped down the hostel stairs. She yanked off her woollen cap, revealing a voluminous bun and glanced ahead to find her son darting towards her.

Both mother and son grinned widely, their eyes flooded with an overwhelming happiness; she bent down and flung her arms around him.

"Aren't you feeling cold with no warm clothes on?" she asked, ruffling his frizzy hair.

"Mom, this is summer!" Ankur, who was clad in a cotton T-shirt and a pair of jeans, reminded her. Selvi wondered how he would react to the scorching heat of Chennai, now that he had gotten accustomed to the hilly climes.

As Ankur turned around to lead her to the hostel, he spotted Trishulpani on his bicycle several yards ahead.

"Trishulpani," the boy called after him. At the same time, he noticed a young man in a pink shirt emerge from an outhouse behind the clump of poplars.

The farmer reversed his bicycle and pedalled towards the boy and his mother. Alighting from his two-wheeler, he parked it against the white trunk of a birch. When they were close enough to make eye contact, Selvi looked straight at him and greeted him with a warm smile. An unsettling sense of confusion lingered around Trishulpani's otherwise amiable expression as he responded to her gesture. Selvi's large, limpid eyes spotted the dents in his forced smile like water finds leaks in a boat. He shifted his gaze to her luggage, which he intended to carry till the hostel door.

"I guess you heard what my in-laws accuse me of."

Before the embarrassed Trishulpani could mumble an incoherent reply, she smiled again and said, "It does not matter what you think of me. We don't know each other. But I like to think of you as a caring and large-hearted man since that's just the way my son sees you. By the way, I'm Selvi, a professor of botany."

It might have been her forthright manner or the fact that there was something common in their professions that extracted a broader smile from Trishulpani this time.

"Since plants interest you ma'am, please come to my garden some time. Besides potatoes, which I grow for a living, I also have a few fruit trees, some medicinal herbs and a couple of flowering shrubs."

"Sure, I will come with my son this evening. And please call me Selvi."

The young man in the pink shirt, whom she hadn't noticed till then, cleared his throat to speak.

"Tamang *ji* has asked me to take you to your room," he said, before lifting Selvi's luggage and gesturing to her to follow.

Trishulpani accompanied the young man, Selvi and Ankur till the birch tree where he had parked his bicycle. Before turning away to mount his vehicle, he said with a smile that appeared genuine — a smile accompanied by the brightening of his eyes, "So meet you in the evening."

The hostel had a few spare rooms, which were rented to the students' guardians during their visits. Selvi, staying in one such room, remained seated in a straight-backed, armless chair for several hours each day, checking answer sheets from the exams that had just ended. The deadline for submitting the mark sheets was such that she could not afford to keep them all piled up till she returned to Chennai.

At the insistence of both the mother and son, Trishulpani would accompany them during their strolls around the village. They would watch the sun disappear in the crook of the snow mountains from the spotless premises of a fifteenth century temple or from the mineral streaked boulders on the bank of river Kanga. Another favourite spot was the Moonpoong Lake. The sunrays toppled over the pointed peaks, soaked the cottony clouds, patched the loose boulders and striated the pine forests that were, otherwise, penetrated only by the sways of chill and drones of camouflaged insects. The semi-round mountain across the lake would turn aglow as a hand closely cupping a diminishing flame.

Not too long ago, beauty used to sadden Selvi. Rumbling clouds would blotch her thoughts, lush forests would seclude her from whatever sense of joy that might have come her way, the churning sea would capsize her resolve to move on and the picturesque hills would tire her. Sleep would elude her as memories would come creeping between her body and the soft surface of the bed. Hunger had no room as she continued to feel bloated with the disappointing outcome of her choices.

Bit by bit, she had been able to disentangle the melancholic evenings and fling them into the waves striking upon the Marina beach in Chennai.

On the second day of Selvi's stay, in the course of their walk, Trishulpani halted in front of a thatched roofed hut. "Munna became a grandfather today. Let's meet the little one," he suggested.

"Munna? You mean the man we met at the temple?" Selvi recalled the farmer tip-toeing up to a bald man who was mopping the temple premises and addressing him as 'Munna.'

"Yes, he is the temple sweeper."

Trishulpani's feet were already on the threshold when she clutched at his *kurta*. Drawing her hand back immediately as he turned to face her, she said with her eyes lowered, "I don't know him, nor does my son. How can we barge in? Won't they feel uncomfortable?"

"Not at all," replied the farmer with a throaty laugh. "They will be delighted if you visit," he assured.

Munna's wife was cradling their new-born grandson, who was as white as the snow on Nanda Devi and peered at Selvi with his tiny red eyes. Keenly observing the baby, Ankur itched to touch his soft cheeks and stroke his puny limbs. Splayed on a string cot, the boy's mother was still in a stupor resulting from the pain and exhaustion of labour. Neither the baby's father nor his grandparents bore any semblance of joy on their faces and they were muttering something in their local dialect. Selvi settled down on an old rug beside Trishulpani and slurped the glassful of rhododendron juice offered to her. Then she took out a crisp note from her purse, rolled it and tucked it between the thumb and forefinger of the baby's grandmother. Before she or her husband could utter a word in protest, she requested, "Please accept it as an aunt's blessing for her little nephew and buy him new clothes on my behalf."

Once they were at a considerable distance from the hut, Trishulpani confided in Selvi, "Munna believes that a curse had fallen on his grandson because he did not scrub the temple floors last Saturday. There was a severe pain in his joints."

"Why? Because of the way he looks?" Selvi rolled her eyes heavenwards and let out a deep sigh, wondering how to politely contradict such an utterly ridiculous line of reasoning.

Trishulpani nodded. Fuzzy clouds hovered over the tips of pine trees. The green slopes were sporadically speckled by red cherries, white pear bloom and purple orchids, and interspersed by frisky streams that babbled under the bridges hyphenating the tortuous road.

"He is an albino. This condition is also found in plants and animals. Please tell your friend that most albino humans live perfectly normal lives."

"I'll tell him, but I'm not sure whether he'll be convinced."

"Haven't you seen or heard about an albino before?"

"Now that you mention it, I think I've read about it in my school textbook. But I've never seen one. There's none like that in Roopar." They hastily moved towards the slope on their right, almost grazing against the rugged rocks as an army jeep roared past.

"Why do they have such skin and eye colour?"

"They lack melanin, the thing that gives colour to the skin, hair and eyes."

Ankur was a little ahead of Trishulpani and Selvi, trying to imitate the chirping of the birds soaring past the clouds before swooping down to their nests. They had almost reached the school gates when the farmer spoke again, "Tell me about the white plants."

"White plants? Oh, you mean the albino plants? For them albinism is fatal most of the time, unlike in human beings as the green colour of leaves is necessary to 'cook' their food. However, there are albino redwood trees that have not only survived but grown to be sixty-six feet tall."

"How?"

"It so happens that the redwood trees grow in circles from a common stump. It is through this stump that the albino trees draw 'food' from the others in its group."

Captivated by a distinct bird song, Selvi took a peek between the sal trees curtaining a steep slope: a bird with a blue plumage was knitting coarse, dry grasses into a shallow cup like nest.

"That's a blue rock thrush," Trishulpani pointed. Engrossed in watching the bird, Selvi was a little startled on finding herself standing so close to him.

Ankur dashed through the gates towards Mr Tamang's pet — Meghlu, a furry dog of unknown pedigree. On noticing his human playmate, he waved his tail so vigorously that it seemed it would fly off.

The week was almost over. The demise of each day was not like the crumbling of a dry flower, but rather, the release of an imprisoned bird that flew away to live somewhere else, far away from the cage of the calendar — the grid of pre-arranged dates. On her last day in the mountains, Selvi put aside the answer sheets and looked out at the sunshine split by the timeless woods into millions of rays and reassembled over the tranquil lake waters. Ankur was happily preoccupied that morning. As all the other boys had left for their hometowns, he had the special privilege of assisting his art and crafts teacher in preparing charts, which would be used for teaching when the school reopened. Selvi tripped to Trishulpani's garden alone. The farmer was so wrapped up in his work he did not hear the grate of her shoes against the pebbles. It was only when he inhaled a scent, which differed from the fragrances of the flowers he grew, that he glanced up to see her framed by the arching branches of two copiously leafed almond trees.

"No luck with the seed?" she asked.

"Not yet." Trishulpani shrugged. Selvi's student had gifted her a handful of seeds which neither of them could identify. She had planted them at various spots including her rooftop garden, the patch of earth in front of her college and in her maternal uncle's farmhouse premises. But none of them had yielded so far. Only one seed remained when she arrived in Roopar. When she told the farmer about the seed, he wanted to sow it in his potato field. "It'll never grow into a sapling if you don't sow it. It's best to give it a try," he reasoned.

"Ankur has been prodding me to make a trip to Baharban," said Selvi.

"But you must set out right now," Trishulpani stressed. "You can't go there after sunset. There are no settlements. It's from Baharban that nature spreads itself to the permanently snow-clad peaks, uninterrupted by humans," he explained.

"Yes, Ankur told me so. I'm on my way to the bus-stop."

"Alone?"

"Yes, Ankur told me which bus to board."

After several minutes of silence, Trishulpani summoned his voice, "Can I come with you?"

The delicate enunciation of the words ensured her it was not just an offer made of rigid politeness.

"Of course, you can. You remain so busy that I was scared to ask," she replied with a tinkling laugh.

The potato field was rippling with green leaves and purple flowers. After two weeks harvesting would begin.

"I better not water them today," Trishulpani remarked, contemplating the cloudy sky.

"Yes, excess water is not good for potatoes," Selvi agreed, unmindfully caressing her cheeks with the wavy petals of a white musk rose she had picked up.

*

Alighting from the bus at Baharban, Selvi stood spellbound, imbibing the magnificence unfurled before her. At that moment all she felt like doing for the rest of her life was gaze at the bluish grey clouds cuddling the mountains and the pearly snow strung across the stark branches of trees. Numerous rapids mingled with the river streaking through the valley, striating the blue-green water with white flecks of current.

A man stumbling along with a bag full of camera equipment accidentally shoved against Selvi. Instantly, Trishulpani secured her fingers between his, so she would not trip and hurt herself against the sharp-edged rocks. The lines on their knuckles rippled like the water before he released her, on noticing the amateur photographer waddle away in the direction of the river. Across the water, bulbous wild flowers draped the undulating hills in shades of scarlet and yellow. The blossoms drooped over each other or raised themselves to sway and converse with the mellow sun.

The loud chatter of some tourists who disembarked from the same bus broke Selvi's trance.

"Let's follow the stream," she said to Trishulpani and stepped on a large, flat rock by the water. Treading the slippery rocks with caution, she reached a gnarled tree that had bent over the water, dipping its forked branches in the shoaling current. She glanced back and found her companion several feet behind, answering to the queries posed by a large gang of youngsters who had sprawled themselves on the bank. She lifted her leg high, crossed the trunk and from there onwards she picked up speed, almost bounding across the boulders. More than a decade ago, she and Tanuj had skipped from rock to rock along a gurgling stream in the wee hours of morning, untouched by fatigue despite a long night of lovemaking. They had broken into a run, throwing caution to the winds and somehow missed not even a single step.

"Aaa." A sound escaped from her lips before she managed to fling her arms and grab a huge rock to prevent herself from falling.

"Are you all right?" Trishulpani called out, hurrying towards her.

"Sure." She turned and smiled, brushing off her jeans; her heart throbbed loudly within, still recuperating from the shock of an impending injury. Her elbow had gotten scraped during the sudden embrace with the rock and she guessed her forefinger would continue to tingle for days, but even then, she was relieved to have slipped from the relentless coils of memories.

Trishulpani knew the area well, having jaunted to Baharban with his friends many times on foot in his childhood. A few metres ahead, the slope was not too steep and they could clamber up to a large boulder, surrounded by the unknown wild flowers and amply shaded by the statuesque rhododendron trees.

The incessant rain at night, leaped off at the broken edge of Trishulpani's sleep, spawning a waterfall down his mottled, semi-conscious musings. Years came splashing upon him and his wife's face appeared, freckled by the lines of water, depicting what she would have looked like had she lived longer. The darkness within his room, something to which he had grown accustomed, suddenly seemed unbearable. He reached for the kerosene, but the lightness of the container surprised him. As he brought it close to his eyes, he discovered that it had leaked and there was not a drop of oil left in it.

The blanket, though musty with age, protected him from the chill seeping through the cracked windows. But since he was not at ease with his face shrouded, he could not escape the rain's scent that perplexed him with its familiarity. He wondered in the morning how long he had stayed awake before drifting off into a dream where he saw himself roam about in his own garden, repeating after Selvi the names of plants and trees as if he was hearing them for the first time.

*

"Be careful, the ground is too slippery," Trishulpani warned, hearing Selvi at his gate. His eyes darted back and forth from his potato plants to her and she guessed he was impatient to show her something. He led her to a portion of his cultivable patch, across slimy mud and treacherous rocks, gripping her by the arm.

"Look at this." He parted a few potato plants to reveal a couple of light green leaves, unlike those of potatoes.

"Is this where you sowed the seed?" she asked, slightly gaping in disbelief.

"Yes," he replied and scratched his chin, wondering at the emotions bubbling within her.

Selvi bent over the tiny sapling, drew the tip of her forefinger along the outline of one of its bifurcated leaves, stroked the firm, erect stem, and then stepped back to gaze at it.

"You said it might grow in your potato patch. Was it just a guess?"

"There was a reason. When you told me about the albino redwood, I wondered whether this seed belonged to a parasitic plant too. The pots where you sowed had no other plants. When you sowed in your garden, you might have chosen a bare patch. Even if there were plants nearby, they were not suitable targets. Its root failed to penetrate the root of another. So, the seed perished before the stem could bore through the soil. But I felt that the potatoes being fleshy roots would be the ideal companions for our stranger," Trishulpani explained. His full lips broke into a satisfied smile and the sunlight caressed the contours of his unshaven, strong jawed face.

"When will you leave for the station?" He had to coerce his lips to shape the words.

"The road got blocked by a landslide last night. The gardener told me first and then the others confirmed," Selvi said slowly as if allowing some time for each word to register in his mind.

Despite the salving sense of relief breezing through Trishulpani, he exclaimed, "That must be terrible for you! You won't be able to leave before next Monday at least."

"That might not be such a bad thing," she said in a calm voice.

For the first time, without the slightest tinge of hesitation Trishulpani bored into her eyes. His own reflections on her pupils appeared to be at peace under the shade of her long eyelashes.

"Nowhere else on earth, would I have loved to be stranded," she revealed, and let out one of her ringing laughs that had become as familiar to him as the chirping of a blue rock thrush.

The New Law

Despite the law concerning the minimum amount of space to be left around a residential building, Naresh and Anil's houses seemed to touch each other like two heads engaged in transferring lice. Their kitchen windows were so close that Naresh's wife Bani could see the spices Anil's spouse Shruti was sprinkling on her curry. "Did you listen to the news this morning?" Bani poked her head out of the window to ask Shruti while skinning the garlic cloves.

Bishu, the teacher, gawked while unfolding the newspaper on the way to his school. Mukul, an engineer, found his co-passengers in the shuttle-car lean over to glimpse the e-paper in his smart phone. Employees of a construction firm huddled in front of the TV in the canteen: irrespective of designations, the uniformity in their interest made up for the unevenness of roads they had built.

"In view of the fact that everyone steals, theft has been made legal based on the universal truth that whatever is acceptable to everyone in the society is beneficial for its progress. Under the ambit of the new law, stealing of money, stealing of property and also stealing of women are allowed. Although the last clause has met with several rounds of protests from both women and men, the fact remains that equating women with property is again acceptable in our society. Abiding by the above-mentioned truth, the attitude of the majority should be recognized by the law in a democratic country such as ours."

The soon-to-retire clerk Sudhir's eyes popped out as the news went on. "The person from whom something has been stolen can retaliate by stealing from others, introducing a system of justice unparalleled in history. This will also diminish the burden of courts reeling under the load of too many cases."

In the following months, even the timidest organisations, which were used to trickling public money into their pockets in the manner of carrying sand that escapes into shoes while walking along a beach, felt no hesitation in scooping in a bucketful. Sanctioned structures for public utility like schools, colleges, hospitals, bridges and flyovers remained on paper. Huge residential blocks came up anywhere and everywhere — clogging ponds, crushing agricultural fields, seizing sold plots, cordoning off playgrounds and evicting the ghosts from the crematoriums as land, both public and private, fell under the category 'property' and thus could be stolen.

*

Clutching his baton, the guard surreptitiously advanced towards a young man, who was standing suspiciously close to the exit door with a pair of blue-tinted designer sunglasses. He raised the stick as the youth took another step in the direction of the door, but lowered it at once when the latter turned to the cash counter. The security guard, who was sweating profusely despite the air-conditioning, after his fifty-second tussle in the day, heaved with relief and retreated to his position by the racks. His friend, who did the rounds in another shop in the same mall, was least impressed on hearing the number of men he had cornered that day: he had himself wrestled with seventy-seven.

Despite goods flying off faster from the shelves, the desired profit eluded the malls. They were compelled to spend a fortune in hiring an army of burly guards to follow every customer around. If someone attempted theft, the item had to be snatched from him or her before he or she could leave the shop. The new law did not give scope to the shop owners to recover their stolen goods with police help.

A bill was underway demanding legalisation of murder, which was defined as the stealing of an individual's right to life. Most opposed such a law, wishing to lead prosperous and comfortable lives, fuelled by a steady flow of stolen money. But a handful of powerful men who pushed for this bill considered themselves too well protected to be bumped off.

*

"Nice one," drawled the man in a yellow shirt, pointing at a young couple cooing under a lamp post. "We can beat up that dandy and go for her. Now that the law..." He left the rest unsaid and jumped down from the parked bike where he had been sitting for the last half an hour.

"No no..." The man in the red shirt threw his hands forward and tried to pull him back.

"But she's a bad woman," his friend argued, taking another step and eyeing the woman with menace.

"How do you know?"

"She's out at night with a boyfriend," the man in the yellow shirt replied with the conviction of quoting a passage from a holy book.

The man in the red shirt threw a glance at the couple. The woman was basking in the attention of her lover. He knew his companion did not care for her predicament. The only deterrents could be a threat to his freedom and a backlash on his family.

"But the law doesn't permit us to rape bad women. We are from good families. We don't want trouble. Do we?" he reasoned, striding ahead to turn and stand in his way.

"Are you sure the law doesn't allow it?" The drunk paused and gazed blankly at the street.

"No, it doesn't." The other man shook his head vigorously, as if to make his point.

"Ohhh." The man in the yellow shirt staggered towards the bike, smacking his lips in disappointment. He was not the only person confused by the third clause. The phrase "stealing of women" left much ambiguity. While most agreed that it did not convey the legalisation of rape as that was equivalent to stealing a woman's right to her body, which was not permitted under the current law, a section of people, including politicians, campaigned for the right to rape saying, "Boys will be boys." Since rape was not yet permitted by the state, the law-abiding men refrained from stealing women. One way the law came into use was through an interpretation that legitimized the binding of women as slaves. So, whenever an institution woke up to the fact that it was falling short of staff, but could not afford more, they abducted women professionals from other organisations to force them to work without payment.

*

In the good old days, pilferage was a sport like golf, where only the experts scored by hitting the ball into the loopholes of laws. The current reality having made such skills redundant, the old practitioners suffered much anguish as there was no longer any pride in being corrupt. However, skills and innovativeness could still be displayed in the manner of protecting one's own wealth.

*

'Best Shine Tutorial,' proclaimed the signboard above the netted ground floor windows of a cream coloured, four-storied building. Leaning back in his chair as he waited for all his students to arrive, the tutor was surprised to spot his professor-friend queue up at the ATM across the street. In fact, he was taken aback by the length of the queue since many people had closed their bank accounts in favour of hiding their wealth in their own homes. They no longer trusted any other person or organisation as a result of the privileges granted by the law.

The tutor was halfway through his lesson when he saw his friend return, a smile of contentment lingering on his lips.

"Anand, here's your book. I'm sorry that I forgot to return it the last time we met," he said, hurrying out of the classroom.

"No problem," Anand said, halting at the door of the coaching centre.

"How come you still keep money in the bank?" the tutor asked the professor.

"The college still deposits my salary over there," replied Anand.

"One good thing about having a bank account is that you can transact at the click of a mouse. Suppose you need to send money to a relative who has suddenly fallen ill. All you have to do is…"

"No, Tarun, not so easy," said the professor and explained the new strategies adopted by the banks. To enhance their profit under such hostile circumstances, they blocked the option of interbank transfer so that the payer was forced to open an account in the same bank as the payee. However, in a bid to attract super-successful clients — those who had made the most under the current law — wire transfer was allowed for an amount equal to or exceeding ten crores. In fact, the banks laid a lot of emphasis on facilitating such transfers in the minimum time possible and were rated based on their ability to do so.

"So where do you keep your money? Within double layered clothes or in a secret hole behind the photo frame or beneath the false floor like they show in the movies?" Anand asked Tarun, partly in jest as he did not expect him to reply.

"I've an original method." Tarun grinned but refrained from revealing what it was. He had hidden a wad of two-thousand rupee notes within a roll of toilet paper. All he had to do was replenish the roll before it became too thin to expose the money concealed within. "But since you are my close friend, let me confide in you. I'm contemplating on opening a fixed deposit account. I'll need the maturity amount to see my son through college... I'm not too good at stealing, you know..."

Before he could complete his sentence, his attention was grabbed by the sight of a robust man hauling an iron safe onto an open truck.

With many people opting to store money in password protected iron safes, the banks had to cut down on their number of employees to stay afloat. The government fulfilled its promise of looking into the grievances of all sections of the population. It gave exclusive permits to the bank employees, who had lost their jobs due to the sudden staff reduction, to install such safes in people's homes.

*

"You mean there will be no Falcon Wings games this year?" The sports minister snapped at Mr Khelnaru, an MP and the head of the Falcon Wings Games Organising Committee.

In response, the latter smiled sheepishly. "You knew this all along, sir. I mean no offence but...but...you also got your share."

"That doesn't mean there will be no games," the sports minister thundered. "After so many years our country is getting the chance to host such an important sporting event. Don't you have even a pinch of patriotism in you?"

Mr Khelnaru sighed as if hurt by the accusation. "I'm the most patriotic person you will ever meet, sir," he claimed. "I surround my entire house with national flags during cricket matches..."

The senior politician straightened up in his chair, bored into the MP's eyes and asked in a cold, grave voice, "Where's the money?"

The FWGOC head, too, looked straight at the minister and replied, "Since the law doesn't recognise my deeds as a crime, I've no reason to hide anything from you. There are numerous things to spend on. I'd already taken my parents around the world but I owed the same to my in-laws. There were things I'd dreamt of buying. The money is spent but there's still something left...to own."

The sports minister noticed the FWGOC chief leering at his diamond studded wristwatch and took refuge in the fact that murder was still illegal. He shifted uncomfortably in his chair for a while before rising to his feet. "I've another meeting to attend. This discussion is not over. We will resume it in the evening."

*

Although there was no fear of arrest on admitting one's corrupt deeds, men and women with party associations would refrain from it as elections had to be won and the party image could not be tarnished.

"The obliteration of poverty is more important than the hosting of Falcon Wings Games. How can we rejoice at a sporting victory when our fellow countrymen are writhing in hunger? Every time you feel disappointed that the FW Games could not be held, think about the lives saved with that money," Mr Khelnaru spoke through the TV screen.

"Bulls**t!" The word shot out like a bullet from Aparajita's lips. Watching the news with her husband Pawan, she seethed with indignation. The last few months had exasperated her to the point of madness and she was often dragged back to the fateful day when it all began.

It was a Monday like any other, when she was rooted to her chamber, barely able to take a sip of water as the incessant flow of patients kept her shuttling between her chair and the clinical bed.

"Next," she called out, studying the latest prescription of the patient in waiting, as the severely arthritic man left leaning on his son's shoulder for support.

Startled by the heavy thud of boots since Aparajita was expecting to hear the nimble footsteps of a sixteen-year-old girl, she glanced up and let out a piercing scream. A bullet shot sent the patients scampering away or compelled them to hide under the seats or lie flat on the floor and shield their heads with their bags. Not one to yield to her attacker without a fight, the doctor jabbed him in his ribs with her elbow, but the man with black gloves pushed her to the chair, clamped the chloroform-soaked napkin on her nose, and released his grip only after she had slumped to one side.

The medical practitioner, in whose chamber Aparajita woke up, ordered her to substitute for him during the lengthy vacation he intended to take. He dragged her to the court for her refusal to abide by his impositions. But she held her position saying if she could be stolen by another person, she also had the right to steal herself from him. This line of argument caused a lot of flutter as the law did not mention who were the ones permitted to steal women; nowhere was it mentioned that the woman could not steal herself. Though impressed by Aparajita's sense of logic, the judge hesitated to rule the verdict in her favour. With outspoken women at home, his foresight did not fail to show him what problems he would find himself in, if women stole themselves from others. So the lawyer hired by Aparajita's opponent got the chance to conjure counter arguments and the case continued. That she was in the first trimester of her pregnancy did not bring her any respite from the summons of the court.

The news shifted from the cancellation of the Falcon Wings Games to a terrorist attack in the Middle East.

"Isn't this Khelnaru the fellow who had tried to bully you into issuing a false medical certificate for his son so he could bunk college for two months?" Pawan turned to his wife.

"Yes, he's the one," she replied, her eyes blazing.

"I wonder why he asked you for it instead of approaching his family physician, when he had never consulted you for any treatment," Pawan said and clicked his tongue on failing to catch the headline that flashed across the bottom of the TV screen.

"I think his son had already duped his college several times using certificates signed by the doctors they visit," Aparajita said with a shrug.

"You're probably right. He was after you for your spotless reputation," Pawan said. "Do you still have his number?" he asked after a pause.

"He used to call me from different numbers," she recalled.

"Do you have them saved?"

"Yes, I'd saved all of them so I know it's him if a call comes from any of them. But hey…why do you ask? Are you planning to outsmart him?" Aparajita rolled her eyes with incredulity.

"I've got an idea. Too vague to tell you now…"

"But this sort of people keep on changing their personal phone numbers," she reminded.

"This sort of people used to change their numbers when they had something to fear from the law. Now where's the need?" he pointed.

As an advertisement barged into the television screen, Pawan's gaze drifted to the shelf and the trophy standing on it, golden with an engraving of a tiger. He recalled that he had not polished his trophies since Aparajita's court cases began and got up from his sofa to search for a loose piece of fabric.

Pawan walked to the shelf with the cloth and a bowl of warm soap water. He clutched one of the curved handles of the trophy and tilted it at such an angle so he could have a better look at the stains and the specks of dust. Observing his face reflected on the metal surface, he wondered how much he still resembled the young man who had brought the trophy home, jubilant at scoring the final goal in a closely fought match.

The budding footballer sprinted to the door and pressed the calling bell while imagining the proud faces of his parents who had been following the match on radio. It was his father who opened the door. He grinned and said, "Freshen up quickly. We have a special menu for lunch today to celebrate your win."

After a refreshing shower, Pawan, clad in clean white shirt and brown slacks, smelling of soap and shampoo, sat down at the dining table, longing to be heaped with praises by his parents. Even the day before, they had remarked that he should curtail the number of hours he spent on sports to devote more time to his studies.

"The way you played today I think we no longer have to worry about your career," his mother started.

Pawan smiled, delighted that he had succeeded in bringing about this change in his parents.

"With a little more luck, I'm sure you'll make it to the state team and get a good job through the sports quota," his father completed.

Choking on the grilled shrimp, Pawan continued to cough; his father leaned sideways from his chair to pat him on the back and his mother came hurrying with a glass of water. Even after the retching had stopped, he gasped for breath, and with a bewildered expression, he looked around. The laminated photos from his childhood glared at him and the fan spun noisily over his head. It became as difficult for him to swallow the tasty food on his plate as the fact that football — his life and love — was just a means of securing a well-paid job for the people who mattered the most to him.

Somewhere along the line, Pawan had let his family's wish take over his own like a raw clay figure slowly melting into its surroundings. He discovered that he was adept at software programming when he enrolled for a computer course to improve his job prospects. However, on being selected for a bank job he felt it would be unwise to turn it down, especially since he wished to marry Aparajita right away.

Pawan had eluded the pink slip so far but the way his friends were shown the door left him with little hope for the future. If job insecurity had increased, so had the workload. The bank had relinquished the service of the software company that had developed its online portals. Whenever the banking software needed enhancement, the management turned to its own employees — the ones possessing programming skills. The most dependable among them was Pawan. The extra responsibility, however, did not bring in any additional remuneration or acknowledgement. Even while juggling with his job, his wife's court cases and learning about the iron safe trade — something he would have to do eventually — he had been looking forward to the FW Games.

The bank employee couldn't sleep much that night as scattered ideas finally amassed towards his objective like strangers flocking around a common favourite. Next to him, his wife thrashed about in her sleep, crumpling the *chaddar* which had gotten pushed to her feet. He slipped his hand under the hem of the mosquito net and reached for the switchboard. Then switching on the air-conditioner, he crawled closer to his wife, drew delicate patterns on her glowing skin, still thinking and working out the details of his next course of action.

Out of the ten cell phone numbers saved by Aparajita, two went on ringing. Seven were picked up by people who claimed not to know the FWGOC chief. The tenth one was picked up by a girl, probably a teenager, who was innocent enough to admit that she was related to him. Still it took a little prodding before she agreed to share his number with Pawan.

"At least, the first hurdle is crossed." Aparajita sighed with relief.

Before calling the FWGOC chief Pawan took a moment to let all other thoughts loosen their grip off him. His eyes glowed with resolve and his lips were taut with the precision of the words gathered behind. His wife sat on the next sofa, quiet but partaking in his controlled tension.

Tring...tring...tring. The phone rang thrice before it was picked up.

"Am I speaking to Mr Khelnaru?" Pawan's tone was crisp and business-like.

"Yes."

"Sir, I'm Pawan Dhupi, an employee of ULMBI. All the leading companies operating in this country have got their employees' salary accounts opened in our bank." Taking a brief pause, he moved straight to the point. "I can share with you the salary account credentials of ten million professionals for a fee."

"Why me?"

"I am looking for a distinguished personality among our oldest customers." Pawan had been thorough with his homework. Mr Khelnaru had maintained an account in ULMBI since his days as an electrical engineer in Goodman & Co.

"I see," came the response.

It was a good sign that Mr Khelnaru had not cut off the call. "What is your fee?" he asked.

"The average monthly salary deposited in each account of our bank is thirty-five thousand onwards. I ask for only one hundred crores out of the minimum three and a half thousand crores you will be making."

"How can I be sure you have the passwords of ten million people?"

Though Mr Khelnaru's tone hinted at his scepticism, the long pause before his query showed that he was contemplating the offer. His thoughts might have been swaying between "yes" and "no" like a swing, and it was this swing Pawan needed to leap upon to cross over the chasm of failure, to his goal.

"We can meet for a demo."

"I cannot allow strangers in my house." The FWGOC chief grunted.

"But the demo cannot take place unless I meet you. I don't mind being stripped and searched by your guards."

"Okay, I'll think about it and call you if I'm interested."

With a jolt, Pawan realised that he needed to take the conversation a little further to gain Mr Khelnaru's trust.

"Just one-minute sir, my demo is simple and straightforward. I'll bring along the login credentials of ten million people. You can select from them at random and log into their accounts to check whether the passwords provided by me are genuine. You can also transfer the money from those accounts into your own account in ULMBI. Only if you are satisfied, you can buy the passwords from me and transfer as much as you want."

"We'll see."

"Take your time, sir. In any case, I'll be very busy for the rest of the month. If you decide to be my customer, I'll suggest that we meet on the last day of this month when all the salary accounts will be full."

The same evening, Pawan drove halfway across the city to drop Aparajita to her parents' home. After a hearty dinner rustled up by his in-laws, he bade them goodbye and bent down to lace up his shoes.

"You still haven't told me what exactly you are doing to that Khelnaru fellow. But I wish you success," she whispered while brushing off a shiny bit of paper from his shirt. Her parents were standing a few feet away.

"Thanks for believing in me. Take care of yourself and the baby," he said, hugging her lightly so as not to press her stomach.

As the alarm rang in the morning Pawan opened his eyes and instantly recalled the conversation with the FWGOC chief. He hurried through his ablutions at record speed, dashed to his desk, shifted the documents cluttering it and switched on the office laptop. It was the 4th of July and Pawan knew he had only twenty-eight days to prepare for the demo and the aftermath.

The weeks were such that Pawan hardly realised when the days stretched and overstretched and finally tore away for the night. The soap would often slip off his fingers and the razor would scar his cheeks. He would upturn a bucketful of water over himself to bathe, wipe his body with two strokes of the towel and wriggle into his formals. Then he would heft the laptop into a bag, sling it over his shoulder and stride past his garage to hail an auto to reach the metro station. Given the uncertain job situation and the fact that a new family member was on its way, he could no longer afford to commute to his workplace by car. After gobbling down his dinner in the office canteen, he would return home by the same route, wash himself and immediately turn to the laptop. With Aparajita away and the task he had embarked upon, his life was so much shorn of domestic bliss that, sometimes, he would be surprised even by the mention of his impending fatherhood.

The thirtieth of July could have been the longest day in the bank employee's life but it sped by, with Pawan just managing to apply the last dash of polish to the arrangements.

*

Mr Khelnaru was sitting in a rotating chair with his back to a curtained window. He raised his eyes from his desk to greet Pawan. The bank employee cast a glance around the room. It included two upholstered double sofas, a glass topped table and a bookshelf. Then he slipped his hand into a flap of his leather bag and fished out a scroll of paper. Unrolling it, he stretched it across the desk. He kept half of it pressed to the wooden surface by weighing it down with a glass paperweight while the other half remained dangling along the side.

"My God, Mr Dhupi! Why didn't you email me a soft copy?"

Pawan ignored the FW chief's reaction. He glanced across the other table and spotted a porcelain ashtray and a fat magazine on current affairs.

"Why do you want to sell the passwords for a hundred crores when you could have kept the entire amount of three and a half thousand crores or more for yourself?"

"I'm not too good at saving or investing money. I prefer a running income and I think the password selling business can ensure one for me," Pawan replied to the question he had expected.

Mr Khelnaru selected a user from those listed on the paper, logged into her account and added himself as a beneficiary through his account in ULMBI bank.

"Are you sure she'll not receive an SMS alert?" he asked.

"I've disabled all alerts," Pawan assured.

"Won't she receive an OTP?"

"I've blocked all that."

"How long will it take for my beneficiary request to be activated? Half an hour?"

"Yes," the bank official confirmed.

Mr Khelnaru continued to choose random users and logged in after typing the credentials provided in the sheet. Pawan took his permission to browse through the bookshelf, but found his thoughts drifting elsewhere every time he cradled a book that caught his interest. He assured himself that his arrangements were fool proof; that nothing could go wrong. But even then, he experienced the pangs of nervousness — similar to the anxiety one has to brave before an operation despite having faith in the physician's skills.

Pawan hoped that the FWGOC chief did not hear his heartbeat when he conducted the first transaction. His fingers remained crossed even after the message "Transaction completed successfully" appeared, and he breathed with relief only when Mr Khelnaru's account showed the enhanced amount correctly. The politician verified the transfer from the other accounts where he had added himself as a beneficiary, and the final balance did not disappoint him every time he checked. Pawan felt more and more relaxed and it reflected in his posture as he receded further into the comfortable lap of the sofa.

When Mr Khelnaru was done with it, he lowered the screen of his laptop and gazed at the beige coloured walls for a few moments before boring into Pawan's eyes.

"You must have got Munni's number from your wife. I think I had used that number to call when I needed a little help from her."

Pawan was least surprised. Twenty-eight days were enough for Mr Khelnaru to carry out his research on Pawan, at least to find out the identity of his wife.

"If I can steal passwords from the bank, why can't I jot down the numbers from my wife's mobile phone?"

"That's true. Don't mind me saying but isn't she one of those childish, righteous types? How did she end up with you?" Mr Khelnaru grinned while taking out a cigarette from its packet and looked around for the lighter. Since he could not find it, Pawan let him use his own.

"She knows nothing about me. Her aunt is my mother's friend. She introduced us. I'm nice to her at home and she's happy with it. Can I have my lighter back?"

Pawan's client gave back the lighter.

"Can I have some water?" Pawan asked, scanning the tables and shelves for a jug or a bottle.

"Sure." The FWGOC chief passed him an aluminium flask.

"I see you are a credible crook, having stolen money from your college mess and also from the Earthquake Relief Fund in your office. In both the cases, the money never got recovered," marvelled the politician, swivelling his chair to move closer to the bank employee.

Pawan's blood had boiled at the false accusations. Ironically, his reputation was turning out to be a boon as if he was destined to deceive. He wondered how Aparajita had always trusted him, never doubted his innocence, and even in this case, she genuinely believed he was spending so much time and effort just to teach Mr Khelnaru a lesson. Unaware of the details, she was waiting patiently for Pawan to elaborate them for her at a time he deemed suitable. Though they spoke to each other over the phone and through Skype, she never prodded him to reveal the underlying brickwork of his designs.

Pawan waited for his client to speak further, but since the latter continued to scrutinise him without uttering a single word, he had no choice but to break the silence himself. "I hope you are convinced that the passwords are genuine. Now, please can I have my payment?"

"I'll give it to you next week, after I've completed transferring money from all the other accounts."

"As discussed in our last conversation over the phone you were supposed to pay me once you were satisfied with the demo."

"Why are you in such a hurry?" Mr Khelnaru's eyes narrowed.

"Password swindling is still a crime even though stealing of money isn't. Otherwise nobody would opt for net banking. I need to leave this country as soon as possible and live under a different identity."

Resting his elbows on the paper strip scribbled with the passwords, Mr Khelnaru asked, "What if I don't give it today?" His tone was so normal he could have just said, "Please drink some water."

Pawan swiftly loosened the cap off his client's flask and tipped it slightly over the edge of the paper. A little more incline would cause the water to spill out on the passwords blotching them beyond recognition.

"How can you be so sure I've a hundred crores with me?" His client's voice betrayed no panic.

"Before becoming the chief of the FWG Organizing Committee, you were part of the Save the Farmers Initiative and several projects under the Mothers and Motherland scheme. And before that, you headed the Mosquito Crushing Drive. The Spit Control Movement was also chalked and carried out by you. Since you have already paid me a compliment, I hope you will not mind if I say you made much more than the mentioned sum of money, particularly in the backdrop of our current law."

"I do not expect you to be foolish enough to think I had not decided my own fees for my involvement in these extremely cumbersome projects. But I hope you understand that the world offers a lot of pleasure to those who can spend. So what makes you believe I still have the money with me?"

"Your son is starting out in life. I'm certain that as a doting father you would like to ensure that he gets to maintain the lifestyle he has grown up with, even if the current law is revoked in the future and the basic freedom of deciding the monetary worth of one's own hard work is snatched. As an employee of ULMBI bank I also know of the foresightedness ingrained in your nature."

"How?"

"You had a salary account and a savings account in our bank during your days at Goodman & Co. Your salary was twenty thousand and you never drew over seven thousand in a month. You drew out all the money except for the hundred rupees needed to keep the account active only after you had established yourself as a politician. So, I'm sure you have a hundred crores to spare at this moment, given you will get many times the amount once all the transactions are done. And if not..." Pawan paused, picking up the magazine.

Mr Khelnaru observed the bank official with an expression that gave no peek into his thoughts. This was the moment, Pawan told himself. Before the FWGOC chief could blink, the bank employee rose to his feet, clutched the dangling end of the paper strip, drew apart the window curtains and flung out a part of the paper. As his client made a grab for the precious passwords, the former footballer blocked his advance and set the magazine on fire with his lighter. The dancing flames twisted dangerously close to his synthetic shirt.

"One more move and your guards will find me on fire. I'm sure this little piece of information will spill out from their guts in the torture chamber of the police," Pawan gritted out the words as his client's fingers inched towards the bell for summoning his security staff.

"See, I've risked everything to get these passwords. I'll not be able to step inside my workplace again nor ever get to meet my family including my unborn child. Aparajita will never accept what I've done... So, if I can't have the money right now, it's better that I die." He waved the flaming papers even closer to his body and continued, "Remember Mr Khelnaru, murder is still illegal. Your fingerprints are on this lighter and also on this paper. If I throw the paper out of the window, it will be blown away. Someone will pick it before you can find it and I'd already messaged my current location to one of my friends. The world will know you have finished me after forcing me to leak these passwords." Pawan's voice was even calmer than Mr Khelnaru's as if he was prepared to meet his end.

The FWGOC chief's placid face shrivelled in horror. He parted his lips, which had turned dry, but found himself at a loss of words. He dug into his trouser pockets to hide his trembling fingers. How could he let his chances of getting richer by around three thousand four hundred crores be spoiled by the extremely desperate man in front of him? The demo was good enough. It would take only a phone call to initiate a wire transfer. The alternative would be the death knell to his career and even freedom. Capital punishment too if the public went crazy.

*

Marching out of Mr Khelnaru's cloistered office, Pawan squinted at the bright sunlight. He hopped into a bus, located an empty seat and gazed out of the window. At a roadside tea stall, milk descended into an earthen cup through the pores of a strainer, in lines parallel to the sticks rooted in the ground around a sapling and perpendicular to the tram tracks and the strokes on the public pool water by the boys practising relay swimming – all these lines framing the picture of a way of life that remained the same irrespective of laws and their interpretations.

Reaching in his pocket to take out the bus fare, Pawan's fingers struck against Mr Khelnaru's lighter — the one he had hidden so that the politician was forced to use his.

For the last few weeks, Pawan's food habits, sleeping pattern, the pace of his movements and even the frequency of his breathing had been altered so much it seemed he was inside a spaceship, but now, the familiar sights by the street assured him he was still on his own planet. Within a few stoppages, he felt drowsy. He dozed off, with his head against the backrest of the seat in front. First, he had written a software program to create ten million fake accounts. Although the passwords were fake, the users had to be real as Mr Khelnaru might have personally known many people with accounts in ULMBI. He could have grown suspicious if any of their names were missing from Pawan's list. It had not been easy collecting all their names from the bank database. The riskiest part, however, was deploying the tampered software program. Luckily for Pawan, owing to the discontinuation of interbank transfer facility, he knew Mr Khelnaru would be compelled to transfer the money to his account in ULMBI and not in any other bank. Whenever there was a transaction from one of the false accounts to Mr Khelnaru's real account, Pawan's software program added the transferred amount to the latest balance displayed in the politician's account without actually increasing it. So, the false transaction seemed a real one. Pawan had to ensure that this piece of modified software code would affect only Mr Khelnaru's account, as identified by his customer identification number, and not impact or incorrectly depict anyone else's transactions and closing balance.

It was the call from Chetan, Pawan's best friend since his footballer days, which prevented him from missing his destination.

"I read your SMS. Setting up a non-profit organisation to support sporting talent is wonderful. But how will we get the money to provide them with the facilities they need?"

"I have the money. I'll tell you the details when I'm back home. Why don't you drop in tomorrow?" Pawan whispered with the mobile phone pressed to his lips. He would take a quick bath and drive to his in-law's house to bring his wife home.

Corn, the seasonal favourite, was being fried golden over charcoal fires in clay ovens set up on the pavements. After the long phase of nausea Aparajita had begun to enjoy her food once again. Pawan selected a medium sized maize for her out of the many laid out in a bamboo basket. He would roast it at home and sprinkle it with lemon just as she liked it.

Barricaded

Devaditya unlocked his steel almirah and took out four ornate boxes. "Your mother-in-law would have handed them to you, but unfortunately the task has fallen upon me," he said slowly, levelling out each word.

Before settling down at his desk with his files and a sheaf of printed papers he spoke again, "Have a look at them at your leisure."

Priya thanked her father-in-law and clasped the boxes to her chest. She gently put aside the pile of letters from her admirers to place her gifts on the teakwood table in her bedroom. She would probably not receive any more fan mail as she had put an end to her singing career with her marriage. But unbearable to her was the alternative — not marrying Devraj. She was as incurably romantic as the imaginary women to whom she had given voice through her love songs that became a rage across the nation. She could not help but accept the marriage proposal from the man who had "stolen her sleep" as the lyrics went, even though he had clearly explained to her the rules of his household. These were rules he was bound to despite his education from a premier institute abroad: they were ingrained in him from such an early age that he mistook their complex, roundabout justifications as the molecular structure of his genes.

The former singer unclasped the lids of the boxes, awestruck by the fine craftsmanship of their contents. She had seen nothing like them while shopping in Singapore — a trip she had gifted herself and her parents following the success of her second music album. Bejewelling herself with the set of ornaments she liked the most, she gazed into the long, oval mirror. She trailed the ruby studded gold necklace with a dainty forefinger and tinkered with the big diamond locket. She swung her head from side to side to feel the dangling earrings oscillate back and forth. As she wrung her hands in a Bharatanatyam *mudra* to admire the full effect of the bangles glinting on her wrist, a knock on the door shook her out of her reverie.

"Please wait a minute," she said, modulating her voice to be just loud enough to be heard beyond the door.

To avoid appearing like a guest in a wedding, in her own bedroom, Priya hurriedly took off the ornaments. She tucked them in her dressing-table drawer and trotted to the door, unaware that her most cherished gift of jewellery till date had been designed for the sister-in-law she had never met.

*

It was during the brief spell when the sun relinquished its heat but retained its light that Devaditya finalised his business deals. He would perch on his favourite chair under the shade of a cherry blossom, poring over the laptop placed atop a marble table. Priya would be in the kitchen, inspecting whether the saucers, washed by the maid, were gleaming enough to reflect the tiny beauty spot above her glossy lips. She had an approximate idea of the time Devaditya took to give the final click and lean back in his recliner chair. By that time, his friend Shankar would arrive, and she was expected to appear at the garden table with a tray laden with brimming tea cups, SugarFree and some munchies. Devaditya had never fancied fried snacks like *pakoras*; cheese straws were more to his taste.

Priya would have her tea alone as her father-in-law disapproved of her presence during his tête-à-tête with his former classmate. No wonder she was pleasantly surprised when he asked her to occupy his friend's chair and have tea with him.

"Shankar's daughter has come to visit him with her son and she'll be here for a month. Today, they had gone for a family picnic. Lucky Shankar." A bitter sigh cut across the trajectory of breaths exhaled by the plants congregated in his garden.

Sip by sip, the tea diminished from the cup like the rays of the sun from the sky and Priya wondered how the garden would have looked in a music video at such an enchanting hour. Her anklets tinkled as she slid her feet out of her sandals and rested them upon the smooth, circular patch of cement under the garden umbrella, which was fixed at the junction of two pebbled paths — one leading to the manicured lawn and the other to the fragrant flower beds. Beyond the strips of flowering plants, the rich brown loam peeped between lush cabbage leaves, sprays from the water hose spangled the pumpkins, tomatoes clubbed together in thin, arched branches and the deep violet brinjals closely overlooked the elongating shadows cast by the herbs. At the edge of the vegetable garden, the mango trees swayed restlessly in the pre-winter breeze, eyeing with envy the ripe guavas hanging in an adjacent cluster. But still something was amiss. A water feature? There could have been a fountain. Given the amount of space, perhaps a swimming pool would be a better idea.

"Your lawn is large enough to accommodate a swimming pool," Priya said indirectly.

"Swimming pool!" Devaditya exclaimed. She regretted saying it as her father-in-law nearly jumped out of his chair. But within seconds she noticed the mellowing of his expression and relief took over.

Why didn't this idea come to him? Or nobody proposed it before? Devaditya seethed with regret. Women in his family were discouraged from learning to swim: it was unacceptable for them to don swimming costumes. Yet Devaditya had relented following his only daughter's repeated insistence. When he was younger, he could have easily taught her swimming if there was a pool in his compound. She would have never joined the swimming club nor come across the instructor.

*

A handful of staff stepped inside the departmental store in the wee hours of morning and switched on the lights. The entire shop — from the furniture section to the menswear, from the lady's wear to the jewellery, and from the groceries to the new section for kids — reverberated with their footsteps as they surveyed the racks. They ensured that no ware was about to tumble and no item was out of line. Devaditya strutted into his shop an hour before its opening and strode through the passages between the shelves, more or less satisfied with what he saw. He pushed back a leather sofa that had come too close to the table, adjusted a shirt to rest symmetrically on the hanger and diminished the gap between two packets of corn soup. He could move faster than men half his age, owing to the daily yoga session and the discretion he made in his choice of food.

Glancing at his watch, Devaditya cantered to the front of the store. As he peered through the glass walls, he found a huge crowd thronging outside and his guards pacing back and forth to hustle them into a queue. Within a few minutes, the people who had flocked to see film star Sheetal filled up the large departmental store. Engaged in promoting an animation film for children, she had been the obvious choice for inaugurating the kids' section. The film on the nearly extinct land phones, where she had given voice to Tring Ring, a female land phone, had already generated a lot of curiosity. The crowd and the publicity were the fruits of Devraj's efforts in reaching her through the layers of PR people and managers who encircled her like the coils of a film reel.

The crowd went into a frenzy as a white Mercedes pulled into the driveway. The security guards took up their positions to avoid any possible stampede. Cell phones clicked in unison as Sheetal stepped inside the store, surrounded by a bevy of bodyguards. Though he averted the cameras, Devaditya looked elegant in his new brown suit, his angular face framed by a trim, silver beard and a pair of gold-rimmed glasses fixed firmly at the base of his high ridged nose. The actress, in her white top and blue denim skirt, posed alone for the paparazzi cameras, against the multihued backdrop of the new section named Play Turn. The youth icon also chose this occasion to mention the children who made her life special — the little boys and girls at Twinkle, an NGO she patronised.

Once Sheetal was whisked back to her car, the huge mass of people started swirling out at a leisurely pace. Many of her fans had come in large groups. The space throbbed with their collective chatter — opinions on how she looked in real life, assumptions about her personal life and the speculations triggered by the forthcoming movie trailers. Some of them stayed on to shop or window shop, soaking in the languor of the weekend. Devraj got into a discussion with the floor manager while Devaditya waited for his niece who had arrived from

Berlin. She was eager to take a stroll in his store before accompanying him for lunch.

A loud crash prompted the proprietor to swivel to his right. A boy of around seven-eight years of age had dropped a glass vase while trying to reach out for a toy from an upper rack. The vase should not have been kept among the toys. Devaditya guessed that it was the work of those perpetually broke college-goers, who fiddled with a lot of items but bought none. However, the boy would have to pay for it as excusing him might discourage others from handling the merchandise with care.

With many pairs of eyes on him, the little boy stiffened, eliciting a trickle of sympathy from Devaditya, who looked at him intently. The boy had almond eyes like the sexagenarian and his hair colour was brown rather than black like his hair used to be before it turned silver.

"Don't be afraid," Devaditya spoke to him in an exceedingly gentle manner, unintentionally using the voice he had reserved for occasions like the gold brooch in his cupboard. "Who has come with you?" he asked, noticing a youngster stealing a glance in their direction. "Just ask him or her to speak to this uncle," he said, summoning the nearest shop attendant.

Among the varied colourful displays in the new section, a toy Bajrang Bali caught the proprietor's eyes. Being an ardent devotee of the monkey-God, Devaditya wondered whether the merchandising of Hanuman dolls like He-man dolls would merit an approval from the scriptures. Nevertheless, he admired the craftsmanship that went into the carving of details such as the tiny rivers, miniature trees and miniscule animals dotting the hill balanced upon the outstretched hand of Hanuman.

The boy had come to the store with two teenage fans of Sheetal, whose collective pocket money turned out to be less than the price of the vase. The shop attendant asked the boy for his parents' phone number. Saddled with the task of arranging the misplaced baby clothes on the correct racks, he instructed his junior colleague to dial and put the phone on speaker.

"Hello." The female voice at the other end of the line jolted Devaditya out of his musings.

"Mrs Sinha?"

This particular Mrs Sinha, among the many hundreds in the city, sounded a bit perturbed about shelling out one thousand rupees. However, she agreed to come and pay, saying it would take her only fifteen minutes to reach the shop.

By the time, the shop attendant hung up the phone and asked the boy to sit on one of the six stools fashioned like dice, Devaditya's senses were no longer echoing the realities of his surroundings. He had the dazed look of a man, slowly gaining consciousness after being hauled from the rubble of an earthquake. Like a thread of glue from a compressed tube, the voice continued to trail in his mind along the edges of torn letters, joining up the anguish-ridden years. Devaditya was overcome by an urge to hug the boy, raise him in the air and shower him with all the brand-new toys in his shop. Never in his life before had he craved to initiate an interchange of words that would go on forever, disregarding the motion in his watch. He could not wait to know which games the child yearned to play and the lands he reached by wheeling along the fluttering pages of his treasured storybooks. Was his school a castle of joyous learning where the children could roll up the walls like the charts depicting flowers and fruits? Or was it an uninhibited playground of bullies or a boring, droning factory of assembly line lessons? He wanted to delve deeply into every other detail stirring or halting, jutting out of or blending in the apparent smooth flow of a childhood.

Devaditya had kept his and his son's names away from the 'Events' section of the newspapers and websites where the inauguration of Play Turn was announced. Few knew who owned the months-old departmental store, the latest of Devaditya's expeditious ventures. Rajeswari might become mad with joy on seeing him after a decade. Would she try to leap into his arms like she used to as a little girl? Would she weep? Stupid, emotional fool she was, no doubt. Otherwise, why would she choose such a future? His employees were unaware about his personal life and he preferred it that way. He would not allow a reunion to occur in front of people oblivious of the separation in the first place.

Unpredictable as she was, she could also try to punish her father with her silence, with her lack of expression or maybe just a glare. Devaditya would not like that either — to present her an opportunity to impose her wordless judgement on him, lest he betray any signs of wobbling under its impact in the presence of his staff.

Still, Devaditya could figure out a way to meet her without creating a scene. What if he waited for her in his car like in those good old times when he used to pick her up from school? Disappearing behind the shelves, he emerged with a shiny, purple rectangle clutched between his fingers. Startled on being offered a bar of chocolate, the boy, nevertheless, stretched out his hand to accept it with thanks, a shy smile flickering at the corner of his lips. Two uniformed lady staff exchanged surprised glances on their way past the stools to a row of perambulators. Their employer retreated to a sofa aligned with the cash counter and the security desk, and observed the boy from a distance.

Devaditya had followed his forefathers and they in turn their antecedents like ribs in the chest. It was their way of grasping the somewhat insurmountable thing called existence. But Rajeswari had untied herself from the rope that fastened her to her predecessors' norms and flung it around to gauge the distance she had travelled so long. Surreptitiously testing, she had chanced upon a soft glimmer of sensations, independent of anything she had known, regardless of everything she had heard. Finally, when she touched the stagnant water and rippled its stillness, it was as good as being washed away by the flood. Too far.

Devaditya clicked his niece's number. "Nishi, I was so busy this morning I had to skip my breakfast. Let's have lunch first. Then I'll show you around my shop."

"If you haven't set out from your house yet, I can come over to pick you up," he offered, after pausing for a moment to hear her response.

Devraj, who was still deep in conversation, emphasised a point to the manager by striking his right fist against his left palm. Tapping his son's shoulder, Devaditya said, "Let's leave for lunch with Nishi. You can resume this discussion later."

Devraj turned to him, his eyebrows raised in surprise. He had already explained the reasons for his inability to catch up with his cousin before 9 PM. Devaditya's glance conveyed to him that there was an important reason behind his insistence. Devraj, who had followed his father's footsteps to many chequered flags of success, trailed him out of their store, a few minutes before the most important woman in his life other than his wife and his late mother stepped in.

With his eyes fixed on the cars ahead and his lips drawn tight as if they would never part again, Devaditya let himself be chauffeured out of the street, neither waiting to meet his daughter nor enquiring about her contact details from his grandson, who sat patiently in the kid's corner of his huge departmental store, licking off the chocolate sticking to the inner surface of the foil.

The Single Bed

She poured the ocean into her pot

Not a drop was spilled,

When it rains, it won't overflow —

Gold cups to be filled.

Hema's close friend Meera had scribbled the lines in black ink on the last page of a hardbound notebook. They were no longer in touch; not that Hema had ever tried to find her whereabouts.

The cushy mattress topping the bed sank under Hema's feet as she stepped on it to reach the box shelf and put back the notepad along with the poetry books she had dusted. It was on the same bed that Meera and her friends would sit and chat on Friday evenings after school, often breaking into peals of contagious laughter. Hema would laugh less but smile more, dazzling those around her with flashes of her perfect teeth. Her expressive eyes would dance in zest whenever they asked her to play the sitar. She knew she was no musical genius, but nevertheless found immense delight in plucking the strings of the instrument.

After an all girls' convent school, it was an all girls' college for Hema. The concept of women's empowerment and financial independence was yet to embrace those institutions. Like most of her classmates, having a career did not fall into her scheme of things. After graduating in English way back in the sixties she had just waited to be married off by her parents.

Stepping down from the bed, Hema flopped on the mattress, weighed down by exhaustion. As she lifted her head slightly, her gaze met her father's in the framed photograph on the wall. Her eyes welled up with tears that polished his memories every so often. Her father, the son of an accomplished barrister, had earned more from renting the spacious ground floor of the inherited house than from his practice as a lawyer. In those days, most couples had several children, but Hema was her parents' only child — her mother had suffered three miscarriages after her birth. Her father had wished for a son-in-law who would match his own father in money and stature. He had wanted his grandchildren to enjoy the privileges that had shaped his own childhood. Unfortunately, such a groom never came along his way and he did not sense the implacable reality even when Hema turned thirty. A sudden heart attack knocked him out of this world when Hema was thirty-four.

Unlike some unmarried women of her generation, who enjoyed their single hood to the hilt, Hema had always looked forward to the thumb impression of *sindoor* as the legitimising signature to the pleasures of conjugal life and the overwhelming experience of motherhood. Yet her upbringing had fed her with the notion that expressing any desire for male companionship was unsuitable for a respectable woman. So, she had never committed the simple act of sitting down with her parents and telling them to select the next decent man they met in their quest for her groom instead of waiting for that elusive prince.

Hema slowly rose to her feet and entered the kitchen. A netted bag full of potatoes and onions was lying in a corner. She bent down to bring out the contents, but turned around with a questioning look on hearing her mother's footsteps.

"I think I have kept my pills here, by mistake," explained her mother, pointing at the kitchen closet.

"You should have called me. Don't you remember what the doctor said? Not to walk for another week." Following her mother's gaze, Hema spotted the small container of white capsules tucked between a labelled bottle of vinegar and a wide-mouthed jar of pickle, and handed it to her.

"There's something else I wanted to tell you," said the septuagenarian, an unusual cheeriness drowning the hesitation in her voice.

Hema stared at her, waiting for her to begin.

"You remember my friend Poonam? She called me yesterday. She is looking for someone to tutor her granddaughter. The child's parents return late from office and there's none to help her with her Maths and English grammar."

She paused. "Go on," Hema said nonchalantly.

"Since you remain free in the evenings, I was wondering whether you will teach her?" the white-haired lady asked, her tone fluctuating between forthrightness and expectancy.

"Me?" Hema frowned. "I've lost touch with everything to do with studies. Ma, are you forgetting my age?"

"The child is only in the second standard," told her mother. "Who knows? You might discover that you enjoy teaching," she added, and Hema would have caught the twinkle in her eyes if she had not turned to the soapstone sink to wash an artificially purpled aubergine.

"Okay, I'll try." Hema sighed. She did not want to pour cold water on her mother's expectations.

The septuagenarian returned to her rocking chair with a smile of satisfaction hoisting the corners of her lips, having succeeded in her attempt to break the monotony in her daughter's life.

*

Hema swabbed the dining table, taking care to wipe off any stains that might have remained even though she had cleaned up after breakfast. She brushed off the dead insects dropped from the incandescent lights above. With the handle of a spoon she promptly scratched out the pinch of wax that had trickled down a candle during the previous night's power cut. The table was bare except for a rotund jug of water and an empty flower vase. She placed her red dot pen in the vase so it would not roll away, settled down in a chair and stared at the cobwebs waving sporadically from the patch of wall above the tube light. Hema had not one but four children to teach, following the first pupil's high score at school, under her tutoring.

The familiar vexation crept into her as the seconds ticked away on the clock placed atop the refrigerator. The children's lack of habituation with her ways irked her like a new pair of shoes that caused blisters for not being accustomed to the feet. Finally, she heard footsteps on the stairs and took a deep breath.

Once the children took their seats, Hema picked up one of their exercise copies and hurriedly jotted down some sentences, drawing blanks, in place of the prepositions, for them to fill.

"You have fifteen minutes to complete this exercise. Then I'll give you some sums," she said, glancing at the clock again. Several minutes had passed, but Tina continued to rummage in her bag. Her friends pretended to be glued to their exercise copies while shifting their gazes covertly to take a peek at each other's work. At last, Tina lifted her eyes from the bag to find Hema glowering at her.

"Aunty, I forgot to bring my pencil box," she said meekly. "Can I borrow a pencil from them?"

Hema bit her lips to prevent herself from snapping. What a careless child! It turned out that none of the children had an extra pencil to lend. The tutor's chair screeched loudly as she pushed it back to get up and march to her bedroom. The pencil she used to list her groceries was not in its stand. She wrenched open the drawers in the walnut chest, raided the multi-chambered cupboard and flung around the embroidered cushions. Stomping around the room, she fingered the window sills and dashed to the living room to survey the central table and the shelves lined with showpieces from her father's youth. But the pencil was not there. She asked her mother, but her words only ricocheted off the septuagenarian's blank expression.

With no place left to search, Hema stormed into the dining room, banged on the table and yelled, "How will you remember your lessons and pass your exams if you forget to bring your pencil box?" She let out a volley of words which she failed to recollect later and slouched in her chair, gasping and panting for breath. Tina completed all her exercises with Hema's red pen, but her tutor refused to validate her answers.

After returning to their respective homes, all the four children received reprimanding for their total lack of interest in studies — their tutor had rung up to declare that she would teach them no longer. Hema found the pencil later in the kitchen, under pouches of powdered turmeric and ginger paste.

That night, no matter whether Hema pressed her face to the pillow or turned to her sides, she found discomfort in every posture of sleep. She reached for the radio on the bedside table, flicked through the channels, but found no program or song that suited her taste. She tip-toed to the living room and clicked on the TV, her thumb ready to press on the minimise volume button so as not to wake up her mother. A semi-clad woman cavorted on the beach to blaring music, cheered by lascivious men in swimming trunks. In a hurry to both reduce the sound and change the channel, her hands fumbled, and the remote slipped off and crashed onto the floor. Switching off the TV, she skulked to her mother's room and parted the door curtains a wee bit to check on her. Just as she had feared, the old lady was wide awake. "What happened, Hema? Did you break something?" she loudly asked.

"No, Ma." Hema rushed to her side and dropped beside her bed. "You must go to sleep." She did not remember for how long she had caressed her mother's silky silvery hair, guilty that she had spoiled her sleep. When the bright sunshine warmed her back, she found herself still in the kneeling posture, her head resting on the ailing woman's lap.

The ground-floor flat continued to be a steady source of income for Hema and her mother, but there was one problem. It so happened that the sizable rooms turned into the cupped leaves of pitcher plants for the tenants, who had shifted to the metro for work. The airy chambers devoured their ambitions, which died like hapless flies. As a consequence, the tenants left within a short span of time and Hema was forced to search for new ones.

The mother and the daughter's shared space was like a napkin neatly folded into half and then unfolded again — the faint crease a line separating their existences from each other. A week before her fifty-fifth birthday, Hema found herself left with the sole inheritance of their quaint little world, populated by square pink cushions and colour coordinated porcelain. She gave away her sitar as her mother loved to hear her play it: yet there was no way she could escape from the ruthless reminders of her loss. Her mother's invisible footsteps marked the floors: she had walked along with Hema not only from the latter's childhood to her adulthood, but also from her youth to near old age.

Hema took up a new hobby — kitchen gardening. She would grow succulent tomatoes and fragrant lemon in the patch of land behind her house. As she shifted the clammy earth, scattered the minuscule seeds and watered the plants, her mother's images would haunt her. Eyes open but looking nowhere, face shrivelled with age and contorted with pain, head sunk into the pillow and tubes snaking their way from various parts of her body. She would still glimpse her chapped feet, stuck out of the stretcher, when her neighbours lifted her into the hearse to be driven to the crematorium. Hema did not have the composure to break tradition and torch her mother's corpse with her own hands. It was a second cousin, the nearest living male relative, who did the needful. Still, she was terrified by what she did not have to see — her mother's beautiful locks slowly being licked, then mercilessly gnawed and finally charred by the ravenous flames.

*

Hema had been planning to sell the ground-floor flat and keep the money as fixed deposit so she could meet the expenses for the rest of her life from its interest. The Singhs, a wealthy couple, whose family mansion had got crowded after their nephews' marriages, were looking for a flat for their son and his bride. Hema zeroed in on them as they offered her the best price, although she was perturbed by the thought of a newly married couple living just beneath her floor. Worse would be the arrival of their baby, which was almost inevitable. In better moods, she chided herself for despising someone who was not even born. One could imagine her relief when she got to know, after the money had already changed hands, that Mr Singh junior had found a work opportunity abroad. Hema secretly prayed that the "few" years he wished to spend in the distant land would exceed the number of years remaining in her life.

Soon the son and his bride bade adieu to their hometown for the foreign shores. Hema would often hear the grating of saws. She guessed the middle-aged couple were getting new sets of furniture made, and looked forward to their stay in her building.

It was on a breezy morning that Mrs Singh appeared at Hema's door. "I was wondering whether you would like to have a look around my flat. There's a little surprise. And the furnishing is almost done..."

"I mean if you are not too busy," she added as Hema threw a glance at the gas stove. The appearance of dimples endeared Mrs Singh's striking features even more. It did not escape Hema's notice how the woman's voice thickened with pride when she mentioned the words "my flat."

"I'll love to," Hema responded, to avoid offending the woman with whom she would be sharing the building for the rest of her life. "But I had been brewing tea... Do you mind having a cup with me?" She stretched her lips attempting a smile.

Mrs Singh agreed, keeping up with the formality. Hema gestured to her to sit on the suede sofa in the living room. "I'll come back in a few minutes," she said.

The cutlery jangled in the old kitchen drawer as Hema pulled it open. She walked up to Mrs Singh with measured steps so as not to spill the tea, and placed before her an engraved spoon, a crystal sugar bowl and a china cup brimming with the black beverage. She had not asked whether her guest, unlike her, preferred it with milk.

Sliding the key into the lock, the new flat owner pushed open the door and shot a glance at Hema who had frozen at the threshold. Prodded by Mrs Singh, Hema stepped inside the flat and navigated through the room by treading on the strips of marble floor peeping between colourful mats that narrated, in pictures, the adventures of the Little Mermaid.

Mrs Singh beamed, mistaking Hema's shocked expression as that of wonderment. "I have always wanted to open a crèche," she revealed, her voice oozing with a sense of achievement.

The contented lady skirted around the stools shaped like squatting frogs and traced the length of a cushioned seat resembling a rather fat snake. She sauntered into the next room, rocked the wooden swing and brushed her hand against the smooth surface of a slide. As she stopped by the inflatable pool to ensure there were no leaks, Hema seethed in fury, but there was nothing she could do. The flat no longer belonged to her. She did not know how she would prepare for the deluge of children in her building. The more she thought, the more difficult it seemed. Like a painting gone wrong that kept getting worse with each intervention of the brush.

The crèche started functioning soon and Hema reacted by minimising the number of times she left her upper floor flat. So, her gardening days were over and she paid the grocer and the fishmonger a little extra to deliver the goods at her doorstep. The TV and the radio were her only companions, but some of their programmes too left her clenching her fists in an unremitting rage.

One afternoon, Hema stepped out of her flat for a visit to the bank. She stuck to the pavement as far as possible, circumventing the wrought iron fences built around the tender saplings to prevent them from being chewed up by goats. Spotting the different shades of gladioli in D'Souza's garden, she edged towards the gates to take a closer glance, but to her horror, Mrs D' Souza's face popped up at the window.

"A packet of safety pins, please," the lady of the house called out. Bewildered, Hema glanced around. A man, carrying strings of knick-knacks over his shoulders trotted to the partly drawn gates. Immensely relieved that she had remained unnoticed, probably owing to a plant which had almost grown into a tree, she kept her gaze straight and hurried to the end of the lane. At the turn of the road, she stepped under the sprawling shade of an enormous banyan and bowed her head in front of a stone Shiva Linga, although she no longer had anything to ask the Lord for. She had just lifted her head when a small boy ran past her, singing a film song peppered with lewd lyrics. The child, about four years of age, was certainly oblivious to their meaning. Yet a bomb burst within Hema. She turned and stomped to her house and showed her wrath to the washed utensils piled on the counter beside the sink. With vehement bangs she put them back on their shelf. She never liked the wooden cabinet in the dining room. She shoved it out with all her strength as if it were a restaurant customer who had not paid for his meals.

Consumed by her own rage, Hema failed to notice her neighbour's shirt fly past her window and the coconut leaves tilt to their left like someone dodging a blow. Minutes later, she found her cheque book lying on the desk beside the window. Utterly soaked! She quickly placed it underneath a fan and pressed one of its corners, which was thankfully dry, with a paperweight.

Rushing to the windows to bolt them, Hema noticed the clouds. She did not remember seeing clouds as dense and dark ever in her life; they were a continuous mass, with no gaps, trapping everything lying underneath in an indomitable darkness. It seemed a new kingdom had sprung up over the teeming city. After shutting all the windows, she scampered to the balcony, almost slipping on the wet floor. Through the hazy screen of descending water she could barely discern the crinkly windows of the adjacent houses. Shiny bubbles dimpling the shallow troughs between the pavement and the wavering edge of the cement road popped at the poke of the impinging raindrops. A smear of orange light appeared in the distance, but with the footpaths encroached and nowhere to retreat, the hapless pedestrians resigned themselves to being splashed over by the car. Unclasping the clothespins, Hema picked her garments one by one till she reached the end of the long balcony and flailed her free arm to shoo the drenched crow who was observing her from the railing top.

The collapse of a neem tree, accompanied by the split of its trunk and the snap of its branches, preceded the loud ring of the doorbell. Hema opened the door to let Mrs Singh in. The weather had turned cold with all the rain, but a few beads of sweat glistened near the crèche owner's diamond nose stud.

"The cyclone is coming at a speed of a hundred and twenty kilometres per hour. I had to promise to keep the children in my crèche for the night. Their parents are stuck in their offices," Mrs Singh explained.

"What can I do for you?" Hema asked dryly, her inherent irritation gaining ground.

"All the shops are closed. I can manage without a dinner but I can't keep the children hungry. Can you please provide us with some food?" Mrs Singh looked straight into Hema's eyes and held her gaze for an answer. Her voice had grown hoarse from answering to the incessant calls made by the worried guardians.

Hema remained silent for a moment, surveying her face, which was still beautiful, though age had made inroads through the pathways of wrinkles despite the expensive anti-aging creams. She could not help feeling sort of vindicated as the crèche had caused her much anguish though none of its wards or staff had ever disturbed her in any way.

"I live alone. Where will I find food for thirty children?"

"That's true. Whatever you can give will be of help."

Hema, a dedicated custodian of her late parents' image, tried her best to shun outright impoliteness, at least towards adults. Mrs Singh was asked to sit on the sofa while she looked for what she could spare. She would not give up her dinner; that was for sure. She scanned the racks and pulled out the trays of the double-door refrigerator that had served her for almost two decades. Within a few minutes, a loaf of brown bread bought in the morning, a bottle of jam, some apples and bananas, puffed rice, a can of orange juice and an intact packet of nutty biscuits were arranged on a table in front of the crèche owner. Hema refused to accept any money for them, listened patiently to Mrs Singh's gushes of gratitude, and mentally prepared herself for a sleepless night, shredded by the fury of wind and the noises made by a large bunch of children.

Mrs Singh called after several hours: though annoyed, Hema was not surprised.

"Sorry to disturb you again," said Mrs Singh. "I need more help. Thirty children cannot sleep in a single room. I've spread out mats for them in two of the rooms. I've been running constantly from one to the other, but it's only nine o'clock. I can spend the night in one of these rooms. Can you please sleep in the other?"

"What about the ayahs?" Hema, who had not faced a worse request for a long time, asked the crèche owner coldly.

"Maya is on leave. Sunita left as soon as she noticed the first signs of the storm. I offered to pay her extra to make her stay, but she told her son was sick."

"So, have you managed the children, all by yourself, since the afternoon?" Hema asked.

Mrs Singh did not fail to detect the mellowing of Hema's tone and replied at once, "Yes. When I came to you to request for food, one of them had hurt herself by jumping from the top of the slide. Now they are too tired to engage in mischief. Please come. Having an adult in the room would ensure safety. It's not that you have to stay awake and look after them. You are like my elder sister: your presence is reassuring enough."

Hema smirked. Mrs Singh knew how to use words. "There are no beds in your crèche. I'll have to sleep on a mat, I suppose?" she asked sharply.

"No, I would never ask you to do that," the crèche owner sounded embarrassed. "I brought in a bed a month ago, in case any children fell sick."

"Where will you sleep?"

"I don't think I'll get to sleep. However, if I feel I won't be able to carry on at all without lying down for a while, the floor will do," she said coolly.

Hema was compelled to admire the unflinching professionalism of Mrs Singh, who had been a pampered housewife just the other day. Once again, Hema's family reputation and Mrs Singh's courteous behaviour prevented her from being churlish. Reining in her dread, she slurped the last drop of her vegetable stew and climbed down the stairs. A few children had dozed off already. The crèche owner requested Hema to pat the rest to sleep, but her unloving palms fell flat on the children's backs like coasters hurriedly put atop tables. Tired of this fruitless activity, she slumped on the single bed near the wall, keeping the children to themselves. The bed felt stiffer than the one she was used to, but she was too dozy to create a fuss.

Sound of footsteps reached Hema, but she pretended to be fast asleep. As the footsteps grew fainter and faded outside the door, she lifted her eyelids fractionally, but they drooped under the spell of unrelenting drowsiness. Before she could sink to the deepest pit of sleep, it occurred to her that she was supposed to keep an eye on the children. It would be a matter of shame if the kid wandered about the house indulging in mischief or worse if he slipped out into the storm for an adventure. In a jolt of panic, she opened her eyes wide and sat upright; then finding her slippers, she rose to her feet and quickly tip-toed out of the room. She peered into the next room, skimming the darkness until she could make out the outline of Mrs Singh, who was reclining on the floor and whispering stories to the children. The crèche owner looked at the door upon hearing the soft rustle of Hema's loose nightgown.

"Any child entered this room from mine?"

"No." Mrs Singh stirred herself from her posture to search for the kid, but Hema gestured her to stay there, fearing her audience might also roam about if she left the room, leading to a great pandemonium that would cost her the entire night's sleep.

Hema plodded across the flat until she found the boy in what used to be the living room in her childhood. He was squinting under the slide and gathering something by the light of his battery fuelled toy watch. She switched on the electric bulbs. Startled, the child swung around.

Round red beads were scattered across the floor.

"What are you doing?" Hema demanded to know.

"I'm picking up the beads of Pooja's necklace," answered the child.

"How did it get torn? Did you have a fight?" Hema asked in a stern voice, narrowing her eyes.

The boy nodded.

"So why are you picking them up?" she interrogated.

"I was feeling bad. I want to make her the necklace," replied the boy so softly that he was almost inaudible.

"How will you 'make her the necklace?'" she probed in surprise.

"I'll learn from my grandmother. She sews garlands for the Gods," he explained.

Sighing, Hema squatted down despite the pain in her knees, to help him pick up the beads faster so that both could go back to sleep.

Soon the boy crawled onto his mat, but the room was not as quiet as Hema had expected.

"So soft! And I love the colour." A voice trickled through the darkness. "It's for my new grandmother."

"Who's your new grandmother?" Another voice lightly ruffled the silence.

"She's my father's aunt. She came to stay with us after I was born. My grandmother has been there before. So, she is the new one."

"From where did you get it? Petro shop?"

"No, I'm not allowed to go there alone. And nobody will let me buy anything for her."

"Why?"

"I don't know."

"Where are her other grandchildren? I mean other than you."

"She has none. They say she has no children. So she came to stay with us after new grandfather died."

"But how did you buy this bag since nobody wants you to get anything for her?"

"A man was selling them in front of my school gate."

"But your mother drops you to school."

"She goes home after dropping me and comes back to pick me up. I bought it during the Tiffin break. He was standing among the *panipuriwalas* and *jhalmuri* sellers."

"Do they let you go outside? That's not allowed in my school." The second voice betrayed envy.

"They don't let us out either. But the gate is full of holes. We can put our hands through them."

Hema guessed that the child was referring to a collapsible gate. Somehow the conversation flowed in rhythm with her thickening drowsiness like a lullaby, instead of cutting across it.

"Where did you get the money?"

"From my piggy bank. They'll be angry if they know there's nothing left. So, I slipped in some pins through the slit. The pins will make noise when they shake it and they'll think there's still money in it."

"Who are they?"

"Everyone — father, mother, the other grandmother, Charu *didi*. Nobody gifts her anything."

Hema opened her eyes partially to glimpse the present, which was luridly coloured and made of fake velvet. One look at the bag was enough to tell her the price: she had a knack for buying pretty purses and handbags in her growing years. She deduced that the child never had much in her piggy bank.

The thunder rolled the house on the curve of its prolonged roar, disrupting the sleep of several children. They shrieked out, driven to a semi-wakeful state. Outside the rain-stained window, the gritty edges of puddles glinted powdery silver under the ghostly lamp posts. Water from the flooded road whirled into a manhole surrounded by fluorescent flags to prevent untoward incidents. The low-lying side lanes continued to resemble canals carrying forth the occasional paper boat behind a flotilla of Thermocol bowls, tangles of rotting garlands and bulging, overfilled plastic bags.

The wall she was facing used to have built-in shelves. A blue cloth, suspended from above, descended like a waterfall in front of the items arranged on these shelves. The edge of the cloth ended just above the six-year-old Hema's reach. She would expectantly watch it flutter in the wind, but it never flew high enough to reveal anything.

"What do you keep on these shelves?" Little Hema used to ask her mother.

"Aladdin's lamps," replied her mother.

"How many lamps?" inquired Hema.

"Oh, there are many of them — one for every member of the genie family."

"Give me one lamp. I want the genie to fulfil my wishes."

"The lamp is not for little girls. They do not know the difference between right and wrong and cannot be allowed to make wishes. If I give them to you, fanged demons will leap out instead of genies."

Hema remained in the dark about what was on the shelf.

It was well past midnight when a soft touch gently rumpled Hema's sleep. A little boy, about two years of age, had climbed up on the bed, possibly in a state of diffused drowsiness. The pace of water streaming down the window panes had diminished and a streak of candlelight fell upon the child's face. Hema realised there was a power cut. A candle burned in a bronze holder, placed on the play table and another one shone from the window sill of the attached washroom — both must have been lit by Mrs Singh. As Hema shifted to ease herself out of the child's grip, he clutched her tighter in his sleep. Light from the steady flame swept unhindered on the child's smooth forehead and spilled over his closed eyelids. It illuminated his eyelashes, which were curved like the wicks placed along the length of traditional clay lamps. His face was softened by the glow of a peaceful sleep and the warmth unknowingly imparted by the elderly stranger.

"It filled the Wells, it pleased the Pools

It warbled in the Road —

It pulled the spigot from the Hills

..."

When Hema was a student, she could recite many of Emily Dickinson's poems from memory. She said a poem must be read by many at different epochs, to be remembered across civilisations. Those who did not read could still listen to the others' recitations, cherishing the words emoted and dipping into the pauses for the ones left unsaid. She had gifted Meera *The Poems of Emily Dickinson* on her sixteenth birthday — the last present before they lost touch forever. She found a new group of friends on entering college who too disappeared from her contact list one by one like trophies from the table at the end of their annual sports day.

The sleeping child stroked the skin on Hema's wrist, probably a habit with his mother curling next to him every other night. Water continued to scribble on the window panes as if in the laborious process of arriving at a decision. There was no more thunder to loudly proclaim the stormy feats, just the sound of drops speaking to each other. Another poem that came to her from time to time like the rain itself — the one her father loved to recite — was by Henry Longfellow.

"Thy fate is the common fate of all,

Into each life some rain must fall,

..."

She tried to recall the next few lines of the poem but an entirely different rhyme latched on to her mind. It went like this:

"Sprouting big fangs, Aladdin's lamp,

A little girl sneezes, and wishes to go damp."

Hema grinned at the ridiculousness of her own words and fell asleep with an arm around the child.

*

The elderly lady woke up startled at not finding herself in her own upholstered bed. Panicked, Hema looked around till her glance fell on the sleeping boy. At first, all the incidents of the previous night came rushing, as if they were competing against each other to unfurl in her mind, trying to knock and send the others hurtling away. Finally, they all managed to reconcile among themselves and glide into her memory, in order of their occurrences. Sitting up in her bed, she softly slipped the pillow under the sleeping boy's head and looked out of the window. Flocks of inky clouds floated languidly to the western skies, biding their time to reclaim their kingdom. The wet jujube leaves, sneaking out of a neighbour's fenced garden, were caught in a benign spell of rejuvenating sunlight. They glistened over the road caked with crumby mud, strewn with long, brown leaves and mottled with pink, gold, silver and blue swirls of spilled petrol.

Hema heard footsteps in the next room and wondered whether Mrs Singh had been able to catch any sleep at all. Bent on finishing her ablutions as fast as possible, she left the bed to make her way to the washroom. She would help the crèche owner get the children ready before their parents arrived to take them home.

The rhyme on "Aladdin's lamp" caught up with her as she firmly squeezed a crumpled tube to let out a blob of pink toothpaste.

"Sprouting big fangs, Aladdin's lamp

Baking me a cake, a dragon in my camp."

Hema improvised on the lines she had composed the previous night and giggled at the mirror with a mouth full of paste, splattering the glass above the basin and the adjacent wall. Even after sluicing her face in the cool water, she doubled over in laughter while wiping off the pink, frothy sprays resulting from her hilarity. As she turned the taps to fill the bucket, another ditty took shape in her mind. She promised herself that she would overcome her inhibitions and recite them in front of the children the next time Mrs Singh would seek her help.

For now, with the door locked behind her and the splashes of water drowning all other sounds, she did not mind singing it aloud.

"Swimming in the bucket a yellow feathered duck

Quacking till the rim it found a way to luck.

Staring at the towel it felt its lathery wings

Then and there decided to fly off with the kings."

Half as Good

The tantalising smell of onion *dosas* and chicken *pakoras* prevailed over the stuffy canteen. Ajay took another puff on his cigarette as the hour hand in his watch touched five. Why did Bela attend every class like the nerds? Well, despite her short skirts, tight tops and high heels, she was a nerd too. Ajay snorted with irritation. If she was any less attractive than what she was, he would have dumped her long ago just the way he had gotten rid of Seema and Parul.

Girdled by his admirers, Rahul was strumming away on his Spanish guitar, a tuft of sleek hair streaking his dreamy eyes. Druv stomped into the room, straight from the football field; the soles of his Nike shoes left striated footprints that looked like the X-rays of lungs. Hearing the crunch of a squashed plastic cup, Ajay glanced around and his eyes fell on the roll of cigarette clasped between Shekhar's lips: he guessed it was cocaine.

Finally, Ajay spotted Bela striding towards the canteen. Neither her face nor her gait bore any signs of fatigue, unlike her girl-friends who looked somewhat dishevelled after so many classes and long lab sessions. She was blooming with a natural glow as if she had just stepped out of her home to board the college bus. Her long hair was neatly set up with clips, her well-fitting blouse tucked into her pleated skirt, and her eyes and lips accentuated with makeup — not too bright but toned down to blend with the college ambiance. The sight of her was enough to dispel Ajay's petulance. He felt no inclination to waste time by asking her what had prolonged the last session or express the peevishness that had pricked him a while ago. They sped off on his bike to Jhilanil Park — their favourite haunt with its sparkling blue pools, the purposefully dim, cosy cafes, the colourful tents doubling as curio shops and the dark-green thatched screen of casuarinas beyond which they could experience the privacy of their bedrooms.

The next morning, Ajay almost bumped into Mili, his senior, on his way to the computer lab as she was hurrying out after her viva. He had already walked past her with an apology when she called out to him. She seemed out of breath and her wiry hair had sprung up to form a whorl around her face.

"I'm directing a play for the fest and I want you to play the lead," she said.

"Thanks for considering me but I don't think I'll be able to pull it off," Ajay responded with a shrug. "Please look for someone else," he added to emphasise his reluctance.

"But Suman told me you stole a lot of hearts as Romeo in your school play," said Mili, flashing a mischievous smile, but Ajay had already shifted his gaze to the laboratory door.

"Mili *didi*, I don't have time for acting right now," he replied bluntly with a backward glance. The truth was that he could not bear the thought of attending rehearsals every evening for an entire month.

An off period followed the Data Structure class. Some students raided the library, some dashed to the playground, but most huddled in the canteen. The college comprised of two buildings, facing each other with a courtyard in between. Ajay and Bela traversed the courtyard to enter the opposite building. Then they took the elevator to reach the terrace.

A paved road — like the performance cutover they would need to cross — separated their campus from the sprawling lawns of the tech hub: Electronic City Complex. Ajay and Bela would imagine themselves working in the offices across the street or in similar organisations in a different city or even abroad. In her mind, Bela would arrange and rearrange her future workplace across cultures and continents just the way her mother would shift their family photographs from the black painted shelf to the brown plywood table, from the table to the pink mosaic window sill and from the peach linen draped stool to the white walls.

Perched upon the cubical water tank, the couple got an extensive view of a classroom. The chairs were empty except for the one occupied by

Rishi, who was bent over his desk, busy scribbling in his long, hardbound notebook. He practised the ritual of noting down whatever he had learnt from a lecture as soon as he could. He said it helped him to remember and get a better grip on new concepts. Back home, he followed up with the day's lessons again. Ajay, who believed anything not remembered was not worth recalling, had spun out a bunch of jokes on Rishi and his habits. His friends, who would roll with laughter at those jokes, insisted that he become a comedian. Ajay had given a good thought to his friends' suggestion until he came across a leading comedian's interview. The man mentioned reading four newspapers daily to gain inspiration for his gags. Who could imagine the king of comedy sitting down with a pile of newspapers and a sharp pointed pen, encircling bits of news and finally linking the circles to get his unending chain of jokes?

Bela slid down the tank wall, tugged at the hemline of her skirt which had gotten crumpled at the back, and peered over the parapet to watch the beautiful cars flitting in and out of the tech hub. Standing side by side, pressed against the wall, was less torturous to Ajay than sitting close. It helped him to cope with the urge of touching Bela, who strictly averted physical contact within their college. His mind drifted to the semester results that would be out next week. Aware that his chances of passing in Digital Circuit were slim, he could not stop cursing Prof Sawhney for setting questions from outside the syllabus. Despite the sporadically bubbling tension, he pursed his lips in amusement. He imagined his friends' expressions when he would share his jokes on the professor with them. Another consolation was — if he scored poorly, so would the others — the questions had harrowed everyone.

*

Ajay was sipping lemon tea and blowing smoke rings outside the college gates when he received a call from Jugal. Prof Sawhney had stepped inside the elevator with a pile of answer sheets. Ajay gulped down the tea and took one last drag on the cigarette. Marching down the cement path leading to his building, he wriggled inside a crammed lift, his heart pounding in his chest as the elevator rose.

Twenty... Seven... The room resonated with the call of Ajay's roll number. Nearing the professor's desk with a couple of strides, he stretched out his hand to grasp the answer sheet. His heart sank as his eyes fell on the total marks scribbled at the corner of the paper. Though he had apprehended such a low score, it agitated him like an electric rod on a circus tiger. A retest awaited him for the first time in his student life. It no longer mattered that there were many others in the same boat as him; after all, he would have to stand in front of his father alone — the only man he could neither ignore nor joke about. Back at his desk, he stared at the answer sheet with his chin balanced on both palms.

"Rishi has got ninety," Nikhil whispered. Ajay looked up from the paper and glared at Rishi's back, his face reddening with rage and wishing if only he could wring his neck...

At the end of the period, many of the students stepped into the corridor to flex their limbs. The department head would steer the next class. Unable to confine his detest for Rishi to the jokes he had created about him behind his back, Ajay stormed towards him when he was returning from the restroom.

"You found out the questions from Prof Sawhney, you filthy slicker," Ajay bellowed.

Startled at being shouted at, Rishi stopped in his tracks. His classmate was glowering at him, his smooth features contorted in fury.

Rishi took a deep breath. "You would have known the answers too, if you had attended his classes. He had mentioned each of them during his lessons," he retorted in an unwavering voice.

His reply flared up Ajay, who stirred up like a vexed serpent and lunged at him, hauled back in the nick of time by Druv and Rahul. Rishi, however, did not budge from his spot.

"Perhaps, you don't know I attend martial arts classes every evening after college," Rishi warned. His voice was calm and his steady gaze met Ajay's glare, despite the pall of unanticipated humiliation shadowing his face.

Ajay himself, a natural in Kung Fu, had been one of his instructor's favourites. He had discontinued his lessons when he began to find them boring: they were not worth sacrificing the booze parties with his friends or romping under the sheets with his then girlfriend Tina. He still practised some punches and kicks in front of the mirror — whenever he was in the mood — especially after watching an action flick. His martial arts skills were just another feather in his cap besides his academic performance and agility in the football field. It also helped that his acting talent, flair for comedy and good looks made him popular among the other young men and much sought after by the prettiest girls around.

"Merely attending classes doesn't teach you martial arts just like mugging up information doesn't make you an engineer," sneered Ajay. Standing a couple of feet behind him, Rahul and Druv exchanged glances, ready to step in if the situation spun out of control again.

"Who said I mug up?" Rishi's voice carried an icy edge, but he was still making an effort to grip on to his characteristic politeness.

"Anyone with eyes," Ajay spat, taking a step forward.

"What do I care what jealous fools say?" thundered Rishi, his composure beginning to crumble. His fists knotted in rage and his face smarted from the unprovoked insults hurled at him.

"Why don't you fight it out with me instead of quarrelling like a girl? Let's see whether you are half as good as me," Ajay challenged, circling his foe.

Before the situation could take an uglier turn, the department head strode into the scene. The two boys had no option but to yank themselves away and retreat into their classroom as none of them wished to risk expulsion. The crowd of students, gathered from the floors above and below, quietly dispersed towards the staircase and the elevator. To Ajay's dismay, he spotted Bela among them — her pace quicker than usual, her face lowered in shame.

After her last class Bela was about to step out of the campus alone when Ajay darted out of the canteen and caught up with her. "You have not seen how he licks up to the professors. I study in the same class and stay in the same locality as him, not you," he tried to explain to Bela, who was a year junior to him, but her eyes flashed with anger and she continued to walk.

"We'll go to CreamCrunch Cafe today. You wanted to try out their chocolate fudge ice-cream," he called after her desperately, as the blood rushed in his veins and the sweat trickled down his face. Two professors passing by them glared at him as if he were a loathsome stalker. The security guard, who was lolling on his bench, leaped to his feet, ready to intervene if the boy continued to pester the girl. Ajay halted, furtively observing the uniformed man, certain the latter would report to the principal if he got into a tiff with him.

"Sorry, Ajay, I need to reach home early today," she replied curtly and marched out of the gates, her high heels clanging on the asphalt cement. He clawed at his scalp in frustration and began to pace back and forth in the courtyard. His eyes fell on Rishi who was standing outside their classroom, speaking to Prof Dash, probably prodding her to clarify his doubts even after she had wound up her lessons. Blaming him for the altercation that had provoked Bela's wrath, he swore at him under his breath till the night guard started his rounds of the campus.

No matter how many times Ajay rang Bela, craving to hear her lively voice, all he got to listen to was the annoying jingle she had chosen as her ringtone. The explanations and apologies he messaged, too, coaxed no reply out of her. She also ensured that he never got to spot her outside her classroom; not even during the lunch break and the occasional off period.

*

Discussing cricket scores outside the college gates, were Ajay and his friends, after the first-class test in the new semester. The electronics lab session would begin in another fifteen minutes. A burly man alighted from his motorcycle and paraded towards a thin, middle aged man selling green coconuts from a cart parked on the opposite pavement.

"How much?"

"Fifteen rupees."

The vendor sliced off the top of the coconut with a clean sweep of his chopping knife and handed it to his customer. The well-built man quickly sipped the juice with a straw, hurled the fruit at the street corner without a glance at the dustbin a few feet away, and held out a ten rupee note.

"I told you it is fifteen rupees," reminded the vendor, annoyed that his customer had forgotten the price he had mentioned just a minute ago.

"You will get only ten from me," the man replied.

"If you don't want to pay fifteen, you could have chosen not to buy from me," the coconut seller retorted, raising both hands above his head in exasperation.

"How dare you argue with me?" His customer grabbed him by the throat. "Do you know who I am? I can kick you out of this pavement any moment."

"*Babu*, if I keep no profit, how will I feed my children?" Though bewildered by the man's savagery, the frail vendor with sunken eyes refused to flinch. Life had dragged him through numerous battles. Many bullies he had confronted before.

"Let me see. Maybe you need to be freed of your children. If you have a daughter..." The ruffian's sentence hung midway as someone grabbed his collar from behind. As he turned to glare, his eyes bulging in rage, a neat punch landed on his broad face. He tried to raise his right leg in a kick but Ajay blocked it with his left hand. The strongman turned away swiftly, picked up the chopping knife from the vendor's cart and charged at the engineering student. Ajay struck hard at his opponent's arm with the back of his hand, prompting the weapon to fly out of his grip. Before the hooligan could gather his moves, Ajay's front kicks flung him away, and he fell upon the road with a loud thud.

Ajay swaggered to the college gates, conscious of the admiring glances from his friends, who had seethed at the stranger's barbarity, but unlike him, had been too scared to protest. Fifteen minutes were over: he was about to step inside the college when a sudden thought struck him and he paused to check his wallet. As he had feared the cherished photograph was missing. Swivelling around to face the road, he glimpsed something glinting on the pavement and made a dash for it. He swooped down on Bela's photograph, and on raising his head he found himself looking directly into the eyes of the lady herself. He grinned sheepishly, running a hand over his head and struggling to find something to say, but Bela, who had watched him fight for the coconut seller, smiled indulgently and came forward. Straightening up, he cast his glance all around as if unable to believe his beloved was right in front of him. Then slowly a tremendous joy filled him up, dispelling the anxiety that gripped him during those unanswered calls. She told him afterwards that she had stepped out of the campus to get medicines for a friend. Later in the day, Ajay learned that the man he had fought was a local thug with political connections.

In the months Bela had shunned him, Ajay realised how much he desired her beyond her body. Looking back, the period of avoidance shone like a moonlit gap between the shadows of leaves cast upon a by-lane, where they found themselves strolling one evening, savouring the advent of autumn. Initially, Ajay had refused to admit to himself that the unrelenting longings of love had afflicted him too like most of his friends. Eventually, he bowed to the indispensability of that one person, without whom all the wondrous sights of the world would not appear as they were; not even bear resemblance to their pictures, but remain as shapes in the dust.

A school, deserted after class hours, sprawled behind the row of trees on their right. On their left, trenches had been dug for laying down the foundation of a building. The stone chip coating had worn off from a short stretch of the road, which was also damp from the water spilled by the workers.

"What astounding effects!" Ajay commented on the movie they had watched an hour ago. He stumbled on something and looked down to find a piece of brick partly embedded in mud. Prising it out with his pointed toed boot, he kicked it sideways.

"The climax gave me goosebumps!" Bela swooned, turning towards Ajay. He lifted his eyes from the road and fixed them on her. The moonlight slid along the curve of her dangling earrings that matched perfectly with her silver bordered black sari, her silky hair cascaded down her back and the leafy trees reflected in her doe eyes. Suddenly her face crumpled in shock and she let out a shriek. Someone had groped her from behind. The miscreant was sitting pillion on a motorcycle that bolted into a lane grazing the school compound. In the simmering moonlight, they recognized the side-parted, slicked back hairstyle copied from a popular regional actor and the thick neck demarcated from the broad shoulders by a gold chain. He was the ruffian Ajay had fought.

Earlier, Ajay would drop Bela home whenever they went out on a date. After this incident, despite her objections, he saw her off at her doorstep even when she returned straight home from college.

*

Ajay was walking home from Kartik's house after a game of chess. He had planned to return two hours earlier to have dinner with his parents, but his friend, with his brilliant moves, had gotten him fastened to the board so long. The streetlights were broken. The road ahead seemed not to exist like the retracted claws of a lion, but the young man was only a stone's throw away from his residence and the clapping of shoes, though far behind, assured him of the presence of other humans.

A sudden breeze rustled the leaves of the fruit trees jostling between the houses and their glass shard spiked boundaries. He shot a glance at the sky and found it tinged with red. Lowering his gaze, he glimpsed a winged creature hovering near the air-conditioning unit outside a top-floor window and wondered whether it was an owl or a bat. Something scurried near his feet. He dropped his eyes to catch sight of a mouse that crawled out of a squishing plastic and scampered across the lane. Then hearing the prolonged gong of a wall clock, he turned to his left and witnessed a mangy cat jump out of a grilled window. It made a dash for the scrawny rodent which was wriggling through the gap of a rusted gate.

The footsteps behind Ajay grew loud all of a sudden. A disquieting suspicion crept into him, but before he could swing around, someone pulled both his arms and pinioned them to his back. A hooded man flicked open a knife. Ajay felt its sharp blade tingle the skin of his throat.

It was impossible not to be petrified. Yet the student tried his best not to allow his fear to leap out of control and crush his presence of mind.

Ajay had no option but to let himself be led by the men, past the shuttered shops, the locked doors and the dusty, deserted bus terminus. All the while, he controlled his breathing so that his assailants could not guess the extent of his fear from the frequency or force of his inhalations. He strained his senses of sight and hearing to reach beyond their limits hoping they would detect the slightest chance to free him, but unfortunately not a single opportunity showed itself all along the way to the vast, desolate field.

The men were three in number. Reaching the middle of the field, they made Ajay stop under the shadow of a banyan tree. When Ajay was four, his *ayah* would threaten to bundle him under this tree if he refused to nap at noon. The nursemaid would describe the tree as a she-demon. The dangling roots were strands of hair she flung around to strangle her victims; the branches were claws designed to disfigure the hapless creatures who unwittingly sought her shade. His mother would be busy, attending to her patients in the clinic, unaware of the means of control enforced on her only child. Little Ajay, too proud to disclose his fears, never slipped out a word to his mother when she returned. It so happened that a couple of years later, his mother cited the example of the banyan tree to instil a sense of humility in him. She explained how the roots of the plant came all the way down to the earth to grow up as separate trunks, acquiring branches and leaves of their own. Similarly, a man must be grounded to learn, prosper and rise. She never came to know her son had developed the habit of turning deaf at the mention of the word *banyan*.

The man wielding the knife took a step forward to stand just a foot away from Ajay. Only his eyes were visible. They had the steady focus of one who unquestionably followed orders, never interrupted by any personal grievances. Then the eyes narrowed in full concentration and the gloved fingers tightened around the hilt of the knife. The banyan tree towered over Ajay, monstrous in its stillness and terrifying with its silence. The nemesis from his childhood refused to draw attention to his plight by unleashing its tenacious roots, juddering its leathery leaves or screaming out through its many pores.

Ajay sensed they would not waste words on him. If he wished to live, this was the moment to strike. He rallied all his strength and flipped his leg backwards, kicking the man behind him. Although it took the wracked man only a few seconds to collect himself, Ajay had succeeded in wringing his hands out of his grip. He leapt off the ground and bringing both his legs together he hit the man in the front, on his chest. The man behind retaliated by jabbing him in the back with his knee. The student bit his lips to hold back a yelp and catch the faint screech lingering in the distance.

Twisting his body leftwards, Ajay slapped his right forearm against the other to shoot out a punch. The powerful sweep of a flattened palm against his fist revealed that the assailants were no novices in martial arts either. He heard the squawking of wheels. The tinkle of a bicycle bell prompted him to split open his lungs for the loudest cry of help he could muster before one of the men clamped his palm on his mouth and another pummelled his stomach to muzzle his speech with gut-wrenching pain.

When his head was inches away from the earth, with eyes stinging in pain from a fresh gash above his brow, Ajay saw a cyclist appear at the edge of the field. The rider turned to the ponytailed figure sitting behind him, who jumped down from the bicycle and sprinted in the opposite direction. The attackers, who were facing the student, had luckily not seen the cyclist. With a flick of his hand, Ajay took out his phone from his pocket, and before the screen went blank with all the stamping, he managed to switch on its torch, praying the cyclist would spot him.

The knife point almost touched Ajay's chest, but he grabbed the hilt and tried to push it away with all his strength. Pedalling furiously towards them, the cyclist had almost reached when the ruffians heard the swish of wheels. The stranger shoved aside the nearest goon and bounded towards the one about to stab Ajay. He twisted his hand to spin out the knife and lobbed it out of all three's reach. The weapon cut a neat trajectory above a cluster of oleander shrubs and fell far away, upon a tuft of wild grass. The man new to the fray pirouetted like a dancer to smite the goon with the Round Kick, and once again lifted his leg high to unfold it and ram a Snap Kick into the man working up a strike from the right. Noticing the third attacker space his hands for a new stance, Ajay sprung upon him with a vault. Simultaneously, he blocked the ruffian's wrist with one hand and clutched his throat with the other by curling his fingers into a claw — using the Tiger Stance. Two against three was not that bad.

When the fight suddenly turned to two against two, the sanguine feeling that the third one had fled for good slipped into Ajay's frenzied mind. The student's shirt was drenched with perspiration, his tough hands bruised, the lady-killer eyes blackened and the long-fringed hair in a mess. The banyan tree was shorn of all stories, neither frightening nor inspiring, just being what it was. In his thoughts blurred by exhaustion, the idea of survival came unaccompanied with cravings for the delights life had offered. Life seemed something he had to strive for without caring where it would lead. And the seconds that ticked away could tip either way.

From both sides, the two assailants aimed kicks at Ajay's ally, but with an instant diverge of his fisted hands he thwacked them both on their cheeks. One of them dived to topple him over, but grabbing him by the arms, he channelized his momentum to catapult him over a branch. The college-goer realised his mistake in assuming he was left with one less opponent on noticing the missing attacker creep up to his saviour from behind. And in a rush of panic, he spotted the knife in his hand. Knocking the man who came in his way with a sudden upward thrust of his elbow, the student propelled himself towards the other assailant and targeted a blow at the hand that held the knife. His heartbeat stopped. He realised he had missed. The knife bored into his ally's back, as his mouth fell open in horror.

Awakened by the commotion, a murder of crows cawed and stirred in their nests. It had begun to drizzle; raindrops pouched in the palm-sized hollows dotting the flat field. A faint slither in the depths of the lowest tree cavity gradually gained perceptibility, but with the growing thud of footfalls, it disappeared among the tallest grass after a brief flash of coils under the intrusive torchlight. Ajay gawked at the figure curled near his feet, his eyes bereft of the ability to blink, even as his neighbours, in various states of undress, swarmed around him. Some hurled questions; they shook him vigorously to elicit an answer. Some others set out in search of medicines and cotton swabs to dab at his wounds. Quite a few had pounded after the outnumbered criminals and at least one had dialled for an ambulance and called the police. The girl who had alighted from the bicycle had brought them along, but unfortunately a few seconds too late.

"Rishi," she screamed upon seeing the youth lying on the dark grass which was darkening further with the ceaseless flow of blood.

"If only I was half as good as you," lamented Ajay, squinting through the hazy lenses of water drops, cradling his classmate in his arms, his breath falling heavily between his words, "you wouldn't have been hit."

Unconfined

Gopal's slight frame was pronounced by the subtle slopes of the huge green blanket. He twitched his left hand, throbbing from the presence of a needle injecting drip. Though a mild tension pricked at the back of his mind as he waited for the surgery, his eyes rambled about. The ward boy lifted the old man off his bed, made him lie down on a stretcher and wheeled him away. The fair, curly haired boy on the opposite bed winced as the doctor pressed the plunger of the syringe, and a plump nurse carrying a bottle of ointment nipped over to the bed at the furthest end of the men's ward.

Calling out of his window to inquire about Gopal's health, Kalipada's next door neighbour Rakhal had warned, "That hospital has gone to the dogs." Though shaken by his words, the former jute factory employee had suppressed his disquiet: nursing homes were beyond his means. Among hospitals, this was the only one with an available bed — with the outbreak of dengue, patients were relegated to the floors in several large hospitals across the city. Gopal's condition was not dengue; the heart ailment he had been suffering from had finally got diagnosed and he needed an immediate surgery.

Kalipada rose from the stool beside Gopal's bed to adjust his blanket so that no part of it hung too close to the floor.

"Why didn't *Didi* come?" Gopal asked. Dark patches encircled his lively eyes and new pimples had erupted beside the old scars on his brown face.

"She wanted to come, but I asked her to study. She'll come tomorrow after her Physics exam," Kalipada replied. "Anyway, you don't have to stay here for long," he assured.

Kalipada's wife Kamala hurried to the bedside after a quick word with the doctor. "Don't be scared. Just listen to the nurses," she said to

Gopal, wiping his slightly moist forehead with her soft fingertips. The clock on the wall ticked its way to the end of the visiting hour. Before turning to leave she promised to be back in the evening. The surgery would take place the next day.

Kamala recalled the days when Gopal was little more than a toddler. While his mother mopped the floor, he would sit on the steps leading to the roof, his gaze flitting across the rooms and lingering on the various household items that piqued his curiosity. Often, he would fiddle with the only plaything he possessed — a plastic frog full of puny balls.

The balcony drew him: he would crane his neck from the stairs, to glimpse the potted plants hoarded on the floor, jostling on the railing top and suspended from the ceiling. The pots were made of burnt clay or plastic. There were even a few glass bottles — delicate tendrils coiled out from their narrow mouths to trail beyond the grilles. Kamala had bought many of the saplings from the annual Rath Yatra fair, where the vendors spread out their wares on a grassy field pocketed with rainwater. The profusion of plants reminded Gopal of the greenery in his village. After his father's death they had to leave it behind and come to the city in search of a living.

Gopal's mother was scrubbing the washbasin in the bathroom when he left the refuge of the staircase to explore the balcony. To avoid the jutting branches, an adult needed to crouch as if he were stepping into a palanquin, but little Gopal found no difficulty in ambling beneath the foliage. He arrived at a barren patch of the floor and spotted a door on the adjacent wall. On realising that there was a tiny room between the bedroom and the balcony, his eyes gleamed as if he had chanced upon a secret hideout.

It suddenly occurred to Kamala, who suffered from occasional bouts of forgetfulness, to check whether she had extinguished the prayer lamp. Rushing to the balcony, she found Gopal tugging at the latch of the door. For a moment her heart stopped in terror as if she had glimpsed a dangerous beast among the thick foliage. Prejudices about caste and birth came crashing down on her as a precariously piled assortment of daggers, swords and spears. Old beliefs, nourished and kept alive through the millennia, scoffed at modern attempts of assimilation as though the latter were a child challenging the authority of an adult.

Kamala screamed with rage. Before the child could react, she stooped down below the leaves, crawled forward and dragged him out of the balcony as roughly as she could. Incensed, she failed to notice how the boy got lashed by the scratchy branches and scraped by the coarse leaves. Pricked by a rose thorn, he let out a sharp cry, but it could not thaw Kamala, who heaped abuses on him and his mother, her voice growing hoarse and the blood surging in her veins until a time came that her words got garbled and she huffed and puffed for breath.

Some workings of the mind, unmonitored by the eyes, are like overlooked toys strewn on the floor. One sees them only after one has tripped. The disturbance within Kamala took time to settle though the swirl grew weaker with every passing hour. By bedtime, the last of the disrupted grains of thought had been carried back to where they belonged, yet traces remained of their displacement. Kalipada put aside his newspaper and switched off the lights, when Kamala, who was lying curled up to him in the bed, tugged at his hand.

"Something happened this morning while you were sleeping," she started.

"Yes, I heard your voice. I guessed that you were furious with Malati, but I was too drowsy to ponder over it," replied Kalipada, who had returned from the factory at dawn.

After narrating the incident Kamala fretted, "What if Malati doesn't turn up anymore? She's far better than all our previous maids."

"Don't worry, we'll see what happens tomorrow," Kalipada whispered, stroking her smooth cheeks with the back of his hand.

Malati, who could not afford to quit her job in the Bhattacharya household, rang the doorbell at six in the morning as usual, but Gopal was not with her.

"Where is Gopal?" Kamala asked softly.

The maid told Kamala she had left him in their hut with the door locked from outside. She did not want him to wander around with the other slum children, who often got into danger. A couple of days ago, a child had crept inside a storehouse and got killed, when a heavy sack had toppled over him. A shiver ran through Kamala, imagining Gopal shut in his home with a few inanimate items and an immense possibility of peril.

"But keeping him locked can also be risky," Kamala told her. "What if there's a fire?" she asked and noticed the maid's face grow pale and shrink in horror at the possibility itself.

"You can bring Gopal along," Kamala continued, and then glancing away from the maid to fix her eyes on the nails driven into the wall, she warned, "But he must not try to enter the room next to the balcony."

Gopal was so young that the memory failed to bore its claws into his mind — the inability to recall about the earliest years being one of the few levellers in an unequal world. But he remembered his mother forbidding him to venture near the room because she had reiterated the warning in the subsequent years. It was Kamala, who found it difficult to forget her own spell of nastiness: she was resigned to her guilt like one burdened with a loan that took ages to pay off.

*

Kamala was peeling potatoes in the kitchen when the bell rang. Some pesky salesman, she assumed. She turned to the door only after dealing with another lumpy potato and binning the last shred of its skin. As she reached for the bolt, the bell rang again — this time it was more prolonged. To her surprise, Kalipada stood before her, his gaze on the floor and fist pressed to the wall.

"You are back so early today!" Kamala exclaimed, her lips struggling with a happy but confused smile. Kalipada pushed the attaché into her hands, pulled at the shoelaces and kicked off his footwear. Without responding to her smile, he stomped to the washroom and all she could hear was the gush of tap water.

As Kamala placed the cup of milky tea on Kalipada's table, the pressure cooker whistled and she had to hurry back to the kitchen. She poured the boiled lentils upon the chopped onions sizzling in a *kadai* and was proceeding to sprinkle *ghee* when it occurred to her that her husband might have drowsed off from fatigue. Tip-toeing to the bedroom, she found him perched on his chair, his left elbow pinioned on the armrest and his right hand dangling, away from the cup.

"You still haven't drunk the tea! It must have gone cold," she said, slightly annoyed since she always took care to serve him a steaming cup as soon as he returned from his workplace.

Kalipada neither spoke, nor turned to meet her gaze.

"I've washed your blue striped shirt. You can wear it to the factory tomorrow."

"Kamala, I cannot go to the factory anymore," he groaned.

"What?"

"It has closed down."

Kamala's head reeled. She clutched the door handle for support. Had she ever wanted anything other than two meals a day, a decent education for her daughter, a couple of new saris for the Durga *pujas* and someone to help her with the ceaseless chain of domestic chores? Was she asking for too much? Why did the Almighty decide to snatch away even the minimal conveniences? She hurled more angry questions at her God till she caught the whiff of burnt *dal* and dashed to the kitchen.

The next morning, Malati trotted to the end of the corridor and picked up the trash can. She emptied the contents of the bin into the municipality sweeper's stinking vat, returned to the house, rinsed her hands and began to sweep the floor. Kamala scuffed close to the maid and cleared her throat. Pitching her voice to be loud enough to spare her the trouble of repeating, she said, "You need not come from next month."

The words hit Malati's ears, bounced and plucked the shine off her eyes. They seeped beneath her skin, spreading an all-consuming, burning sense of gloom that erupted from the depths of uncertainty. Bleak were her chances of finding a new job: her endeavours to find work to supplement her income from the Bhattacharyas had been unsuccessful so far — the families she had inquired about through acquaintances already had maids. Tossed by her dejected expression, Kamala's guilty conscience shot up like mercury during a high fever. With her husband's face, too, shadowed by the same curse of joblessness, there was nothing she could do for her maid.

*

"Offer these flowers at the Lord's feet," Kalipada instructed Madhav and his wife, and sprinkled the holy water over their bowed heads. As the lady busied herself in arranging the *prasad* in Thermocol bowls, out of the corner of his eyes Kalipada glimpsed the crisp currency note peeking from the householder's pocket. He used to visit this mansion in his childhood, accompanying his father who was a full time Hindu priest.

"If you give me just ten minutes to finish my breakfast, I can drop you home," Madhav offered.

"Thanks. It will be fine if you drop me at the bus-stop." Kalipada smiled, touched by the gesture.

"Would you like to have *parathas* with me?" Madhav asked.

Kalipada smiled again but shook his head, although his stomach growled with hunger that the meagre *prasad* could not combat. He also realised it would be impossible to stop for a bite on his way to the school if he had to reach it on time. The new priest diverted his mind by thanking his Lord that the headmistress was considering Rupsa's admission in mid-session.

"Madhav *babu*, I need some advice on investments," said Kalipada.

"Sure. Go on," the accountant replied and gestured to the chair next to him.

A week later, with a heavy heart, Kalipada collected his daughter's Transfer Certificate from the principal's office, rushed past the glass walls of the computer lab and scurried out of the gates of her old school.

Later in the evening, when the priest had settled down in his chair to calculate the day's expenses, he overheard a conversation between his wife and his daughter in the next room.

"How will I meet Ridhima?" Rupsa asked her mother, while trying on her new uniform — a sky blue *salwar-kameez* with a white *dupatta*. It was clear from her tone she had already begun to miss her.

"We'll take you to her house sometimes," Kamala promised.

"Ohhh, that means I'll get to see her only once in a while," lamented the daughter.

The sharp disappointment in her voice drove a wedge through Kalipada's heart. Given his circumstances, he had no choice but to admit her to a school with lower fees. He hoped she would soon make new friends and stop missing her former classmates so badly.

The Bhattacharyas somehow beat their hunger, paid the electricity bill and the school fees, and served the deities who resided in the room forbidden to Gopal and all others from his caste. Within three months, Malati found employment as a cook in an affluent home, much to Kamala's relief though she was still coping with the uncertainty looming over her own family.

*

Kalipada's late great-grandfather had unearthed the idols from a field adjoining their ancestral home in Bankura. It is said Lord Mahadev Himself had told him about the idols in a dream. The rock carved deities were seated on a throne: Mahadev's arm encircled Parvati's slender waist, the snake around his neck contemplated its surroundings with beady eyes and the hefty bull Nandi playfully tucked his snout between his feet. The crescent moon rested at a strange angle on the tangle of Mahadev's hair as if the Lord had caught it in time during a tumble in space to prevent its disappearance in the infinite. Parvati's large, petal shaped eyes exuded such power that no occurrence in the universe could escape her gaze. She was bejewelled with gold earrings, bangles and necklaces bought by Kalipada's forefathers and the householder himself during better days. They believed the idols were a thousand years old. To Kalipada and his ancestors, their value lay not in their history or craftsmanship, but in the belief that Lord Himself chose to reside in their home.

The calling bell and the alarm clock had followed the electric-kettle to the heap of junk. Shoved out of her sleep by the loud banging on their door, Kamala glanced at her husband's wristwatch and panicked. It was 7:30 AM. Her days began at five. She would attend to the deities, mop the floor and dust the furniture before confining herself to the kitchen to rustle up the breakfast. After breakfast, it was time to cook lunch. She tried to catch some sleep after lunch, but more often than not, some chore or the other cropped up and snatched it away.

Kamala lumbered towards the door, struggling to shake off her drowsiness. She was awake till late in the night, nursing a quivering, feverish Rupsa. Unlocking the door with the key from an antique, silver key ring, she scrutinised the familiar looking boy and exclaimed, "You, Gopal!"

It had been ages since Gopal was last seen in the Bhattacharyas' house. Yet his stare, carrying the blankness of unmemorable years, exerted a kind of continuity. He must have been twelve but was short for his age. He wore an oversized shirt and trousers that ended two inches above the ankles. His eyes were red from excessive rubbing, skin roughed by the struggles of the street and hair matted from the dearth of an urge to comb or wash. He broke the news of his mother's death while gazing at the staircase to the roof.

Gopal was willing to perform any kind of work in exchange for a meal and a shelter. Turned away by his mother's recent employers, he looked up to the Bhattacharyas as his last hope. Saddened by his former maid's demise and moved by Gopal's plight, Kalipada scratched his balding pate, but it took Kamala only an hour to make up her mind. She insisted, "We can't turn away an orphan. We'll keep him. Our Lords will see to the rest." Little did she know what her words actually meant.

*

"Be careful," said Kalipada, pulling close the door as Kamala and Gopal bade him goodbye. They strode out of the gates and took the lane running past a ramshackle saloon.

After trotting through several alleys, they arrived at the building with the signboard 'St Peter's School.'

"Stay well and listen to your teachers," Kamala said, affectionately pressing her chin on Gopal's head. He stepped inside the free school, run by the Christian missionaries. She emerged from the lane to take the parallel one and walked for fifteen minutes to reach the two roomed building, rented by an NGO. A silver-haired lady sat at a small, polished table, pouring over a leather-bound register. Kamala walked up to her, unclasped her bag and unfurled the handkerchief she had sewed the previous night. After minutely examining the embroidery of dancing peacocks, antlered deer and fluffy rabbits the elderly woman nodded in approval. She pasted a numbered sticker on the kerchief, tucked it away in a drawer and jotted down Kamala's name and the allotted number in a notepad.

Kamala wondered whether the money she would make at the month-end would suffice the expense of the new member. At least, she did not have to worry about the cost of his books as he could use Rupsa's, who was only two classes senior. Much of the text followed by his school curriculum were the same as those she had studied.

Gopal was kept away from all time-consuming chores so he could study and indulge in the games of his choice. His duties were simple: he unlatched the door when somebody knocked, served glasses of water when guests arrived, and helped Kamala tidy the bedrooms and prune the surviving plants in the balcony.

*

"Ma, I finished my homework," Gopal said, passing by the kitchen. The word 'Ma' pounded in Kamala's heart with an undefeatable force. Soaring in ecstasy, she turned off the gas, loped out of the kitchen and saw the boy approach Kalipada, who was buried in a newspaper.

"Baba, here's the letter I found in the letter-box," said the teenager, handing over a sealed envelope. Kalipada closed the newspaper with a snap, flicked off his plus power glasses and gawked at the boy for a few seconds. His thick moustache began to twitch. Kamala could not remember the last time she had caught such a dazzling grin on his ageing visage. A year had passed since Gopal had come to live with them. Though the Bhattacharyas had been referring to themselves as his parents for months, it was the first time the boy called them as such.

Before the factory's closure Kalipada and Kamala had prayed for another child. The wish that had floated around their minds only to be forgotten like a game of yore, finally found fulfilment through Gopal. They did not consider the option of a legal adoption, lacking the means to face the hassles. But everything that belonged to the Bhattacharyas was also Gopal's, except the prayer room. The couple discussed time and again whether to open it for him, but certain notions clung despite the tussle. Arguments brought along with them counter arguments stringing a chain that bound them to the replica of the previous day.

*

The couple sat on a cushioned sofa in the sparsely lit antechamber. The air-conditioning was such that Kamala had to reach for her pallu and wrap it tightly around herself. Kalipada, too, shivered and knotted up his legs. Lack of sleep had weakened their resistance against such unfavourably low temperatures.

Gopal's illness came into his foster parents' notice about a month ago. After returning from his school the boy sat down on the freshly wiped floor, next to Rupsa, for a warm meal of fish and rice. Several times, she jogged his arm on noticing his head loll from side to side.

Lowering her plate into the sink, Rupsa remarked to her mother, "Gopal is so sleepy today." It also struck her that he had left his soiled plate on the floor — something so unlike him.

By the time, Kamala came looking for him to ask whether he was unwell, Gopal was in bed, his limbs wrapped around the side-pillow. She leaned over the headboard to call him but held back as all the sleep, robbed off from several insomniacs, seemed to have descended on him.

Gopal avoided his textbooks for several evenings, complaining of excessive fatigue. At first Kamala suspected that he was just being naughty, conjuring up imaginary problems to escape from his studies. A flashing memory prevented her from admonishing him, but she explained to him why he should study to grow up and get a career.

*

Kamala hurried back from the NGO, somewhat disturbed by Gopal's continuing disinterest in his lessons. His friend Nikhil was rapping at their door.

"Aunty, we haven't seen Gopal for days," he said, his eyes crinkled in concern. Before Kamala could reply the door unbolted with a click.

Kamala entered the house and called out, "Look Gopal, who has come."

There was neither any verbal response nor the patter of footsteps.

"He's sleeping," Rupsa, who had opened the door, whispered.

"Gopal, here's Nikhil," Kamala called again on nearing his bed.

The sleepy boy's face lit up as he opened his eyes and saw Nikhil. Rolling away the oblong side-pillow, he sat up and patted the staid grey bed sheet, gesturing to his friend to sit near him. Kamala drew open the curtains. She clinked open her sewing box and uncoiled a bit of green thread.

"Won't you play with us today?" Nikhil asked. Kamala squinted to locate the eye of the needle.

Gopal shook his head. "I don't want to go outside. Let's play Chinese Checker today," he mumbled, his words slurred by drowsiness.

The needle slipped off Kamala's fingers and rolled into the junk stowed under the bed. She dropped to the floor to search for the needle, her face suddenly warped. She knew he enjoyed cricket too much to avoid, unless there were some pressing reasons.

"May I help you, Auntie?" Nikhil offered, noticing her in such a posture. His words, though picked up by her ears, were debarred from reaching her brains by a clamping foreboding.

Kalipada took Gopal to a general physician who referred him to a cardiologist. The little smiles curving along the pillars of the Bhattacharyas' inner temple were ironed out the day Gopal's chest X-Ray reports came out.

Before accepting the most undesired means of procuring the money for Gopal's heart surgery, the Bhattacharyas had tried all other options. They appealed to everyone they knew. Kalipada visited each house in which he or his late father had conducted *pujas*. Many pledged their help, but derided him behind his back for fostering an urchin when he could provide so little for his wife and daughter. Some contributed as per their means but the sum was too meagre to meet the combined expenses of hospitalisation, doctor's fees and vital checkups after the surgery. Sleepless nights steered Kalipada to the streets. His familiar lane was dark as a cave tunnel and the shadows of temple spires like pointed stalactites. A patch of light from an illuminated billboard seemed the only opening.

*

The idols, which had to undergo antiquity authentication tests, were found to date back to the eight century. Kamala and Kalipada bowed their heads and touched the sacred feet of the ancient figurines for the last time before they were carted away to another room. The celestial couple appeared as serene as ever; stones and Gods indistinguishable in the lack of agonising attachment since such a trait was only for those between. The Bhattacharyas dashed out of the antique dealer's office lest they froze, unable to sever themselves from the idols. They strode along a thronging pavement in complete silence before boarding a bus to reach the hospital.

Words resurged in Kalipada when the bus conductor asked him about his destination. To their own surprise, the Bhattacharyas were slowly infused with peace as the bus roared down the roads. A decision no matter how tough, once nailed and sealed, brought along a lulling effect. Kalipada wondered whether the Lord and His Consort had come to his ancestors for this day and this purpose? Who could guess what goes on in Gods' and Goddesses' minds?

The bus braked twice at the same signal. A pair of competing kites seized the attention of the jaded passengers; the sun's last glow sponged the patch of sky hoisted by a church steeple and frilled by the coconut leaves. Nearer to the crossing, swept by a cool blast of wind, a shirtless man, dripping with sweat after a football match, swaggered among flying shreds of glazed paper. Framed by her fluttering *dupatta*, a petite woman intercepted a tide of students for signatures to her petition, while an eunuch, donning thick mascara, found her way to the cars.

Kalipada and Kamala had read it in religious texts and heard from the words of saints, propagated to them through many people and many ages. They had yearned to believe in it, waiting for some sign to put contradictions at rest. But for the first time they were experiencing it — Shiva and Parvati — everywhere.

Higher than the Hills

"Two small packets of Lays, a packet of local chips, three Kurkure, two bottles of Pepsi, two Seven Up, one Limca, three Thumbs Up," Akash said aloud while jotting them down in the notepad along with their respective prices. His employer would scrutinise the listing next morning. Now he was in his other shop overlooking the road that brushed against the eastern edge of the lake before leading on to the settlements. As the rowers looked around, munching on chips and sipping cold drinks, Mala whispered, "This is your chance."

Akash picked up a one-rupee coin, curled his fingers and closed his fist. When his fingers flew open, there was a fifty and a ten rupee note and a five-rupee coin in his palm. In total, sixty-five rupees — equal to a dollar.

"Teach me this. Won't have to pay a fortune to buy dollars if I get to travel on-site for my client," joked a young man, wiping off his sweat.

Akash grabbed a discarded packet of chips and rubbed at the tear below its upper edge. The tear faded as if it were a new packet. He nicked it again and reached within its depths to bring out a bunch of carnations. He repaired it for the second time with a twist of his hands and punctured it with a pen to spill out a handful of soap bubbles. Then he pried out a folded fan from the empty Thumbs Up bottle, followed by a string of glittering beads. Akash's gaze seldom wavered from Mala as he pretended to perform these tricks only for her, but his real sights were set on the customers who had travelled all the way from the cities to hone their skills in rock climbing, rappelling, cave crawling and rowing.

Mala prodded Akash to show her the 'No Smoking' trick. He lit a match and inched it towards a cigarette. The flame vanished. He repeated the trick to confirm that the flame's disappearance was neither a coincidence nor by an inflow of wind. Spellbound, the group of men and women stood rooted to the shop floor like a bunch of pencils in a stand. He moved on to the 'Fish Pond' act. He poured water into Mala's cupped hands and joined his own palms over hers. Leading her to the edge of the shop, he asked her to part her fingers and waited for the loud gasps with a silent chuckle. The reactions from his audience did not disappoint when the fish leaped from the curve of her palms and disappeared in the lake waters below.

As usual, before leaving, several customers asked for Akash's cell phone number, forgetting there was no mobile tower in his village. Or anywhere near. The shopkeeper wrote, in his best handwriting, his full postal address and the number of the nearest phone booth; something he had already done for many groups of rowers. Only one among them had ever called, but just to jabber away.

Akash packed the props in a box and set the shop in order, refusing to take any help despite repeated insistence from Mala, his employer's daughter. Eventually she left. Long, loose strands of hair played around her face as she cut through the sunlit spot of the lake, sweeping away the water with the wooden oar. It was the same way she would mentally distance herself from any gesture she might have unwittingly made to beguile Akash. No matter what her feelings had been for him since adolescence, she tried her best not to cling to them. She swung her arms faster to pick up speed: she needed to prepare for the Har Shakti puja, a localised version of Shiv Ratri.

Often Akash was all by himself in the shop, the vast stretches of uninterrupted water cocooning him in a magical world of its own. Flakes of thoughts spun around, enticing him to reach out and grasp. He kept toying with their silhouettes until he could imagine their vividness. Spurred on by his repeated attempts at visualisation, they would finally shed their veils and unleash their spell, new tricks shimmering up.

The instructors and the boat owners always discouraged the amateur rowers from hitting the waters in the dark. Akash shut the shop and returned to the mainland before the pinkish rays of the sun ceased to be perceptible like a cream massaged uniformly over a face.

Back in his home, Akash sat down to eat next to his brothers on a bamboo mat. The wooden floor reverberated with the footsteps of his youngest sibling and his friend as they frantically chased each other across the cluttered rooms. Though annoyed with their propensity to trip on textbooks and utensils, scatter stationery and drying clips and knock off bottles and containers, Akash's mother was largely relieved that they were not out in the open as leopard sightings were not uncommon.

Before any household errand could tether him, Akash rushed out of the house with the promise to return soon. Since there were no cell phones, he tried his best to reach the meeting spot on time, zigzagging through the pine forest, a stick in one hand and a lantern in the other. Emerging on the recently constructed road, he raised his lantern to locate the rock with a hole in its middle. He stepped on the rock next to it, then the one below, and descended the slope, treading each rock with caution. In another couple of minutes, the silhouette of a braided and shawl wrapped woman appeared at the edge of the road. He clambered up the boulders and held out his hand. But Tiya trotted down to the bank on her own as usual.

Tiya handed Akash the newspaper she had borrowed from the library. He rolled it and tucked it between two dry boulders. He would carry it home to keep abreast of the news. The news he read in the papers would influence his acts. When Akash was thirteen, he chanced upon a magazine subscribed by Mala's English tutor. Captivated by the colourful illustrations, he had leafed through the pages and come across an article captioned 'Real Wizards,' accompanied with the sub-title 'Remembering the Legends.' After racing through the one-page long tribute to great magicians like Harry Kellar and David Devant, Akash had paced about his room in feverish excitement. He realised that the tricks he performed with kettles and matchboxes, if innovated further, could propel him to the peak of worldwide fame. But even after so many years, the way to recognition remained an incomprehensible puzzle to him. Like the secrets behind his tricks were to his handful of dedicated spectators.

Tiya and Akash settled on a wide rock, facing the stream which was a moving, white mass of sheer speed, giving a visual representation to all the uncounted seconds and ignored minutes of their lives. Flickers of light spangled the woolly darkness swathing the hills across the bank. A faint shadow crept upon Tiya's dimples, although her lips curved into a genial smile.

"What is it?" asked Akash, fiddling with her waist-length braids.

After several long minutes Tiya parted her lips to say, "I heard Mala had rowed to the island again to meet you." There was hesitance in her manner as she was reluctant to come across as insecure. But the disquieting stirring within her, comparable to that of a clock-hand approaching the time of alarm, refused to die down.

"You know that we are friends. The whole village even thinks we are like siblings," he stressed, though aware that his easy-going fondness for Mala was far from being a manifestation of brotherly affection. But it was Tiya who reigned over his thoughts and fantasies; she filled his life with a certain sweetness, which he wished not to lose at any cost. "And would her father keep me alive if something was going on between us?"

Tiya did not reply but the crinkle in her eyes and the restrained stretch of her lips conveyed that she was still not convinced.

"We will get married as soon as I start earning enough for the two of us," Akash promised, drawing her so close that she could loosen her shawl and warm herself against his body instead.

Among all the criss-crossing ideas of an emerging adulthood, there had been a thought that originated from an even tinier speck of thought, but spread all over Akash's mind like a flood, like fame, reaching every corner, surpassing every hint of conflict, till it emerged as a full-bodied emotion. More special moments followed the earliest moments of realisation, assuring him of the way ahead. Tiya, on her part, had been flattered by his attention. The not-so-secret fact that another girl vied for his affections stroked the dormant aspect of her competitiveness, bringing about the heady feeling of a winner. She could not pinpoint exactly when that initial rush of excitement had transcended to a deeper level of ardour.

Before the year came to an end, Mala's marriage was arranged with a city-based businessman. He was smitten by her photographs which had come into his possession through a match-maker. Among all the villagers including Mala's ageing parents, the person most relieved by this development was undoubtedly Tiya. Freed from the last tentacles of anxiety, she glowed as much as the bride-to-be in the run up to the wedding.

Mala's relatives from far-flung pockets of the country started trickling in a month in advance. With the rooms thronging with people and the furniture rocking with laughter, she would invite Akash to her house to perform, usually at dinner-time. Seated on round stools or warm rugs, the guests would take mouthfuls of gravy lapped rice. Their eyes would swivel to follow every flick of his hands. Their ears would be attuned to the arresting click of his fingers.

On the auspicious day, marigold wreaths ringed the casements of Mala's house. Strings of pink and green electric lamps garlanded her father's shops. "Beautiful!" gushed the guests, gazing at the illuminated shop across the dark ripples of the lake, the shehnai emanating a continuous melody to connect the unpredicted sparks felt by some of them. Conscious of the many eyes riveted on her — some exuding happiness, others envy or indifference — as her groom drew a neat line of vermilion across her forehead, Mala sensed Akash slip effortlessly into the inevitability of his own choice.

*

Tiya wistfully eyed the electric blue earrings dangling from a rod in one of the many makeshift stalls, in the grassy expanse between a clump of rhododendron and the river. She had already bought a pair of anklets and gathered all her resolve to restrain herself from splurging any more. She needed to save most of the money she had earned that day.

While moving away from the fairground she recognized the man striding before her by his tall, broad shouldered frame and the salt and pepper hair encircling a bald patch.

"How are you Ramnarayan *ji*?" She greeted the elderly villager.

"I'm fine, Tiya. How are you?" He halted and turned to her.

"I'm fine," Tiya replied with a smile.

"Anchal told me you had set up a stall..." he said.

"Yes," Tiya confirmed. She drew back the strings of her *potli* bag to reveal the tiny silk saris, the crisp dhotis, shiny vests, beaded blouses and elaborately pleated *ghagras* she had sewn for the pint-sized idols worshipped at homes. Noticing just a packet of *papad* in his hands, she asked, "Haven't you bought any saris for Anchal *ji*? There were nice ones in the stall next to the pottery shop."

"Where's the money left after spending on food and medicine?" He sighed and gave a wry smile. "Even in the year Mala got married, I remember buying so many toys for Anil and Megha. In two years, how difficult it has become to make ends meet..." he bemoaned.

Tiya spoke no further and glanced down, slightly embarrassed by her casual question. The same lament rang in her home, in the fields, in the shops and wherever else the villagers gathered.

"I'm so glad that Mala could get away from this place," he continued. "I've heard her husband's business has picked up really well, especially after the birth of their son."

After returning to her house Tiya took out the reels of orange and green thread, and pulled the chair next to her sewing machine. Though she had an innate sense of design and her creations stood out for the appropriate use of tassels and sequins, only a few had gotten sold so far. But she clung on to the hope of making a proper entry into the market soon.

The bobbin was ready on the spindle. Rotating the handle of the machine, Tiya continuously shifted the piece of cloth under the needle as the stitches appeared, hemming the *ghagra*. She heard the swish of a sari at the door, but determinedly kept her eyes fixed to the cloth.

"Rajan's elder brother has come to visit him and will stay in our village with his wife and son for a week," Rani *bhabi* began. Tiya caught a whiff of something that smelled like manure. Before stepping out of her home in the morning, she had seen her sister-in-law flatten the lumps of cow dung and slap them against the walls to dry. They would fuel their clay oven at dinner time. Tiya guessed Rani *bhabi* had been waiting all day to speak to her and in her haste, she had not noticed the dung still webbing her fingers and caking her nails. "The son is a government officer. They will come to meet us tomorrow. So you must not leave the house," she commanded.

Aware of where she was heading, Tiya responded, "I'll love to meet them, but you know I'll not marry anyone other than Akash."

"And remain the oldest unmarried woman in the village," hissed her sister-in-law.

"*Bhabi*, I'm only twenty-two," Tiya reminded, without shifting her eyes from the needle.

"So what? No woman in Pirpahar remains unmarried at twenty-two," fumed her brother's wife. Tiya knew her intention was not to deprive her of a place in her father's home. Rather it was a reaction to the social pressure mounted on her husband by the other villagers.

At last Tiya turned to meet Rani *bhabi*'s gaze. "I don't want to spend my life copying others. I can't love anyone else the way I love Akash. Please understand."

"Wait till your brother comes home," Tiya's sister-in-law roared and stormed off to the cow shed, her anklets clinking loudly.

With a deliberately unperturbed expression, Tiya inspected the partly sewn *ghagra*. Suddenly, her forehead throbbed. The constant squabbles were taking a toll on her health. No longer did she get the chance to meet Akash in the evenings. He had to supplement his meagre income from the shop by arranging bonfires and music for the adventure sports enthusiasts, who wished to unwind once the darkness thickened.

Before slipping beneath his snug blanket next to his brothers, Akash would sit, with his legs partly folded, on a worn carpet spread on the floor to cover up the space left by the bed. He would fiddle with a ballpoint pen, contemplating the items in his room and mulling over new magic tricks. Outside the window the hills sloped towards the lake, bristling with conifers and ringing with the persistent courting calls of insects.

*

No sooner than he finished counting the notes from the day's sales, Akash's employer handed him a card adorned with pictures of babies. Surprised, Akash flipped it open and immediately recognized the slanting handwriting. Mala had invited him to perform as a magician at her son's first birthday party. Barring him and her parents, the only other invitee from the village was Tiya. Her inclusion did not surprise him. He understood Mala's concern for his ease during the brief stay in her house.

Mala had booked their train tickets as well. "I'll have to shut my shops for six days! Just imagine. That crazy daughter of mine won't listen," he muttered. Akash wondered how he would take Tiya along. It was not acceptable for an unmarried couple to travel so far. And he knew better than to expect Tiya's family to challenge such norms.

*

"Hurry. We can't afford to miss the first bus to the railway station," Akash whispered, standing outside the gate, a woollen cap covering his ears. The couple knew the village elders would censure Tiya for her elopement. But luckily, since most of them were not against her choice of a husband, they would allow them to stay here if they could return as man and wife.

Tiya tip-toed out of her courtyard and noiselessly pushed the bamboo gate behind her.

She glanced repetitively over her shoulders in alarm, clutching her bag tightly over her heaving chest. Her heart leaped at the crunching of leaves under her feet. Her cold, reddened nose itched, but she took a deep breath to control the irresistible urge to sneeze. The sight of the purple geraniums sneaked in a tinge of regret. Did such pretty flowers ever bloom in the crowded plains? The sky was exposing its paleness; the hills surrounding the lake were like lips drawn in for whistling.

*

The cab that fetched the foursome from the railway station whooshed through the opened gates of an apartment complex, trailed along the cemented path running between rows of similarly designed high-rises and groaned to a stop next to the block marked as C. Spotting them from her bedroom window, Mala streaked down to the premises. After touching her parents' feet, she turned to Tiya and drew her in a tight hug as if she had missed her too. Finally, when she took a step towards Akash and beamed, he noticed that she had changed little — just put on some weight, though not in a bad way by the yardstick of his gaze.

"*Namaste*. I hope you had a smooth journey," Mala's husband enquired, rising from his cane chair as the party from Pirpahar entered his duplex flat. The baby, coaxed out of his favourite hideout underneath a mahogany desk, scrutinised the new faces from a distance.

Tiya was gazing at the shops crested with colourful hoardings, and at the cars racing down the flyover when Akash strolled into the balcony. He glanced back at the door and crept closer to her. His eyes fell on a lone, fragile sapling resigned to its place between the towering buildings like the commuters trapped in traffic. On a different occasion, he would have missed the rocks and the stream. "Can't wait for the party," he gushed instead, entangling his fingers with hers.

Mala's parents slept in the guest room overlooking the lawn. Akash shared the adjacent room with two of Manoj's friends while Tiya was directed to his sister's room as expected in an Indian household. The magician could not help but smile ruefully, guessing the scandalous speculations back home.

*

Wrapped in a richly brocaded silk sari, Mala sashayed into the large rented hall. Her hoop earrings caressed her round shoulders as she tilted her head, to contemplate the effect of the fuzzy festoons swaying from the top of the windows. Her long, shampooed hair, twisted in a bun, allowed a view of her slender neck as she lowered her gaze to fix it upon the Jumping Pillow, then on the rocking horses and the huge teddy bear which was large enough for three children to snuggle in its lap.

With long feathers tucked in their hair, five little girls capered about in the performance area, demarcated from the rest of the hall by a strip of ribbon tied around two knee high poles. At the first beat of the music played from an I-pod, the children lined up and clasped each other's shoulders. Then they hopped back and forth in a perfect rhythm. A teenage boy's stand-up comedy drew a scatter of laughter and finally, it was Akash's turn. Donning a shiny turban, he strode to the performance area and stood in front of the mike.

"Good evening, I'm Akash from Pirpahar," began the magician, not only thrilled at the sound of his own amplified voice, but also a tad nervous on glancing at the hall full of strangers.

"I will start with a magic called Simplification," Akash said after taking a deep breath. Two five-year-olds alighted from the rocking horses and ran to the chairs arranged in a row in front of the performance area. Akash picked up the elaborate labyrinth he had made with cardboard, raised it for everyone to see and placed it back on the table. He unfolded a tablecloth, flung it over the mini maze and hovered his hands over it. Then he simultaneously drew away both his hands as if he were swimming - pushing apart the water on either side. When he flipped the cloth away and bowed, a plain rectangular box stood in place of the labyrinth. Akash spotted Mala nudging a reedy, bespectacled woman to follow his performance. The lady's gaze lingered, for a few seconds, on the magician's getup and mannerisms, but soon drifted to the heap of scrumptious fries on the caterer's tray.

Next in line was a trick called Arctic Oil Spill. Akash upturned a tumbler to let his audience know it was empty. Pouring water and then oil into it, he slid it into a bare box and brought down the lid. He beckoned a girl who had been running across the hall, chasing another child with a serpentine balloon. Caught by surprise, she stopped in her tracks and scrutinised the magician with interest. Keen on a new experience, she scudded to the stretched ribbon, slipped through the gap between the pole and the wall, but scuffed towards the table with some wariness. Put immediately at ease by Akash, she readily yanked open the lid of the box as he instructed. The magician gaped, pretending to be as startled as the girl. There was no tumbler, just two glasses: one with oil and the other with water.

"If only we could deal with the Arctic Oil Spill like this," Akash beamed and rounded off the act by gulping down the water to prove that it was unspoiled. A dozen men and women, standing not far away from the poles, hooted at the punch line of a risqué joke. Another gang, parading across the hall, regarded the props with interest before whizzing out of the door to light their cigarettes.

Akash pulled back his gaze to the table and then shot a glance at Tiya. Shadows chipped at her forehead. One half of her face caught the light. The hair cupping it shone like a crescent moon. Her mountain skin glowed. She nodded and her eyes brightened as she met his gaze. Her lips quivered and then bloomed into a most divine smile, urging him to carry on. The magician arranged two empty clay cups on the table and in front of them he placed a framed photograph depicting picturesque mountains and sparkling streams. With rapid movements of his hand, he picked up an urn, whisked it behind the photo and tilted it. After putting aside the photo he picked up each cup and drained its content into a bucket. Water had collected in both the cups as if it had branched like a river while falling from the urn. When he kept three cups, the water filled up all three; in case of four cups, it split into four. After five bowls had been filled Akash looked up from his props, his glance sweeping across the expressions of the guests. His jaws clenched as he watched them chattering away while licking the creamy cake off their fingers, spearing kebabs with toothpicks or clinking at the bottom of the bowls with their spoons for the last dregs of soup. The varied insentient delights in the hall kept the children preoccupied. While juggling with her roles as an alert mother and an attentive hostess, Mala managed to catch snips of his performance through the pauses between her conversations with the guests. Like a prisoner reaching for her beloved through the gaps between bars.

Through much of the night, sleep waited outside the ambit of Akash's consciousness. As a bright splash of sunlight warmed up his bed, his eyes, which had closed not too long ago, flew wide open and fell on a Roman numbered clock. Next to it, stood a lacquered flower vase choked with a bunch of dry roses. Akash recalled the flowers being brought fresh from the florist on the day of his arrival. One of the men who shared the room with him was bent over his travel bag.

The magician forced himself to rise to his feet, then hobble to the bathroom. Staring at the outlet of the spotlessly clean washbasin, he took a deep breath and let the cold water trickle down his face, wetting the crinkled collars of his shirt. He unravelled the towel from the rod, wiped himself and frowned at the brass rimmed mirror. The glass infuriated him with its inability to reflect the difference, the transparent material opaque to the true appearance of his visage, which he imagined being an assortment of broken pieces balanced on each other, like a lamp that has just cracked, but not flung apart as yet.

Akash was spared more despair as the day surged at breakneck speed. "Since Tiya's parents are not here, will you do the *kanyadan*?" Akash looked at his employer expectantly. As planned while journeying to the city he would marry Tiya in a temple before boarding the evening train.

"Of course, I will," Mala's father replied, resting his palm on Tiya's scalp. Like most villagers in Pirpahar, he had longed to see them married.

Thick garlands of tuberose interspersed with red roses. The *pandit* solemnising the union poured two spoons of *ghee* into the fire, which crackled and instantly shot up as if to burn down the invisible limit constraining their passions. Flames swayed at a steady tempo, fanned by the teenager assisting the *pandit*. The couple intently followed the priest's instructions and repeated the *mantras* after him. With his dhoti tied to her sari, they circled around the fire seven times, reliving the scene they had seen in innumerable daydreams. With the two pairs of shiny pupils pinpointing to the unforgettable moments of realisation and reciprocation, of vitalized desire and its fulfilment, Akash drew the vermilion across Tiya's forehead. To Mala, it was like the cinematic interpretation of a story she had read long back in a book.

After the ceremony Tiya implored her husband to accompany her to the lanes behind the temple. No matter where she went, she always carried a few samples of her needlework in her handmade cloth bag. She wished to explore the demand, if any, for her creations in the tiny shops that smelled of incense, tinkled with devotional bells and shimmered with the prayer lamps from China.

"Don't be too late. I'll take you to my favourite restaurant before you catch your train." Mala waved to them with the calm sprightliness of a school girl who had scored well in a tough examination. She had just witnessed the moments which she had considered in the past to be a challenge to her mental strength; a test of her composure. Her husband drove away for a meeting after bidding goodbye to the newlyweds. She strolled towards a boutique with her parents and her son, who chomped on her thick golden necklace, his eyes brimming with mischief.

The illegally constructed shops on the pavement forced pedestrians to walk on the streets. The couple had just taken a few steps when a rickshaw swerved, blocking their way. Akash, too used to his life in the hills, uttered an indecipherable word in exasperation and threw back his head to stare at the sky. Tiya nudged him to look in front. There was an excited urgency in the manner she jogged his chest. Lowering his eyes, he noticed a poster encased within the tarpaulin flap at the back of the rickshaw.

Hocus Pocus

The Biggest Competition for Magicians

In the Country

To be judged by the King of Magic N.C. Sircar

Guest Judges from the world of films and sports

Venue: Suryadeep Auditorium

(beside Chitralekha Centre of Arts)

Date: 1st September, 2022.

For details please call 97865432567

Or

Visit www.hocuspocusmagiccontest.com

Tiya captured all the details with a click of the camera they had received from Mala as a wedding gift. As the *rickshaw-wallah* started to pedal she dragged her transfixed husband to the side of the street to let the honking vehicles accelerate to their destinations.

Dilemma

Padma could feel the warmth of the noodles in her hands as she wrapped the square, pink Tiffin box with a checked napkin, knotted it and tucked in a blue plastic fork. She picked up the red water-bottle with the green strap and shook it to check whether she had filled it up already. As the clock chimed from the dining room shelf, she rushed to her bedroom mirror to mask the shadows of her fatigue with a few strokes of the blusher. Then she punched a *kalka* shaped *bindi* on her forehead and drew out her leather purse from the unlocked wardrobe. Only a few ten-rupee notes were left in it. Those were enough for the day. She would ask her husband for some money when he returned at night.

Anshu pricked her omelette to pull out a piece of green chilli and held it aloft before Aryan's eager eyes. Aryan, elder to her by three years, snatched it from her fork. Slipping a finger underneath the top bread of his sandwich, he added it to the tiny rings of chilli sprinkled on the white fibres of boiled chicken and chewed his breakfast with relish. He hated eggs and Anshu could not stand the taste of chicken.

"Hurry up," Padma called out while unzipping her children's school bags to check whether they had packed all the books and exercise copies as per their respective timetables. She did not want them to suffer the humiliation of standing outside the classroom for an entire period as punishment.

Piles of soiled utensils crammed the kitchen sink. She would tackle them after dropping her children to school. Her in-laws lacked faith in school buses. At least, she did not have to spread old newspapers near the school gates and sit there for hours like many other Moms, who chaperoned their children back home. Her younger brother-in-law, who was still enslaved by sleep, would be ready by then. He would mount his bike and whizz to the school to pick them up.

As usual before leaving, Padma faced the corner of the room where a small, burnished, cuboid projected out from the wall like a balcony. It was from this wooden block that the Gods and Goddesses surveyed her family. The smell of incense still hung in the air. She joined her hands to seek their blessings. Then clutching Anshu's hand, she hurried towards the bus-stop, often on the verge of tripping while trying to keep pace with Aryan, who almost galloped along the bustling street.

They did not have to wait long for bus number 22. Reaching the door of the vehicle, she paused to watch her children climb safely into it. Then a sudden excitement gripped her as she hitched up her sari a wee bit to raise her leg and land on the steps of the bus. Will he be there today?

The seats always got filled up at the bus terminus itself. Padma and her children squeezed themselves between the front seat and the partition behind the driver's seat. Extricating Anshu from the bulky schoolbag, her mother looked expectantly at the seated passengers near them. A bespectacled lady caught her gaze and nodded with a half-smile. Padma placed the bag on her lap, and with her arms encircled around it, the woman closed her eyes and dozed off. Padma stole a glance at the passengers jostling at the back of the vehicle and spotted him through the many human figurines pillaring between.

He was tall, with his luxurious crop of hair almost caressing the bus ceiling. Strong too. During the nasty brakes, he would stand steadily, his fingers lightly resting on the back of a seat, while the other passengers lurched forward.

Padma recalled the previous bus rides. They were standing close by. He had bent down to squeeze Anshu's cheeks. On another day, he had offered her children toffees — chocolate coated ones wrapped in polka-dotted cellophanes. They had thanked him, eyes widening in surprise. Padma, who never allowed her gaze to linger on unknown men, had smiled courteously, with her eyes lowered. Anshu had twisted the edges of the wrapper to slip out the toffee and sucked it with relish while crumpling the cellophane. The little one had fiddled with the wrapper throughout the journey before disposing it off in a military green dustbin near her school. The day after, Padma had beamed at him out of politeness. This time looking him in the eye, and he had flashed a good-natured grin. Padma never understood what was in his smile that spellbound her and shrouded her in a confusing cloud of bliss and painful longing. With his chiselled face, height and lean physique, he was attractive, no doubt. But with so many handsome men Padma passed by every day — even her husband was not bad looking despite the bald patch — she had no clue why she was reacting to him.

Passengers straggled towards the door as the bus approached another stoppage. With the human curtain between them thinned, he noticed Padma and her children at last. As she had expected, this time too he greeted her with a radiant smile. Her lips parted at once and for a few priceless moments she remained connected to him through their smiles — the two curves like two valleys in time — while the same-route buses adamantly competed, the tucked away mobile phones rang out raucously, crowds swelled in the muddy, open markets and queues meandered across the paved bus terminuses. The sting in her heart stretched on, reaching a sharp point till she found herself ripped off by an unrelenting onslaught of desire.

Padma imagined herself with him in Fiona Cafe, a stone's throw away from Care Home Hospital. Once in six months, she would treat herself to the crunchy cutlets and piping hot cardamom tea on her way home from the healthcare centre where she had worked as an admin staff — a job she had quit years ago to accommodate the ever-increasing demands of homely duties. She could almost feel the softness of the round, velvet cushions against her overstrained back as she spoke to him in hushed tones between sips of flavoured tea. Then an image of a curtained room sailed into her mind but it instantly quivered like a boat in a storm as she succumbed to her shyness. But it left her with a bright smile which she promptly hid under the folds of her pursed lips lest she was mistaken for a crazy woman smiling to herself.

What if she were marooned with him for an entire day? Or even an hour? A transient but overwhelming gift from fate for all the dishes she had rustled up at an unnerving speed, the towering piles of utensils she had rinsed and the mounds of dumped clothes she had washed. Couldn't she enjoy a reward for all the sleepless nights she had nursed her ailing in-laws, even though she knew they would abuse her again after regaining enough strength to unfurl their viciousness? What about a brief escape from all the tantrums thrown by her children every day? Compelled to fit in more chores in the limited span of time, each day twisted up like a wrung cloth. What about a balm for all those insufferable weekend afternoons when her husband tried out the tricks he learned from porn sites? He would not accept she did not enjoy them as his friends claimed their wives did.

The bus screeched to a halt behind a car with an L pasted on its back window. Missiles of abuse from her co-passengers flew past her ears as the lady in the driver's seat took time to start her brand new car. But weren't her children her greatest rewards? A raspy voice gave the final spin to the questions churning for a long time. Withdrawing her hand from the rod, she pulled out a plain, unembroidered kerchief from her bag and wiped off the sweat from her face. The raspy voice picked up pitch — wasn't she stepping beyond the line that distinguished between need and greed? The voice gained and gained in volume till it was as loud as bomb explosions, scattering away even the most resilient thoughts. As the gleaming car finally glided ahead, the bus once again geared up with a growl for the race.

The "reward" would also have a mind of his own. More streams of sweat trailed her throat as she wondered how the man would react if he guessed her feelings. Though Padma had ceased to be the babe she was in college, sometimes light and shade would creep up in an unique patchwork to haul her out of the rubble of overspent years. Before any hope could spurt that he might fancy her too another thought burst into her mind. For whom was he carrying those lozenges? Just like her, he might be someone's spouse and someone's parent too.

Noticing a lady with henna-dyed hair stir up in her seat, Padma grabbed her daughter's hand and collected her school bag from the dozing woman's lap. She surreptitiously inched towards the place being vacated, unwilling to alert the other passengers to it. As the middle-aged lady, burdened with two heavy bags, stood up and wriggled past a man, her face creasing with the effort, Anshu promptly slid into her place. Now Padma was so close to him she was even scared to look in his direction lest he suspected something. Instead, she turned to the nearest window. Her eyes fell on a white temple with a sharp pointed spire, and pillars that widened at the middle and were etched all over with intricate carvings of lions and clawed birds. Although there were no bus-stops or traffic signals nearby, the bus braked suddenly. The passengers sitting at the front followed the driver's gaze to spot a black cat languidly ambling down the road. Though Padma passed the temple every day and always caught a fleeting glimpse of the stone idols inside, for the first time her gaze arched along the curve of the bloodied scimitar and knocked against the severed heads garlanding Goddess Kali. What if she brought upon punishment to herself with her unbridled thoughts? What if the chastisement came in the form of something terrible happening to her children?

As the bus raced to another stoppage, Padma felt many brushes — most of them unintentional — against her pronounced derriere. Men, women and children shoved their way towards the door. She knew one of the moving bodies belonged to her fancy man. Out of the corner of her eyes, she had seen him shift from his position to take a step towards where she was standing. In his case, she was doubly sure that the scraping of their clothes was purely accidental. The figure blazing in her ardour could not be a molester.

Two stoppages later, she would alight, one hand clutching her daughter, the other clasping the slightly frayed handbag, her eyes fixed on her son, her buttocks still tingling with the guilty thrill of an accidental brush, and her mind curdled by fear, perforated by searing questions, swamped with unchallenged beliefs, yet fuzzy with an inexplicable desire.

The Scimitar

Ramesh and Kissan dashed to the cars pulling into the parking lot common to both the palace and the temple. Kissan crept near a Tata Sumo while Ramesh set his sights on a Force.

A tall, elderly man peered out of the Tata Sumo's front window before stepping down from the car. Two middle-aged men bearing resemblance to him, and a woman, slightly younger to them, vacated the middle seat. The back door flung open, jumped out a jeans-clad youth, followed by two girls who sent Kissan's heart aflutter. One of them, dressed in a tight salwar kameez, brushed her hands casually over her cropped hair to adjust the windblown curls. The other girl reached for her ponytail that traced the length of her spine, swung it over her left shoulder and slid out the band holding her hair together to let the dark locks sway in the wind.

As Kissan spotted other tourist guides in the vicinity of the vehicle, he shook himself out of his trance and trotted towards the elderly gentleman. Before his contenders could catch up, he cleared his throat and asked, "Sir, do you need a guide?" Pretending not to hear him, the white moustachioed man marched onwards.

"Amazing places, aren't they?" Kissan asked, turning around and positioning himself such that the entire family could see him. "I can tell you why they are even more wonderful than what meets the eye. I promise you will not regret my company." He poured out the words he had practised, in the tone he had perfected.

The middle-aged lady regarded him with interest and the pretty girls too gave him curious glances. Never failing to notice such signs, Kissan said with a smile, "You can pay me whatever you like."

"Okay, come along. But remember, as you said, we will pay you whatever we consider appropriate. You must not bargain," stressed the patriarch, fixing his steely gaze on him.

"Of course, sir." Kissan nodded, barely able to suppress his grin.

They passed by a star-shaped fountain: the water split into six sprays to sprinkle its six corners. A small *mayurpankhi nao* — the boat with a bow curved like a peacock's neck — ferried children beneath these six arcs of water. Aromas wafted from the delicacies filling up the trays in the food stalls. A couple halted to look at the lockets embossed with the face of Goddess Kali. Gopal, who was selling them, had spread out his wares on a clean white cloth unfurled between two gold dust coated benches. The street outside the wide gates of Raja Chand Palace had been his daytime address since he lost his right leg in a truck accident.

Queued up outside the ancient Kali temple, Kissan narrated the legend of Raja Indrasurya. The great lake at the centre of the city — its only source of water — had dried up. The king had engaged his strongest men to dig up the bed of the lake. They drilled and drilled, but failed to reach the water table. When people were dying of thirst, a man met the king, claiming to know a solution. Though none believed him, he went on insisting that the water would gush out from the bed if struck with the scimitar of the temple's presiding deity — Goddess Kali. Left with no other option, the king, though sceptical, extricated the weapon from the hand of the stone idol and struck the parched earth at the bottom of the lake. To his surprise, little spurts of water burst out from the lake bed, wherever it came in contact with the blade of the weapon. Still there was a problem. The founts were drying out before anyone could drink from them or even hold their cups against them.

"To retain the water, the happiest man in the kingdom must shed his tears upon the spurts," the stranger said.

"But how will the happiest man cry?" the king asked, his forehead creased.

"Make him peel onions," the man suggested.

"Onions! Now where will I find onions?" A shadow fell upon the king's visage. "My people consider them to be impure as they grow under the soil. They don't farm or sell them." He let out a prolonged sigh.

"I've grown a few in my kitchen garden," the man whispered. The kings' eyes lit up; he was suddenly blessed with a new lease of life.

The happiest man brimming with joy, despite the acute thirst clawing at his sore throat, squatted on the lake bed and started peeling an onion. As soon as his eyes moistened, the king thwacked the hard chunk of earth to ensure the new spurt of water mingled with the falling teardrops. Like a firework, the water shot up, sending the three men hurtling to the lake's edge.

The gush continued even when the grasses curling over the lake's edges found themselves in the middle of a vast water body. Soon, the water barged into people's homes, filling up the rooms, wrecking the belongings. The water, with its sheer volume and unparalleled pace, would submerge the kingdom in an hour.

Confronted by the new calamity, the king again turned to the knowledgeable stranger for advice. The man was prompt with his explanation. "The Goddess is angry as you have taken away her scimitar. She wants it back immediately. But the scimitar must be used to kill a human before it is returned. Otherwise it will fly out and fall upon any random man, woman or even a child."

Reluctant to subject anyone to such a gruesome end, the king offered to sacrifice himself.

"Whoever kills a king with the holy scimitar must be the one to succeed him to the throne. Or the weapon will kill the next king," the stranger warned.

Unaware of his vested interests, the king believed him as his words had come true so far. The man knew no other person in the kingdom would agree to kill the king and as expected, the task eventually fell upon him. The king proceeded to explain a few aspects of his governance, but stopped as the wails of his people, struggling through the deluge of water, reached his ears. He prayed to God to infuse his wife and young children with the strength to cope with his absence and bless the new king with the wisdom to rule well. As the sly man raised the weapon with his gaze fixed on the king's neck, a radiant female form suddenly appeared and snatched it away from his hands. She was Goddess Kali herself. With her three eyes blazing and her hair clouding all around, she kicked the reprobate out of the land. With a couple of strokes of the scimitar, she drew two parallel lines through the remaining dry patch. Then she directed the excess lake water within these lines to create a canal, which flows even today pouring its water into the Ganges at a pilgrim spot several districts away.

"This story is already written on the board," the short-haired girl pointed out, the disappointment in her voice shattering Kissan.

"Come on, you are our guide. What do you know about this place which no one else does?" the other girl interrogated with an unmistakable taunt.

"He knows nothing else." The middle-aged woman's whisper was loud enough to be heard by the guide.

Kissan's face shrunk. The Department of Tourism had put up boards near the entrances of all heritage sites to enlighten tourists about the facts and myths associated with them. The guides would churn this information in their own imagination to serve up an incredulous concoction to the tourists. Kissan had also slipped in a few figments of his mind into the legend, but somehow that had not impressed his clients.

Ramesh was at the tube well, sprinkling water on his face and arms for respite from the heat. He filled up a mug for Gopal as the ground was too slippery for him to tread.

Without mentioning the context, Kissan wondered aloud in front of his friends, "Isn't there anything we know, other than what's written on the boards by the Tourism Department?"

Ramesh was in no mood to speak: he had failed to convince the occupants of the Force and all the other tourists he had approached to hire him.

"I'm sure that the Tourism Department has no inkling about the stories we've heard from our grandparents," Gopal said. "Like the legend of the golden snake."

After a hasty lunch in a packed eatery, Kissan and Ramesh strolled to the parking lot while Gopal made his way to his wares. A tea seller, who carried out his trade from the steps of a tomb, guarded them in his absence.

"I'm so drowsy," Kissan said, splaying himself on the bonnet of a Taxi.

"Me too, let's take a walk," Ramesh responded with a yawn.

They trudged along the pavement in the direction of the fountain, but stopped and glanced back on hearing a bus screech to a halt.

The automated doors of an air-conditioned Volvo parted. An ebony-complexioned couple stepped down from the bus and trooped to the pavement. The man, sweating profusely, put on a baseball cap to shield his shiny bald pate from the blazing sun. The woman brought together her frizzy hair to shape up a bun and fastened it with clips procured from the pocket of her denim skirt. From the same pocket, she brought out a map and unfolded it. Seizing this opportunity, Ramesh loped towards them, and a minute later he turned around, a glow of relief tinting his face. And then he trotted to the palace, followed by the couple. While showing them around the palace gardens, he sighted Kissan in the distance, surrounded by a large group of backpackers. Kissan spotted him too as he looked past a marble maiden. The two friends waved to each other before drawing their attention back to their clients.

Deep bowls with engraved lids clustered on the royal dining table. Flanked by

gold-embroidered napkins and sparking crystal glasses, the spotless plates reflected the chandeliers above. The arrangement exuded a feeling that at any moment the royals would slip into their velvet-cushioned chairs and turbaned men would step forward to serve.

A cupboard occupied an entire wall of the room. It was stacked with china cups and saucers of every size and design. Miniature palaces, forts, frolicking princesses and galloping horses were etched on the stately teapots. The saucers were inlaid with gold, the handles of cups and spoons encrusted with gems and the sugar bowl resembled a lotus with nested rings of silver petals.

The tourists gaped at the grandeur before them. Kissan sought to impress them further. He narrated the tale of the golden serpent, and on reaching the end of the saga, he purposely fell silent, waiting for them to exclaim in wonder.

"Cock and bull story! Not an iota of fact," muttered one tourist as they emerged from the dining room and headed towards the library. Crestfallen, Kissan somehow managed to complete the tour of the palace, often lapsing into absentmindedness, inviting grimaces from some and hard stares from the rest.

*

Kissan tipped an enveloped letter into the mouth of the letter box before taking a lingering glance at the nearby sweet shop. Wiping off the sweat from his brow, a man dropped pyramidal mounds of potato stuffed flour in the oil that bubbled in a huge, steel *kadai* and fried them into *samosas*. Kissan patted his shirt pocket. There were a few crisp notes, but he wanted to save them for some other day. He knew the wallet in his trouser pocket would be almost empty by the time he finished buying the essentials from the marketplace.

The unpaved path led to the fishmongers' shades. At the junction of two muddy tracks, he had to stand on his toes to peer over the crowd. A couple of men and a woman, wearing straw hats, were digging a patch of earth. He heard from the onlookers that two gem studded daggers had been unearthed, fuelling the guess that there were other valuables buried near the spot.

Towards noon, Kissan and his friends swiftly occupied a bench in the busy eatery to gobble down their meal of rice that had lost its warmth, *dal* that had squandered its taste to the excess water and a vegetable curry abandoned by spices.

The excavators sauntered into the shop and paused at the counter to buy cold drinks.

"I think the daggers belonged to Kulbhusan III," one of them surmised, drawing the other two into a long discussion.

"Imagine if we could find the legendary scimitar..." the woman said wistfully.

Kissan, who was pulping the vegetables in the remaining rice, suddenly turned still as if struck by the weapon.

"Do you believe in the myth?" her colleague was sceptical.

Kissan hung on to each word they spoke and nudged his friends to listen.

"Can't comment on the myth," replied the lady, "but the temple has stood for over five-hundred years while the scimitar in the Goddess's hand dates back to two centuries only."

*

The three friends peered over the edge of the high parapet around the terrace of a monument as the settlements swayed below with lives and livelihoods. It was Gopal's first visit to the roof of the twenty-storied structure. The government had recently gotten it repaired, and a lift installed. The new localities had developed in such a way that the lake mentioned in the myth was no longer at the centre of the town, but nearer to its eastern fringe and an artificial island built upon the waters served as a picnic spot. A strip of canal, stretching behind a row of residences and fenced parks, was the rein holding the town to the galloping past.

The question posed by the pretty girl and the conversation between the excavators swirled about in Kissan's mind. This was his chance to find something beyond the reach of all, including the archaeologists.

However, he could not exclude his two best friends from the quest after sparking their interest with his own exuberance.

"Two hundred years ago, this town fell under the reign of Sultan Mir Mohammad, who respected all faiths and exalted the skyline with both mosques and temples," Kissan quoted from the information he had mugged up to work as a guide.

"We need to find if something unusual had occurred during his rule," Ramesh said.

"Why don't we ask Jagdish sir?" Gopal suggested.

"That's a great idea! But you must take the initiative. You know why…" Kissan left the rest unsaid. He was drifted to the memory of a classroom with long wooden tables and backless benches. Jagdish was solving a sum, his chalk squeaking against the blackboard. As the ongoing murmurs grew perceptible, he suddenly turned around and glared at Kissan through his black-framed glasses.

"One more word and I'll throw you out of the classroom," he thundered before resuming to write.

Face reddened on being caught, Kissan sat up straight and tried to listen intently to each step of the sum that Jagdish explained. But as he approached the concluding step, his father's drunken slur rang in his ears instead of his teacher's clear baritone. The day before he had witnessed a brawl between his father and elder brothers. His mother too had been dragged in and beaten.

Jagdish gave his students similar sums to solve. Kissan proceeded with the first problem. Stuck in the middle, he raked his brains to guess the next step, his eyes closed and face screwed up. But the silence around him was invaded by the clatter of utensils crashing on the floor, thuds of furniture flung across the room and screams intermingled with the tinkling of jewellery.

Kissan fidgeted in his chair and bore the vicious silence until he could take it no longer. It felt like the press of clammy fingers on his throat. At the first word that slipped from his lips, Jagdish, who had his ears trained on him, grabbed the duster, and with aim perfected through years of practice hurled it at his forehead. A spiking pain captured Kissan's senses. It seemed his head had split.

Expectedly, Kissan did not see Jagdish over the weekend. On Monday, as usual, the students rose to their feet to wish him, "Good Morning," when he strode into the classroom and took off his cloth bag. They were surprised to find his unruly curls trimmed and his stubble shaved off. He returned the greeting with a wide smile and gestured for them to sit.

"How many of you have heard about the city of Chittoor?" Jagdish asked, scrutinising the young faces before him. Some boys raised their hands, and some others flaunted their knowledge without waiting for their turn. Instead of appearing vexed, the teacher listened to all with an indulgent smile. Finally, when they finished speaking, he described the Chittorgarh Fort and forayed into the Battle of Haldighati. The students, aware of his grasp over a wide range of subjects, listened with rapt attention. Slouching in a corner with his eyes to the floor, Kissan too was swept in by the narration.

Kissan had no clue how many minutes had flown by before Jagdish fell silent, cast his eyes on his table and then shot a glance at his watch. "I'll give you ten sums," he said, "The first one to get them all correct will win a prize." He turned to the blackboard and scribbled down the problems at a furious pace.

Despite smarting from the welts inflicted by his father, Kissan was brimming with a new sense of pride. The night before, he had armed himself with a shovel and stood up for his mother. He confidently tackled the first problem and pounced on the next. While struggling with the fourth, he had not noticed when Gopal had walked up to the teacher's desk to hand over his exercise copy.

Kissan had no option but to submit his answers when the bell rang. He doubted whether he had got any of the sums correct except for the first one.

Jagdish trudged inside the classroom the next morning, his cloth bag heavy with the submitted exercise copies. He stacked them on the table and rested his palms atop the tallest pile.

"Now for the winner." He winked. All eyes swivelled towards him and the room sunk into pin drop silence.

"Gopal, please come forward and collect this envelope containing my entire stamp collection." Jagdish beamed, holding out a sky-blue envelope amidst thunderous applause.

In the next couple of months, Gopal busied himself in sorting the stamps according to their countries and pasting them in neat rows in an old diary. He left home the day he found the shredded pages of the diary buried among the ash in the kitchen stove. He immediately knew it to be the handiwork of his father, who considered his passion a waste of time.

Gopal lived up to Jagdish's expectations by capping his school final results with over eighty percent score in three subjects. Encouraged by his teacher, he got himself enrolled in a BSc course in the evening section of a local college. However, his education came to a standstill with the accident. He could not appear for his part one examination. Once he recovered from being a nearly dead man to a man without a limb, he had to take up whichever job came his way to pay off the debts arising from his medical expenses.

*

Clutching the rails, Gopal pinned the tip of his crutch to a stair and hauled himself to the next step. Faced with three doors at the landing, he knocked at the one partly concealed behind a hanging of embellished seeds. He could not wait for the second to pass as he heard the creak of a latch, and then his favourite teacher appeared at the door, his curls longer than ever, his eyes bulging with bewilderment. Jagdish's face broke into a wide grin as the initial disbelief wore off.

The teacher either did not have a living room, or he considered Gopal too close to be led to the room designated for outsiders. Instead, he asked his former student to relax in an armchair next to his bed in a room occupied by not one but four cupboards that almost touched the ceiling, with titles after titles from the lowermost to the uppermost shelves exuding their spell through the glass doors.

To his former student's relief, Jagdish did not dwell much on the accident. Unlike many others, he refrained from letting his gaze shift from Gopal's face and stray near the missing limb.

"Do you have any books on the history of Mirmeetpur?" Gopal asked, admiring the collection in the cupboards.

"Sure, I do." Jagdish sprang from the bed where he had been sitting and in a flash of a second, he brought out the book from among hundreds of others.

An hour sped by over cups of tea and vignettes from each other's lives. Finally, as Gopal began to fiddle with his crutch, Jagdish guessed that it was time for him to leave.

"When will your students come?" he asked, referring to the schoolchildren Gopal tutored.

"Within thirty-five minutes. I must leave now. Take care, sir." Mounting pressure on the crutch, he straightened himself, and said, "Unfortunately it is no longer possible for me to touch your feet."

"Don't bother. My blessings are always with you," Jagdish assured, patting him on his head. "Come again."

"Sure, sir. It was great talking to you. And once again thanks for the book."

Reaching the door, Jagdish asked, "Shall I come down with you?"

"No, sir." Gopal smiled. "I came up on my own."

*

The three friends huddled on the monument's terrace.

"Two hundred years ago, a communal riot broke out in Mirmeetpur. Some outsiders, jealous of the prevalent harmony, had instigated the Muslims against the Hindus. This led to a temple demolition spree," Gopal summarised what he had read.

"But the Kali temple was not destroyed. Only the scimitar got lost. We must find out how…" Ramesh pointed out, scanning the roofs of the newly constructed lodges.

"The priests and devotees might have fought to protect the temple and one of them could have used the scimitar as a weapon…" Kissan speculated, fiddling with the few facts they had got.

"And the scimitar slipped from his grip when he was defeated," Ramesh completed what Kissan was about to say.

"In a different chapter of the book, the author mentions that in those days only the priest's elder son could succeed him to the job. What if this practice has continued?" Gopal wondered.

"You mean, if the current head priest of the temple has descended from the one who held the position two hundred years ago, he might have information on what happened during the riot. Assuming he knows his family history." Now a smile of hope curled Ramesh's lips.

No matter how many times the two young guides had visited the temple, they never had an occasion to interact with the priest. It was almost time for the temple gates to be locked when Gopal's tutoring session wrapped up for the evening. The beggar woman crouching at the temple gate counted the coins dotting the outspread rag before knotting it up. Coins jingled as the saffron clad man sitting opposite to her thrust his misshapen bowl in the nook of his left elbow, clutched his *ektara* and turned towards the road. The three men found their way across the temple compound by the flickering flames of clay lamps encircling the potted *tulsi*. Apprehensive of not reaching the Goddess's shrine in time, Gopal asked his friends to move ahead.

The main chamber was illuminated by lamps while the three turrets at the top were in complete darkness, against the black sky as if the night, unable to find enough space to spread itself, had formed three pleats. The guides took off their shoes at the designated shed, rinsed their hands and feet from a long-spouted tap, and ran up the stone steps.

Humming a tune, the priest glimpsed at the watch he had kept atop a wooden box. He appeared relaxed as the rush of devotees had ebbed for the day. The two young men quickly offered their prayers with folded hands.

"My friends and I come to this temple often," Kissan began. The priest adjusted the sacred thread across his chest and smiled with his lips closed.

"Every time, I wonder how you manage so many devotees, right from the crack of dawn," Kissan continued.

The priest smiled again and shook his head in humility.

Kissan introduced himself and named his parents, siblings, and also an uncle who was in the police. In response, the priest spoke a little about his family, mentioning his wife and ailing parents. Finally, Ramesh interjected to ask whether his father too had been a priest at the same temple.

The old priest grinned, revealing his gums, and said, "The people who came to excavate also asked me the same question. Yes, my father worked here before me but not my grandfather, who came from the hills to settle in this town. You wanted to know whether we had been here for generations, didn't you?"

"Yes," Ramesh replied, his face shrunken in disappointment.

The priest's young helper stepped out of a small chamber on the left, as Gopal entered the temple to join his friends.

"I met someone who claimed his forefathers had served this temple as priests. He had come to offer *puja* to the Goddess like everyone else. This was around....nine months back," the junior priest recalled.

"Do you know where he stays now?" Kissan asked, his dampened hopes roused with a click.

"He said he is staying in America."

"America? You mean the USA?" asked Gopal.

"He only said America."

"Must be the USA. A person staying in South America or in Canada or Mexico will tell the name of the country and not just say 'America'", Gopal reasoned.

"You met him in this temple? How come I didn't hear a word?" The senior priest frowned.

"I think he was wary of disturbing you. You were arranging the offerings for the Goddess. Since I was sitting nearer to the steps, he spoke to me."

"Did he say anything else?" Aware that many Indians were immigrating to the USA every year, Gopal wondered how they would trace him.

"Anything else..." The young priest racked his brains. "Yes, he had introduced himself by name..."

Kissan's eyes instantly lit up as if a star had sprung down before him.

"But I can't remember it." The fellow was most apologetic on noticing the gloom eclipse the devotees' faces.

"One thing I remember. In fact, it's impossible to forget. His middle name was Iqbal."

"Iqbal!" Gopal exclaimed. Ramesh's mouth fell open and the senior priest seemed to freeze, with eyes wide open in shock.

"But his ancestors were priests of this temple...." Kissan mumbled after several minutes of silence.

"He had a Hindu first name, a Hindu last name but a Moslem middle name."

"The last name must have been a Brahmin surname as in those days only a Brahmin could become a priest," Kissan derived.

"Yes, a Brahmin surname," the youth confirmed.

"Don't you remember what it was?"

"No...but it was a common one."

After leaving the temple premises, the young men huddled near a streetlamp to untie the thread and unwrap the *prasad* from the dried sal leaves. Breaking the sweet into three pieces, they touched them against their foreheads before savouring the taste which lingered in their mouths even after the last speck was gone.

"So, some clue to proceed." Kissan felt optimistic.

"But how?" Gopal failed to muster much hope.

"I can think of a way... We have to try..." Ramesh did not reveal further.

Kissan and Gopal were stumbling in the dark, hoping to tread upon a way that would lead them to the scimitar till Ramesh took them by surprise one day. Unlike Kissan and Gopal, who had never used a computer, Ramesh found himself at ease in social networking sites. Initiated to the charms of the web world by his friend Ravi, who worked in Bangalore, Ramesh would visit a cyber cafe whenever he could afford it to keep in touch with the girls he met on Facebook.

Ramesh had searched with the combination of "Iqbal" and each Brahmin surname prevalent in this part of the country. Many US citizens named Iqbal had Hindu surnames, owing to the comparatively less social restrictions on cross community marriages among second or third-generation immigrants. However, in the long list of search results only one fulfilled the criteria of a Hindu name preceding "Iqbal" and a Brahmin surname succeeding it. He had promptly messaged the stranger on Facebook, mentioning that he was from the town of his forefathers and wished to know more about the Kali temple. Mr Mishra, pleased to be contacted by someone from his ancestral town, replied within a day and readily agreed to a video chat with Ramesh at 10:30 AM US time, which would be 8:00 PM in India. Since the cyber cafe closed at 9:00 PM sharp, the young men knew they would have to be quick with their questions.

Covered with glossy advertisements of computer courses, the door swung open on Ramesh's gentle push. He walked inside and held it wide open for Gopal. Kissan entered after them and glanced around. His gaze roamed across the computers separated by white partitions to the robust complexioned owner sitting at a plywood table, his right cheek bulging with a *laddoo*. Inhaling the incense wafting from the shelf, Ramesh flopped into the chair in front of the nearest computer and hit the keyboard. Gopal and Kissan drew their chairs close to him to get an unobstructed view of the popping pages.

Ramesh's friends keenly observed his clicking fingers as he sent out a chat invite to Arvind Iqbal Mishra. The priests' descendant instantly responded, and a blurred view of a room filled up the screen. As the haziness gradually diminished, they discerned Arvind's angular features, cleft chin and soft eyes. Behind him there was an unlit fireplace — arched and made of brick, like the ones they had seen on TV and dolls, undoubtedly brought from India — possibly from Rajasthan, posing on the mantelpiece in sequined ethnic wear.

"Hello," Arvind Iqbal Mishra greeted them with a smile. The three young men introduced themselves.

"Tourist guides! That's interesting," he remarked. "I'm a doctor. My wife Adela is a cookbook writer and we have two lovely daughters," he said.

Before the young men could frame the first question he spoke again. "You want to know about my ancestors who had served the temple?"

"To begin with, we are curious about your middle name."

"That's a long story. I found it out from my ancestor Pratap Mishra's memoir, which was handed down to me by my father..." Arvind was interrupted by his younger daughter, who came bouncing to him in a Halloween mask and hooked her fingers to resemble claws. The doting father let out a low scream, knotted his fists and pretended to shiver with fright. The child broke into a giggle and skipped to another room, reciting a spooky rhyme.

"Two hundred years ago, on a day in the middle of autumn, my ancestor Mahadev Mishra, the head priest of the Kali temple, stepped out of the inner sanctum on hearing a commotion. A mob of men came charging with swords, their bloodshot eyes spewing malice, and it was clear that their intention was to destroy the abode of our Goddess. Mahadev darted inside the shrine, prayed to the Goddess and reappeared at the entrance, armed with her scimitar. You must have heard of the legend revolving round this scimitar?" The men nodded and Arvind continued, "Headed by Mahadev, many junior priests, devotees and servants of the temple entered the fray with whatever they could grab — knives for slicing the fruit offerings or heavy metal utensils emptied of the cooked *prasad*. Mahadev thwarted the mob with all his strength, often tapping into his presence of mind."

Kissan glanced meaningfully at his friends to remind them of his earlier speculations, some of which tallied with Arvind's account of the incidents so far.

"While Mahadev was fighting off the mob, more Hindus poured out of their homes, equipped with hammers, sickles, sticks or kitchen knives to barricade the temple with themselves. The depraved ones among them grabbed this opportunity to break into Moslem homes and pounce on their women. A profusion of smoke clouded visions and assailed nostrils as engulfing flames shredded the skyline.

A Moslem, whom Mahadev had helped in his hour of need, came dashing to reason with his community. By the time he reached the paved road that led to the temple, the priest had died. His mangled body was lying at the edge of the canal. Across the lake, the rioters surrounded the dead priest's twelve-year-old son, who was returning from the *pathsala*, unaware of the sudden communal frenzy tearing apart the town. Mahadev's Moslem well-wisher rushed to the spot, his soles aching after the long run and heart beating with the echoes of the unforeseen catastrophes. As there were no witnesses to narrate what happened between the time he found his friend dead and when he came across the latter's son, I have imagined a sequence of probable occurrences.

Overcome by grief, he kneeled next to the dead priest, his bent head clasped within his palms. A gang of Hindus leaped upon him and tried to pin him to the ground to slash him apart. Wriggling out of their grasp, he picked up for self-defence the scimitar that was lying beside Mahadev, and swiftly blended into the mob of Moslems to escape. It suddenly struck him that Mahadev's son might be trapped in perilous circumstances. He slipped off at the first chance to rescue him. On the way to the village school, he learnt that his apprehensions had come true. The boy had been cornered by murderous men.

Going back to the words penned by my ancestor, the Moslem man informed the boy of his father's death with the words, 'Dead by water...wound...weapon,' and tried his best to convince the bloodthirsty men to put an end to their killing spree. But the men were drunk on violence. They scorned at his persuasions and labelled him a *kafir*. The lone man still carried on his argument, prising out a chance for the priest's son to sneak away into a clump of trees. Once separated by a safe distance, the boy peered through the leaves to find his saviour felled down by the strike of a sword. He escaped to his uncle's house, where he grew up along with his cousins. Many years later, on a visit to Mirmeetpur he came to know how his father had died. He had no siblings as his mother had expired soon after his birth. When he had a son, he made Iqbal his middle name, Iqbal being the name of his saviour, whose sacrifice had ensured his survival and perpetuation of Mahadev's bloodline. The boy was Pratap Mishra who had asked his son to pass on his memoir to the next generation along with the middle name."

Before the chat ended, Arvind added, "When I was a little boy, I used to be embarrassed by the reactions my middle name provoked and introduced myself only as 'Arvind Mishra.' However, my father would insist that I always use my full name to honour the great man named Iqbal. And to respect my ancestor's sentiments in making it a part of our identity. Gradually I stopped being uncomfortable with the eyebrows it raised and now I just love my name for its uniqueness."

*

The three friends were lolling on the grass outside the gates of a public garden. Ramesh was sucking the petiole of a flower fallen from a creeper growing along the top of the garden fence.

"Few people show interest in the battlefield of Dhanshpat," Kissan remarked as he shared the day's experiences with Ramesh and Gopal. "But this family was an exception. As I took them to the site, the man began to describe the battle to his wife and daughter. I wondered who the guide was. Me or him? The daughter, barely four, was more interested in the remnants of a bird's nest inside the old cannon than the exploits of the soldiers."

Kissan spotted a man in a skullcap ambling down the street, accompanied by a veiled woman and a child. Nudged by the woman, he halted to survey his surroundings and then shook his head vigorously to disagree with something she had said. Catching the guide's helpful smile, he stepped upon the grass to ask for directions to the old Moslem graveyard. Kissan instructed them to take an auto to a stoppage called Bhigpur, cross the street, take the first turn after passing the Unani clinic and walk towards the lake. As the family trotted away, Kissan turned towards his friends to resume the conversation, but Ramesh's eyes had lost focus. He had escaped somewhere else.

"What's the matter? Are you all right?"

"Dead by the water... remember what Iqbal had said to Pratap Mishra?"

"What about it?" Kissan asked, his eyes narrowed as he tried to recall the details.

"He was referring to the graveyard," Ramesh replied.

Kissan goggled at him. "It makes sense," Gopal exclaimed, clapping his hands.

"It seemed odd that Iqbal would choose that moment when Pratap needed to concentrate on his own survival to tell him about his father's death. He would come to know of it later in any case. So, I suspected that he meant something else. Now that you said it, Ramesh...dead by water can also mean the graveyard by the lake," Gopal explained.

"Aware of the significance of the scimitar to the Hindus, Iqbal hid it for the priest's son," said Ramesh.

"Dead by water...wound..weapon." Kissan repeated Iqbal's words. "What about the word 'wound?'"

"Let's go to the graveyard. Maybe we'll be able to shed light on that also."

Gopal dragged his crutch towards himself, rammed it into the ground and stood to his full height. The trio leaped into an auto that whisked them away from the tourist attractions, and zipped past the teeming playground, the hushed school and the emptying post-office.

The year — 1605 AD was carved into the middle section of the cemetery's rusted gate. Spreading their canopy over the high boundary walls and the thorny bushes within, the gulmohar trees celebrated the blazing sunset with their red and yellow blossoms. None had been buried here in recent times. No space was left for new graves. Though the entrance was unguarded, the young men hesitated before stepping in, wary of running into the family who had taken directions from them. They crept to the gate, craned their necks and scoured the thickets, but failed to spot a single soul. Slowly they tip-toed inside and pussy-footed along the boundary, letting their eyes dart across the graves that were separated by overgrown bougainvillaea shrubs. Finally, they glimpsed the family kneeling around a grave, almost screened by the copious pink flowers. The friends bunched behind a bush, counting the seconds gonged by their beating hearts. From time to time, they exchanged glances, the sparkle in their eyes pooling to create a millpond where they could just dip and touch the mysterious bed of the past.

By the time the family had stepped out of the cemetery, pulling the creaking gate behind them, a sliver of moon had sailed into the sky. The darkness shrouding the nearby houses indicated a power cut. Rippled the black lake water through the missing bricks of the western wall. The youths trod between the burials, wondering where the scimitar could be or whether their latest deductions would be proven wrong.

Ramesh did not fail to notice Kissan's repeated backward glances. "What if something emerges from the shadows and pounces upon you?" he teased.

Reluctant to convey his fear, Kissan played along, "What if a skeletal hand shoots out from one of these graves and grabs at your feet?"

"Actually, there are such rumours about this cemetery," Gopal interjected.

"What? You should have told us earlier. We would have come at midnight," Kissan exclaimed as if in glee even though his heart skipped a beat. He would find such stories amusing in a different environment, but a graveyard in the growing darkness was bound to scare. He was sure that his friends felt the same too though none would admit it.

"There are cracks in certain gravestones. That's how these stories spawned," Gopal explained. "I think someone carrying a grudge against the buried men desecrated them," he continued, groping for a reason that bypassed the supernatural.

"What good would it do when your enemy is already dead?" Ramesh remarked.

"I won't rule it out. There are all kinds of weirdos," Kissan said, his shaky hands tucked in his pockets.

"I heard of a man who travelled from central Asia to exact revenge on a cheat. But the fellow had died. Deprived of a chance to hurt him while he lived, he galloped straight to the cemetery to wound his grave..." Gopal narrated.

"Wound? Wound...weapon... Remember?" Kissan's eyes gleamed.

"Let's look out for graves having cracks."

"There's still a possibility that an arm will appear out of the crack to drag you underground." Ramesh grinned mischievously.

"Why me when he can find a friend for eternity in you?" Kissan retorted.

Since none of the three youngsters carried any torches, the faint moonlight was their only aid in the search. Ramesh and Kissan bent over each grave, their eyes knitted in inspection, their fingers probing till dust caked them and their palms itching from the brush of unknown flowers. They spotted a few slits, but they were too small for a scimitar to be inserted.

Squeezed against the boundary was a grave flecked with crinkled leaves. Gopal balanced himself against the wall to examine the floral engraved slab. He noticed that the portion furthest from him was bare of any droppings. With one swipe of his crutch, he let the leaves rain inside the grave, disclosing a fissure. Kissan lunged to thrust his hand into the gap since the suspense was too much to bear, even superseding the lingering sense of fear. Extending an arm to stop him, Ramesh plunged into his pocket to bring out a matchbox. "We must check whether there are any snakes or scorpions inside."

Kissan inched towards the crevice with a lighted match stick. When he found no signs of movement within the gap, he bent closer, almost pressing his eyes to the opening. He was certain he saw some metal glinting in the flame. Convinced there were no dangers lurking in it, he slowly let his hand follow his eyes and felt the hilt of a weapon.

The crescent moon glided out of the clouds, slathering the sky, and tethered itself to the tip of a minaret across the lake. A fragrance fleetingly teased the men's nostrils. They sniffed to catch another whiff, but it had already effaced its trace from the abode of the dead. Dry leaves crunched under their feet as they hurried away from the grave and a low, grating noise escaped through the narrow tunnels of wilting grass. Lifted off the earth by a sudden breeze, the fallen gulmohar petals continued to swirl in the air like nocturnal insects. The men had almost reached the gate when the breeze picked up drastically in strength as if to haul them into the events of the past. But they had nothing more to fear with the Goddess's scimitar shimmering in their hands.

The Ventures in a Locked Study

Black and white sketches of famous scientists hung on the walls of the science coaching centre. Ruby threw a glance at the classroom where lessons were going on. Though down with fever, her son was impatient to know the results of the mock test he had sat for the previous week. Aware of Ruby's reputation as a prominent scientist in WCBS, Mr Acharya hurried out of the class to meet her instead of just letting her collect the answer sheets from the front desk. As he pulled out the stapled sheaf submitted by Robin, she glimpsed the total marks scribbled against the left margin. She sighed with relief, imagining the satisfaction on her son's face when he would see his score, which was even better than the results of the previous tests.

"Robin speaks highly of you," Ruby said to Mr Acharya. "I'm glad I'd brought him here. It's heartening to see him do so well."

The tutor blinked, flattered by the praise.

"It's not my credit alone. After all, he has got your genes, ma'am," he replied humbly.

Ruby smiled at him. A middle-aged woman entered the room to enquire about the tuition timings and expressed her wish to enrol her daughter. Expectantly, Mr Acharya was unaware that Ruby had brought Robin home after a prolonged tussle with the rules and regulations that make it difficult for a single woman to adopt a child. It had been an arduous journey bringing him up on her own. Often, she had to rely on nannies and on some days even on unwilling relatives when the nannies failed to turn up. She admitted him to a coaching centre, when his school teachers found it impossible to answer all his queries in a class of three scores students. She regretted her inability to tutor him herself as on most days her research left her with little or no time.

Propped up against a soft, cotton pillow, Robin was watching a movie, when Ruby plonked herself down on a chair beside him. She would go back to her assignments after he went to sleep. She could work from home, sometimes at least: a concept unheard of when Robin was a little boy. The last few months had involved a lot of brainstorming. The date of her current project's first presentation was drawing near.

Robin delved into his English textbook as the end credits rolled while Ruby took a peek at her office email before leaving for the kitchen. Half an hour passed before he heard her footsteps. She entered the room with a tray laden with a bowl, a plate, a spoon and a salt shaker. His appetite reared its head from the growling pit of his stomach despite the fever induced sour taste in his mouth. He drew the bedside table near his bed before she placed the tray atop it.

"What did you decide about Sweta?" Ruby prodded him about the newest girl in the long queue of females vying for his attention. Sitting down in the chair, she scrutinised her son's expression with a smile suppressed between her lips.

"Not again, Mom. I don't want a girlfriend now. I would rather concentrate on my studies," Robin responded, sounding irritated, while dipping a piece of buttered toast in the steaming soup.

"Robin, I know how determined you are about reaching your goals. A girlfriend won't be a distraction for you, believe me. And she can bring some balance to your geeky routine," Ruby assured, without shifting her gaze from the frown on his face.

"Look who's talking," Robin retorted, stirring his soup too fast.

Ruby detested the idea of discussing the reasons for her single status, and a shot of annoyance would not spare her even if her son slightly touched upon the topic. To avoid the turn the conversation tended to take, she told him, "Going out with a girl is much healthier than the sites you visit."

Robin, who had raised the spoon to take the first sip of soup, cast his eyes on the floor, his ears turning red. He recalled in utter embarrassment that the last time he had been to an adult entertainment site, a phone call had interrupted and he had forgotten to delete the link from his PC's History.

Robin's natural intelligence, polished further by Ruby's nurturing and coupled with the good looks inherited from unknown parents, made him irresistible to girls. The female attention he had been receiving since he was barely into his teens was becoming a bit tiring, not that it did not boost up his confidence levels. While bundling his shirts and trousers for the laundry, the number of love letters she had chanced upon surprised her. It elated her that nowadays girls felt free to express themselves. But she sensed something primitive about them flocking around a boy hailed as brilliant. It seemed like a continuation of the age-old tradition in which women were expected to marry accomplished men rather than achieve something on their own. She thought women belonging to the younger generation were leaping through the rings of fire only to bang against a heavy shield at the end.

The next day, a surprise awaited Robin as he stepped inside his flat after returning from school. Occupying a corner of his mother's study, stood a model of a city — dotted with buildings and criss-crossed by streets. At the extreme right of the model was a cylinder with a hole in its base. Water dripped from it into a long channel that meandered across the thick slab of earth in which the "city" had been planted. The "river" skirted the office buildings and lapped gently against the high boundary walls of the university before flowing into a circular face-mirror like "lake." Robin guessed that hidden by the layers of soil, there was a tube channelizing the water back to the cylinder to ensure a steady circulation. Moss blanketed the barren patches of ground and lush saplings shaded the housing blocks. Eight-seater motor boats were anchored along the river bank, sliding-pane buses parked under a glass-panelled shelter, sleek cars locked in the sprawling garages of multi-storeyed residences and a twelve bogie train waited at the start of its serpentine track. Robin noticed that all the transports had tiny solar panels fitted to them. He slipped a finger through an open window of the school and felt the smooth surface of a diminutive desk. While exploring the interiors of the hospital, his thumb sank into the foam mattress of a miniscule bed.

"How did you create all these, Mom?" Robin asked, brimming with admiration.

"I didn't build this model," Ruby replied, picking up a notebook. "Do you remember my professor, Dr Shanky? This was his creation, a prototype for an energy efficient city. His wife requested me to keep it in my house as their pet cat was trying to destroy it."

"But I love cats too. I was thinking of adopting Mini's kittens," Robin protested. Mini was the street cat who had given birth to four kittens in Mr Singh's backyard a week ago.

"Don't worry. With people like us around, they won't go hungry," his mother assured. "But don't bring them into the house. You don't even have time to toilet train them," she reminded, turning to a page in her notebook, where she had scribbled several diagrams indecipherable to Robin.

"These have furniture," Robin said, pointing to the buildings in the model. "What's the point in putting them where none can see?"

"The person who could have answered your questions is missing," Ruby replied, fidgeting with a pen, her face partly shrouded by the shadow of a shelf.

"What? Has Dr Shanky disappeared? How did he vanish just like that?" Robin gaped.

"Mrs Shanky and her two daughters had gone for a mountaineering expedition to the Himalayas. As mobile phones do not work in such remote places, they could not contact the professor for ten days. On returning they found no trace of him. The police have not yet succeeded in throwing light on his whereabouts," explained the scientist, absentmindedly jagging a fresh page of her notebook with the pen.

*

Robin saw very little of his mother for the next few days. During breakfasts and dinners, her eyebrows remained knitted, her gaze seldom lifted from the plate of food in front and loose strands of hair flew in to tickle the bridge of her nose. Robin had never seen her so withdrawn before. Whenever he got a chance, he would put his arm around her shoulders to comfort her, guessing she was unsettled by the disappearance of Dr Shanky, her former teacher and closest friend in the professional circuit.

By the time Robin's seventeenth birthday arrived, the equations and formulae had strung themselves in his mind like party streamers. Ruby had found out the exact date of his birth from the staff at the adoption home. Every year she took a leave from work on this date to be with her son.

For the twelfth grader, the birthday started like all other days. Robin flipped open his book to the latest chapter taught in school and probed the pen stand for a pen with a new refill. Thuds of heavy utensils reached him from the kitchen, and soon enough Ruby appeared, holding on to a steaming bowl with a pair of prongs. As she lowered it on a place mat spread across the top of the bedside table, Robin took a glance at it, but drew his eyes back to the book. Forking one of the pieces of chicken surfacing in the thick golden-brown gravy, she blew at it till it was no longer capable of burning her son's mouth and placed it on a small bronze plate.

"Happy birthday," she wished, approaching his chair.

"Thanks." He turned and smiled widely, his cheeks breaking into dimples.

"Taste this, son. I've prepared it for dinner," she said, bringing forward the plate.

"So soon?" Robin's eyes widened in surprise. On his birthdays, Ruby would start cooking an hour before dinnertime so he and his friends could have the food fresh and warm.

"Didn't get leave. Might be away in the evening too. There is a critical assignment which could not be shifted to a different date as many highly placed people wanted to get it done today," Ruby explained with a sigh. "Anyway, I promise to be back before dinner. The food will grow cold by then," she said regretfully.

"Don't worry. I know you wouldn't be going to the institute today, if you could help it. And please don't worry about warming the food; I or anyone can do it. By the way, the chicken preparation is fabulous," Robin complimented, savouring every bit of the morsel.

"My mother's recipe," Ruby revealed with a nostalgic smile, before adding, "Breakfast will be ready in another hour."

Completing the sums, Robin opened his geometry box and busied himself in swivelling the compass and adjusting the alignment of the protractor. Sometimes he had to erase the imperfectly positioned arcs to come up with more accurate ones. His concentration had just begun to yield to hunger when Ruby called him for breakfast.

A combination of mouth-watering smells swept over Robin as he uncovered the plates laid out on the table. Buttered toasts shared space with a chicken omelette — neatly folded and garnished with potato chips and fried tomatoes. In another plate, mutton cutlets were arranged, interspersed with cucumber slices and strips of cheese. The custard waited in its bowl, decked up with cherries and nuts and towered over by a glass of liquid chocolate.

It was a Saturday. On holidays, Robin, who woke up at the crack of dawn to study, took a short nap after breakfast. The sumptuous meal made his yearning for a spell of repose even more pronounced. He had lied down on the bed beside his desk, when Ruby waved goodbye and drew the door close.

Woken up by the precisely timed squeal of the alarm clock, Robin put on his slippers and headed towards the washbasin to chase out the lingering drowsiness. While traipsing by his mother's study his eyes fell on the floor and he happened to notice a trickle of pale blue liquid under the door. He rubbed his groggy eyes, squatted down and peered at the almost negligible gap beneath the door to locate the origin of the flow. Ruby would lock her study whenever she left the house. Even though she trusted her son, she was under an agreement to take every possible step to protect the confidentiality of the files and documents related to her research, present in the form of both hard and soft copies. Robin, being mature enough to understand why she needed to abide by such rules, harboured no misgivings about it.

"My God, your hands are shaking," Robin heard someone say as he pressed an ear to the door. "The spilt fluid is of no use. It loses its properties on coming in contact with the floor," the man panicked.

"Don't worry, there are other bottles," another male voice assured.

What were these people doing in his mother's study while she was away? Did they come to steal something? Did they break into the house through the window? How was that possible in broad daylight? What could be the fluid? His mother had never worked with chemicals before. Robin put his eye to the keyhole, but could discern nothing. He folded his arms and looked up at the skylights, prodding his grey cells for an idea. With his mind swarming with questions and possibilities, he suddenly recalled glimpsing LED lights for sale in Ali's shop, although Christmas was still a fortnight away.

Robin yanked open a drawer and rifled through the wrapping papers till his fingers traced out the outline of an envelope. He pulled out the crisp note he had received as an advanced birthday gift from an aunt and hurried towards Ali's shop. Though he maintained a nonchalant expression, he was not only bogged down by anxiety concerning his mother, but also charged with a juddering sense of thrill. Armed with a string of fairy's lights, he approached the mango tree that brushed against his mother's study. Gripping the railings of the ground floor balcony, he planted his right foot between a pair of lower grilles and lifted his left leg. Just then, a stout, bespectacled, grey-haired woman — the domestic help of the ground floor residents — rushed to the veranda with a bundle of wet clothes. On noticing Robin scale the grilles, she stopped in her tracks, her eyes wide in bewilderment, her lips alternately parting and clamping as she struggled to decide what to say. He jerked his left shoulder to draw attention to the coiled wire slung on it and pointed at the tree to clarify his intentions. As the maid went about her business of hanging the clothes to dry, he clambered to the upper grilles and from there to the lowermost branch of the mango tree.

He silently thanked his mother's cousins for inviting him to their countryside home during the summer vacations. The tree climbing skills he had acquired in their orchards were rarely found in a city-bred boy like him.

The birthday boy trailed the wire through the forking branches, pretending to decorate the tree. His breath fell fast as he furtively inched towards the study window. Concealing himself behind a mask of long mango leaves, he raised his head for a glimpse inside the room, his hands trembling in apprehension and excitement. He blinked, startled beyond his wits on finding the study jam-packed with men and women. Many of them were attired in office formals. Some were carrying bags and the others light briefcases. Dr Shanky, whom he had last seen on his twelfth birthday, was still recognizable due to his shining bald pate, green eyes and grey goatee.

"Ruby has already gone inside to check the lab facilities at the university," Dr Shanky informed a tall, short-haired woman.

"I see that your city lacks restaurants," a clean-shaven man in a black suit joked.

"If we eat there, we will feel hungry once we return to our normal sizes. Let's keep them outside the city. In any case, they do not consume as much energy as say, offices," Dr Shanky reasoned.

What were those people talking about? Robin wondered aghast. Where had his mother gone? However, he thanked his lucky stars that the window had been kept open. The reason might have been to prevent suffocation. He guessed Dr Shanky had not expected he would be overheard as the flat was on the fourth floor while the neighbouring houses had no more than two floors.

"Ladies and gentlemen." Dr Shanky's voice boomed. "We have already learned how it feels to resize ourselves, when we were sneaked into this house in Ruby's carry bag. We will do it again in a couple of minutes. On behalf of the institute, I would like to express my gratitude towards all the teachers, professors, doctors, nurses, drivers, engineers, plumbers, bank officials, accountants and mechanics assembled here today so that we can find out whether this city is well equipped to carry out all the essential functions expected of it."

"It would have been impossible to build this city without my colleague Ruby, who had worked out every detail from a vague idea I had shared with her and a few others," he continued. "Let's make this city a success as the future of our world depends on it. It is needless to mention how much energy consumption we can reduce by diminishing our needs without compromising on any of our necessities. Let us consider the example of a classroom in a school. How much energy is required to fan a room the size of a shoe box? A vehicle run on solar power will be too expensive for most, but how about a solar powered toy transport? This project is also a perfect marriage of physical science with medical science since without Dr Patry and his teams' Shrinkage Dose, the city would have remained a collection of dolls' houses despite our best efforts. Please remember that nobody other than those gathered here must know about the city before the trial period ends. After that it will be announced by the government and replicated in innumerable locations across the world. In fact, the reason for congregating in a private home to carry further this project is that a few people in the institute are suspected of leaking information. Time is running out. Let's start."

Robin gripped the branches tightly so as not to fall off. With his eyes leaping to touch his eyebrows, he witnessed the volunteers raise a small bottle of pale blue liquid to their lips before they vanished into thin air. He would have failed to notice them, even afterwards, if one of the men had not let out a groan upon bumping against a black butterfly shaped object, which Robin recognized as Ruby's hair clip. Turning to the sand coloured mosaic floor, he saw him clutch his waist and trudge after his companions — men and women as small as Robin's little finger. He gaped as they scurried through the entrances of the offices, school, university and hospital in the city he had mistaken as a mere model.

Some of them boarded buses. Some hopped into cars. The others bustled towards the train or squeezed into one of the motorboats to reach their destination. Robin's eyes darted from one transport to the other as they made their way through the paved roads, the incessantly flowing river or the gleaming railway tracks. He watched the cars pull into the office premises and the buses halt at various stops indicated by boards with colourful graphics. His gaze followed the boats all along the course of the river as they dropped the passengers at designated spots on the bank marked out with differently patterned flags. For the first time in his teenage years, he found himself transfixed by a train as it startled the semi-curled saplings swaying coyly along the tracks before shooting into a tunnel. He remained glued to the diminutive city till all the men and women had disembarked from their vehicles and disappeared inside their workplaces.

Robin climbed down the tree and went back to his flat. From time to time, he pressed his ear to the door of the study, wondering when the tiny people would emerge from the "city." He wished for his friends to arrive late, but the bell rang before long. Every year, it was his classmate Anita who brought the birthday cake, slightly annoying Ruby for hijacking what she considered her sole privilege.

"Happy birthday," Anita beamed, handing over the box of cake to Robin.

"Happy Birthday," Sunny wished and patted Robin on the back.

"Thanks a lot." Robin smiled and stepped away from the door to make way for them. Sunny bent down to untie his shoelaces. Anita, who was familiar with the flat, skipped to the balcony, plopped into an easy chair and waved to a chubby cheeked toddler staring up from the window of the opposite building. Robin dragged two more chairs to the balcony and settled down between his friends.

"Where's Ruby?" Sunny asked with a quick glance at Anita, who shook her head to convey that she too had not seen her.

"She was forced to go to work today but she'll come back," Robin replied, studying the line of ants scurrying along a branch of the mango tree he had climbed just hours ago.

The balcony soon got crammed with chairs procured from all the other rooms. During an ongoing game of Dumb Charades, Anita nudged Robin to suggest the word they would whisper into their friend Neel's ear. But the birthday boy found himself besieged with images of the model and the pint-sized volunteers. Whatever he had witnessed departed from his mind only to come back - like his much-adored stray cats, who ventured to the variety of street life, returning time and again to those who fed them.

Anita arranged seventeen candles on the round chocolate cake and lit them up — each little flame representing an entire year's light in Robin's ten plus seven years of existence, like the prototype in his mother's study perhaps exemplified the future of city life.

"Hello Ruby," Robin heard Neel say.

The birthday boy glanced up from the cake to see his mother smile warmly at all his friends. At their insistence, Ruby posed with him for a couple of photographs. She had changed from the cotton shirt-blouse she wore in the morning to a simmering silk gown; her tresses were rolled into a series of dark brown waves. She would always dress up for her son's birthday, but never before had she gotten her hair curled. Robin suspected that tucked away among the different buildings, there was a beauty parlour in her tiny city.

"I must bring the ice cream," Ruby excused herself after Robin had cut the cake.

"I need something to carry so many ice-cream cups on my way back from CreamBlock," she explained, noticing Robin's gaze linger on the lidded cardboard box in her hands. She quickly adjusted the position of her palms, probably to hide the three little orifices on one side of the box. Flashing a smile at Anita, who was observing her newly curled hair with admiration, she trotted down the stairs, her car keys clamouring in her purse.

Robin could visualise how she would spend the next few minutes before turning up with more than a dozen cups of vanilla ice-cream and a spring in her step. She would drive to a desolate spot and tweak open the box. The scientists and other volunteers would scale the walls of the box, peer over its edge and climb down the stems of grass flowers. They would huddle around a dew, unable to draw their eyes away from their reflections in the water. Some would squat down, cloaked by the shadow of the car and dip their hands in the water drops to rinse their faces.

Once the sense of bewilderment sunk in, they would shake hands with each other and head to their homes after resizing themselves.

Silver Jubilee

It would be the twenty-fifth year of Natyamadhura folk theatre group. Muralidhar knew they had to put up something eye-grabbing for its silver jubilee celebrations to keep the group afloat to see its twenty-sixth birthday and beyond.

In the last few years, they had to compete with not only the television sets booming in many village homes, but also a spate of new folk theatre groups. Some of these groups could afford to flaunt opulent sets and hire big stars from the regional film industry. Muralidhar's village had almost become unrecognisable with numerous shops between the panchayat office and the railway station. It was not uncommon to find balls of crumpled pamphlets and brochures tucked in the grass, discarded grey mobile phone sets camouflaged among pebbles, and plastic packets lying around the ponds and swelling in the wind to acquire the roundness of pitchers. In the absence of offices and similar establishments, night still came early; the edges of placards obtruded the silhouettes of trees like the way an arm in a sling juts out from the body

Twenty-five years ago, Muralidhar was starting his career as a schoolteacher when he, his friend and colleague Binoy, the folk musicians Radhashyam and Benimadhab came together to form Natyamadhura. They would rehearse wherever they could find a place to stand — sometimes in their own courtyards and sometimes in common spaces. Few houses had television then. The actors would often notice the villagers, especially the children, peer through the fences or perch on trees to watch their rehearsals. Since its inception many colourful characters had joined the core team for brief spells like a heady mix of myths added to the undisputed portion of a biography — the kind of plays they liked to perform on stage.

Months got piled up with aborted ideas, and all that remained of the discussions were the dregs of tea from the innumerable cups consumed.

Mohan, a former swimmer, suggested they have a water drama in the largest pond of the village.

"What? In the water during the monsoon? When they become full of snakes?" Kiriti's lotus like eyes dilated in horror.

Laltu wanted to introduce raunchy dialogues to draw in the crowds. "Don't be shocked. I've heard it has become a norm in the theatres staged in the city," he defended his proposition.

"You say that to Muralidhar. We'll see whether he allows you to stay here after that," Sridhar challenged, his thick, bushy eyebrows crooked in disapproval. Everyone knew how miffed Muralidhar was with Laltu's cheekiness and would have dropped him from the troupe, had he not excelled in playing Shah Jahan in a drama based on his romance with Mumtaz Mahal.

One evening, pulling open the gate of Murali's courtyard, son-in-law Shiva saw the other actors squatting in a circle and munching on puffed rice sprinkled with mustard oil and chopped green chillies. Only a month was left for the twenty-fifth anniversary.

Shiva sat down and leaned forward to reach the large bowl from where all the others were helping themselves. He, too, picked up a fistful of puffed rice.

"People of all ages like to watch mythological films and serials. Why?" he brought up the question.

"They love the special effects," he provided the answer himself. "An idea came yesterday when I met my friend Raghu who had been in a circus. The circus had wound up a month ago, and he is searching for a new job. We can hire acrobats like him who would perform mind-boggling stunts. In fact, we can stage a special effect filled Ramayana with no technical wizardry!"

Murali had always been sceptical about Shiva's ideas. The young man, besotted with his former teacher's daughter, had joined the theatre group five years ago, with the sole purpose of winning his approval. Two years had passed since Murali, impressed with Shiva's genuineness, gave his consent and got his daughter married to him. However, he was yet to respect Shiva as a competent actor: he found his histrionics far below average. Even lesser was his faith in his son-in-law's pragmatism given Shiva's day job in an ice-cream factory did not match up to his qualifications.

"Your intention of finding work for your friend is noble. But this is the wrong place. As you know, there was nothing left to share among ourselves after our recent shows," Murali grumbled.

"I really believe this will work," Shiva stressed. Then silently said to himself, "I certainly have an idea on what works on people. Otherwise, I would not have been your son-in-law, today."

"We can make it convincing if we focus on the details. Before that we need to chalk out the places where we can introduce acrobatics," Binoy responded, considering the idea.

"But that man needs an income and we have no money to pay him," Murali reminded.

"Don't worry, I'll look into it," Binoy assured. The next day, with his wife's consent he pawned her jewellery, hoping to get back the ornament if the play was a success.

Shiva had asked Raghu to meet Murali and Binoy in the latter's home. Sitting on a bed with their legs folded, the friends were engrossed in discussing the script.

"Someone has come to meet you," Binoy's wife called out from the courtyard.

"Ask him to come in," Binoy said, his eyes fixed on the script.

As the sound of footsteps grew louder, Murali reluctantly put down his pen and turned to face the door. Scrutinising Raghu from head to toe, Murali decided that he and Shridhar were of the same size and would be indistinguishable in masks to the audience. So Raghu could take over from Sridhar, who was playing Hanuman, in the scenes that required stunts.

"You can set real fire to my tail in the Lanka Dahan scene," Raghu suggested.

"What?" Murali gasped.

"We cannot risk a mishap on our stage!" Binoy exclaimed, jumping down from his bed in shock.

"Don't worry." The new member laughed pleasantly. "I have performed many fire tricks for the circus."

Murali and Binoy glanced at each other. Then Murali nodded and said, "Let's do it since he is so confident."

The senior members also accepted Shiva's idea of not confining the play to the stage, but involving the natural features of the villages where they would perform. They would stage the forest scenes under the shades of the adjacent trees and the big canal on the village outskirts would be the "sea" that Raghu, as Hanuman, would cross with a single leap.

The actors had gathered in a mango orchard in the wee hours of morning to have one round of rehearsal before leaving for their workplaces. Shiva was given multiple bit roles — Mahadev who gives a boon to Ravan at the beginning of the play, King Bali who is killed by Ram's arrow, and a demon in Ravan's kingdom. After mouthing his lines for the first scene, Shiva had retreated to the shade of a tree, when Champa commented, "If we can have a real fire, why not a real snake around Mahadev's neck?"

"Real snake?" Shiva was horror struck.

"What if we hire a snake catcher to play Mahadev?" Champa wondered aloud.

"Snake catcher to play Mahadev?" Kiriti exclaimed.

"Not a bad idea. There are many in my maternal uncle's village that fall within the territory of a jungle," Murali said.

As usual, Murali accepted Champa's suggestion. She had been an indispensable member of Natyamadhura for the last five years. Murali remembered the late Sunday afternoon when the actors were rehearsing in an abandoned cowshed. On realising Mir Zafar had betrayed him, Radhashyam, in the role of Shiraj-ud-Daulah, paced about, seething with rage and digging his fingers into his hair in despair. Distracted by the crushing of leaves, Murali turned and glanced at the supine mango tree felled by the previous night's storm. A woman stood, clutching a baby to her chest and flapping her free arm to ward off mosquitoes. Assuming she wanted to watch their rehearsal to pass time, Murali continued to focus on Radhashyam's acting. However, as the crunching of leaves grew louder, he was compelled to shift his gaze for the second time. The woman crossed the lying tree trunk, stepped inside the shed and walked straight towards Murali. As she came nearer, he noticed that there was no trace of vermillion on her forehead or in the parting of her hair.

Champa had introduced herself as a poor widow, but everyone whispered that she was a whore from the by-lanes of Rupahaata. Impressed with her acting, Murali was determined to include her in the group, irrespective of others' opinions. To those who questioned her character he would retort, "I don't care where she came from. Now she is my daughter."

"But will a snake catcher be able to act?" Kiriti was sceptical.

"It's a brief role, and he only has to put up a placid expression." Champa argued.

"Champa is right." Murali backed her. He chuckled to himself. "If Shiva can do it, so can a snake catcher."

"But where's the novelty in it? Villagers see snakes all the time," Radhashyam pointed out.

"Not on the stage," replied Shiva.

"I think having a real snake will be a big plus point," Binoy said, and added, "None can deny the impact a snake has on the human mind. The more something repels or scares when seen in proximity, the more it fascinates when viewed at a distance."

"It's the same psychology that makes horror fiction and movies so popular," Laltu remarked.

The rehearsals started with Kiriti and Binoy playing Ram and Ravan, respectively. Champa slipped into the skin of Sita. They also finalised the casting of Lakshman, Bibhisan and Sugriv while Murali sent Shiva to recruit a snake catcher from his maternal uncle's village. Champa was asked to accompany him as Murali could not rely on his son-in-law's judgement alone. With Sita unavailable for the day, the rest of the cast geared up for the battle scenes between Ram and Ravan.

Scanning the trees at the outskirts of the village where Murali's uncle lived, Champa could well imagine the snakes coiling around the thick branches, flicking their forked tongues, crawling along the grainy barks and exploring the tangle of roots. The snake catchers would manoeuvre through the constricted space between the trees like Murali's theatre group had continued along the limited spare time of its members.

Champa selected the most handsome villager, named Afzal Mohammed. "See, he has longish eyes. He looks just like the Mahadev drawn in the calendars," she defended her choice. As the play needed a lot more actors, especially for the battle scenes, the troupe recruited more snake catchers who either played demons in Ravan's army or monkeys in Ram's infantry.

Seated at the teacher's desk in his classroom after school hours, Murali was making a list of things that still needed to be taken care of. Radhashyam inspected his flute while Benimadhab was bent over his *dholak*, scraping it with sandpaper. Champa looked on as her son ate his dinner from a steel Tiffin case. Kiriti and Laltu were working out the details of the scene where Indrajeet would battle from his chariot, up among the clouds. It was a common technique in theatres to engender a foggy effect by vaporising a mixture of glucose and water. They had employed it in some of their earlier plays. Dragged by men dressed as horses, Indrajeet's chariot would climb upon a transparent ramp surrounded by the artificial fog to create an illusion of flying. They would deploy the same fog effect and ramp when Goddess Durga would appear to grant Lord Rama a boon.

Sridhar strode into the room to say, "I've been toying with an idea ever since the snake catchers joined our troupe. I was wondering whether we can incorporate the scene where Indrajeet hurls arrows that get converted to snakes. I think it can be done since the snake catchers play Ram's monkey soldiers. They will not mind a few snakes hissing near their feet till Afzal dressed as Garuda, the nemesis of snakes, arrives to take them away."

"I agree such a scene will awe the audience. But how to show arrows turning into snakes?" Benimadhab asked.

"I'm sure we can hit upon a way if we think about it," Radhashyam said, staring at the blank blackboard, his forehead creased in concentration.

Champa accompanied her son to the corridor and waited while he walked to the washbasin at the corner and stood on his toes to turn it on. She wiped off the water from her son's face and fingers with the edge of her *pallu* and scrubbed the greasy Tiffin box before returning to the classroom. Her son stayed back in the corridor to watch the snails crawling on its floor.

"I've just got an idea on how to make this work," she declared, looking at Sridhar although she could feel Kiriti turn to her in surprise and sense the glow of admiration on Afzal's face.

*

They publicised the play a fortnight in advance. Its colourful posters proclaimed: 'Ramayan like you have never seen before. Real fire, real snakes and many more surprises.'

As the date neared, not only Binoy, but Muralidhar too was sighted at the jeweller's shop.

"Can you please lend me some money," said the schoolteacher, digging into the large pocket of his *kurta*.

Mangaldeep, who was adding milligram weights to the pan of a tiny golden balance, shot a quizzical glance at him. Muralidhar brought out a little red box from his pocket and handed it to the jeweller. He opened it and keenly inspected with a magnifying glass the wedding ring it contained. Satisfied, he put it in the sample pan of the balance, in place of the bangle he had been weighing earlier. He took a few minutes to contemplate its price, and then he unlocked a steel box and held out a wad of notes for the school teacher.

Shiva had also pawned a ring and a necklace, but from a different village to escape his father-in-law's wrath. Champa had parted with her pair of silver anklets — the only costly piece of jewellery she had ever possessed.

They would stage the first show in the core team's village. Prior to the beginning of the play, they sprayed the barren land where the audience would sit with bleaching powder to prevent any untoward incidents. Binoy's son, Sridhar's cousin, Mohan's brother and Radhashyam's mother were entrusted with the duty of selling tickets. Carrying loose change and bunches of tickets, the young men went up to the spectators as they settled down on the ground to enjoy the performance.

"This family has just arrived." Radhashyam's mother nudged the other collectors. Sridhar's cousin manoeuvred his way to the couple and their children, who were squeezing themselves between the bordering guava trees. With eyes as sharp as ever, the eighty-four-year-old lady never failed to notice any additions to the audience.

In the start itself, the viewers could not avert their eyes from the defanged cobra coiled around Mahadev's neck. As the play progressed, the tricks and stunts drew more and more applause, not to mention the superlative acting by Kiriti, Champa, Sridhar and Binoy. When Ram, Lakshman and Sita were gathering leaves to build themselves a home in the forest, Champa's son, clad in a rabbit's costume, jumped out of a bush to prance around them. Watching him, his friends in the audience bounded towards the shady trees where the scene was being enacted.

"Come back, Chintu. Come back, Golapi," called out their mothers in utter embarrassment and came panting after them.

"No problem. No problem," Shiva said, as he sprinted towards the audience and stood with his arms outstretched, between the children and their parents. "It'll be wonderful to have an interactive play. Please take your seats," he urged the harried guardians.

Septuagenarian Sadanand's eyes moistened with tears as Radhashyam and Benimadhab, dressed up as residents of Ayodhya, belted out a hymn on Ram to the beat of *dholak* and cymbals. The folk musicians sang many other melodies at the various turns of the narrative, carving out or enhancing the different moods of the epic. Two-year-old Putul shut her eyes tight when the grotesque demons of Lanka stomped into the battlefield. Murali's elder daughter had stitched their costumes out of old clothes and scraps of shiny paper, and her sister — the one who had married Shiva — had fashioned the masks out of dry leaves and slivers of bamboo.

The next spot where the troupe planned to stage the epic had been stalled in its metamorphosis from a village to a town when the promised factory never got constructed. This semi-village lacked the greenery of the countryside as well as the glamour of a city. There were no malls, restaurants, clubs and only one movie hall, and the people who had made money through clever associations were clueless about how to spend it.

The tickets were kept cheap to draw the maximum number of spectators possible. The troupe had calculated beforehand that even with the low-ticket prices, they would make a considerable profit if a certain percentage of the village population watched their play. Encouraged by the size of the audience, vendors parked their carts and food sellers tinkled their bells. Munching masala *muri*, chomping on chutney dipped *telebhaja*, biting into crunchy *pakoras* or sucking canned drinks, the spectators looked forward to a few hours of wholesome entertainment. Some young girls sported new earrings and bangles, bought minutes ago from the vendors who jostled with each other to sell their merchandise. Toddlers brandished their balloons or cuddled furry teddies. Children who were slightly older fiddled with toy bows and poked the unfortunate people in front with the blunt tips of arrows until their guardians took heed of this activity and threatened to drag them home.

The play was progressing well. The monkeys, fuelled by their unwavering loyalty towards Lord Ram, fought fearlessly against the daunting demons. By the time Ravan's son Indrajeet flew into the arena in his cloud traversing chariot, the battlefield was strewn with weapons and shields of the dead and the wounded. One of these dazzling silver shields was nothing but the lid of a basket embedded in the soil — a basket teeming with snakes. It was this shield that one of the monkey soldiers picked up to defend himself from the rain of arrows hurled by Indrajeet, releasing the snakes at the same moment when the projectiles hit the ground.

"Snakes. Snakes. The arrows have turned into snakes!" exclaimed another soldier in shock.

Gasps escaped from the audience. A spectator who sprang up from his seat in excitement had to flop down when admonished by those behind him. Doubling over in pain, Ram's soldiers called out his name before collapsing on the mossy earth. Creatures that had crawled out of the hidden basket moved about in their serpentine gait, like the narrative of the two-hour long play snaking its way round the turns of the epic poem. The audience members craned their necks to get a better look at them although they were easily discernible, hissing next to the spread-eagled soldiers' heels, coiling around the detached wheels of chariots and meandering along the grasses patching the battlefield.

The monkey-soldiers pretended to be unconscious. It was necessary that the snakes did not perceive them as threats. Several times, they had rehearsed with the snakes and performed the scene to perfection in Murali's village. Kiriti's voice boomed out of his chariot, parked a safe distance away from the slithering reptiles. "My friend Garuda, my army has been attacked by serpents. I seek your help in vanquishing our common enemies."

The sound of fluttering came in response. Garuda arrived flapping his wings, his claws ending in curved talons. Just then, a conglomeration of noises from yelling men and barking dogs assaulted the actors and spectators. The men on the patch of land, selected as the "stage" did not need to trouble themselves to discover the source of sound. Those causing the mayhem almost leaped upon them, forcing them to dart in different directions. The audience revelling in the silent terror of watching the legless reptiles was suddenly entreated to a deluge of legs, as a group of hooded and masked men bounded across the ground where the play was being enacted, followed by a pack of livid dogs.

"Thieves, thieves!" shouted the audience. The thieves, emboldened by every slip they had given to the police, found themselves at a loss of wits, challenged by creatures, who seemed to spend a better part of the day lazing in the sun and sniffing for bones. In a panic, one of the pursued men dropped his window grill cutter and pelted towards the makeshift bridge built across the canal. No doubt remained that the gang had attempted burglary, taking advantage of the fact that people were away from their homes, watching the play. Bintu, the leader of the canines bared his teeth and growled, his eyes flashing with the wrath of the wronged hero who punishes the villains at the climax of a film. However, it was Duglu, with patches of furless skin and a mangled right ear, who would go down in history as the true saviour. He bit off a piece of cloth from a thief's trousers, instilling in him and the others a fear that could permanently freeze their criminal proclivities.

Flanked by his friends Neeranjan and Pratap, Bodhisattva, the panchayat leader, began humming a *bhajan* and swaying merrily to its rhythm. He could not thank the dogs enough for preventing the theft as the plunder would have dealt a heavy blow to his reputation. He was also grateful for an opportunity to open his mouth, after being nudged into silence by his wife, not once, but several times during the play.

"You must run and catch the thieves." He heard one of his neighbours tell him.

Bodhisattva, was not only on enviable terms with the political bigwigs, but had gained popularity among a section of villagers by punishing those who married outside their caste or religion. He was about to put the man in his place for exhibiting the audacity to order him. But then, he was confronted with a sea of voices urging him to capture the thieves. In fact, the entire audience had turned towards him. His name was being chanted as if he were a sports star striding into the field.

Suppressing his glee, he said, "But the dogs are already after them."

"The dogs can only chase them away. They don't have hands to grab and pin them down. The burglars will remain free to tiptoe back into our village and attempt another theft," whispered his wife urgently, who was sitting behind him along with his sisters.

"Neeranjan, come with me." Bodhisattva stood up.

"I hurt my right foot yesterday. Didn't you see me limping on my way here?" Neeranjan responded.

"Pratap?"

"I've just recovered from a stroke. I won't be able to run."

Bodhisattva wondered why his friends had not mentioned about their ailments earlier.

"The thieves are getting further away." A frail man with bright, coin-like eyes pointed out.

"We will join you. How will we proceed if you don't lead? What will we do without you?" A wispy haired farmer, who had opened a betel shop after losing his land, asked with his gnarled hands folded and voice choked with emotion.

After racing for a quarter of an hour, Bodhisattva stumbled against a stone and halted, his heart thudding loudly from exhaustion. He turned to his left and swivelled towards his right. The men who had gotten up to join him in the pursuit, including the *paanwallah*, were nowhere in sight. He tottered along, panting and drenched in sweat, wondering whether it was even possible to catch up with the thieves, whom he could see no longer, and the canines, which were now just specks in the distance. Then the unthinkable happened. One speck grew bigger and bigger till he could make out its four legs and even its wee little tail.

As soon as he had inhaled Bodhisattva's scent, Ghogol, born of a mongrel and the panchayat leader's politician-friend's bulldog, had somehow lost interest in the thieves. With his ears pricked up, he turned a hundred and eighty degrees and fixed his eyes on Bodhisattva. Before Bodhisattva could understand what was going on and take to his heels,

Ghogol came for him with the speed of a gale, his yellow eyes flaming, the pitch black fur glistening, the white fleck on his forehead resembling a pupil less extra eye, and every detail of his menacing appearance drilled into the panchayat leader, who had seen the dog earlier in the streets, without noticing him as such. Standing on a dusty, unpaved road flanked by two fishing ponds, Bodhisattva eyed the cane, aware that he would never succeed in hitting anyone with it other than those tied up by his henchmen. However, holding it out like a spear, he took two steps back, wondering which would be the safer bet — to make eye contact with the dog or not. It had been hours since the fishermen had rolled up the nets and left for their homes. The moon, nudging the silhouette of a temple across the water body on his left, was not bright enough to dazzle but not too faint either. A few inches above the surface of the pond, the dragonflies busied themselves in snagging mosquitoes. The skies had remained sealed for the last couple of days. Missing was the drip of rainwater that slipped off the tips of trembling reeds. Even the frogs did not bother to croak. Ghogol tore into the silence with the grinding of his razor-sharp teeth and glared at Bodhisattva, his eyes now tinged with red, and parted his saliva dripping lips.

Perhaps, the panchayat leader would have been rescued by his people if he had scampered towards the audience. However, flustered by the danger that suddenly cropped up and was looming over him, he dropped the cane and made a dash for the school building. He was not seen for the rest of the evening, nor was his pursuer Ghogol.

As soon as the chaos subsided, with the men and the dogs — other than Ghogol, plunging into a grove at the edge of the semi-town, Muralidhar said, "You have already enacted the scene involving the serpents. No point in repeating it. Afzal must collect the snakes. Afzal...where is Afzal?"

The snake catcher had rushed to the spot even before Muralidhar had spoken, but as far as his eyes reached, there was not a single snake slithering about. Using his presence of mind, he told Ram, who returned to his chariot, "I have freed your army from the snakes. Please bid me goodbye for now."

Though all the actors remained tense about the disappearance of the snakes, they did not let it show during the rest of the play. The play concluded as planned and rehearsed with Ram's victory over Ravan and his reunion with Sita. It allowed a happy ending by snipping Sita's trial by the fire and her subsequent banishment into the forests.

On the way to the changing tent, Sridhar said, "We had sprayed bleaching powder on the grounds where the audience had sat. The snakes can't be roaming there. And if they did..." Sridhar paused to scratch his head. "There would be ear-splitting screams...the villagers were huddled so close that the snakes would have to crawl over them."

"They are not on the football field." One of the snake catchers came running to inform, gleaming with sweat after a thorough search.

"I think they crossed the pond and crawled inside the buildings," Kiriti panicked.

"That's terrible," Champa shuddered and bit her lips.

The actors were in a hurry, changing into regular clothes, scrubbing their makeup and packing the props into bags and trunks. They would leave for another town by the night train. The sound of collective footsteps rose from the area where the villagers had amassed earlier to watch the play. Laltu whispered, "I hope they don't blame us."

Before anyone else could speak, the actors overheard a man, outside their changing tent, loudly tell another, "It's not their fault. I'm sure they had practised well. How would they know that thieves and dogs would interrupt at such a crucial point?"

"We cannot stay in our homes. My wife found a snake coiled around the clothesline. By the time I reached the balcony, it escaped, probably to someone else's house," complained the other man.

"Yes, we will wait here till the men from the forest department arrive."

Before the villager completed the last sentence, a snake catcher named Kartik, popped his head out of the men's tent. "We can capture them...in exchange for a small payment," he offered.

The villagers muttered something amongst themselves, but did not seek help from Kartik or any of the other snake catchers. "This village is a stronghold of the newly elected ruling party. With their immense faith in the government, they are relying on its forest department," guessed Sridhar.

"They probably think we will steal their valuables if they let us into their homes," Afzal pondered.

"They might be still in shock. Some of them would have been robbed this evening, if not for the dogs," remarked Tipu, another snake catcher.

The inhabitants of this village, whose vegetation had long been stripped, had no clue on how to deal with snakes. Unable to stay within their homes, the people demanded another play to be staged. Natyamadhura had performed Mahabharata many times and its actors, except for the new recruits, knew the dialogues by heart. Unwilling to be left out, Raghu, Afzal, Kartik and Tipu fitted themselves into various roles. While Raghu enriched the characters with his impromptu tricks, Afzal shone with his natural flair for acting.

The end of Mahabharata approached. The Pandavas and Draupadi were climbing a mound — imagined as a mountain — to reach the heavens. Their backs were to the audience when they heard a sudden cheer. They turned their heads with a simultaneous jerk and blinked in disbelief. A dog had joined them just like Lord Yamraj, in the guise of a canine, had accompanied the Pandavas in their final journey in the epic. The dog had black fur, a white spot on its forehead, a bulldog's snout and tail but a fox's erect ears.

"Ghogol! Ghogol!" the audience erupted.

Surpassing the noise, twenty-year-old Bablu's mobile phone rang resoundingly, much to the irritation of the middle-aged ladies behind him who tried to hush him into silence.

"It might be a call from the forest department. Didn't you know it was my son who got in touch with them?" Bablu's father glared at the women who shrank like pricked balloons.

"Baba, the forest department cannot send men as its snake experts are being held up somewhere else." Bablu turned to his father while staying on the line.

The former irrigation officer snatched the phone from Bablu's hand and bellowed into it, "What took you so long to convey this message?"

"They mumbled something about lack of information." He huffed after disconnecting the line. With his son sitting next to him, he was forced to swallow the swear words tickling his tongue.

Kartik, in the garb of Janmejay, had just taken off his crown and was heading towards the tent, when many of the householders, led by Bablu and his parents, came running and surrounded him.

"Please catch the snakes and take them away from the village. We cannot return home while those creatures are around," implored a young woman in a sugary sweet voice.

Kartik frowned, annoyed with the previous snub. "How will we enter your houses?" he asked gruffly.

"We will take you to our houses. The women and children can wait here. And if your group can stage another play for them...." Bablu's father said, glancing at his wife who nodded in approval.

The snake catchers entered the village homes, led by the householders while the other actors staged the play Taj Mahal for the women and children. The reptile seekers scanned the walls of the houses, upturned the empty pitchers, peered under the beds and combed every patch of green. After inspecting the first three floors of the four-storied school building, the men reached the topmost floor, and found no snakes but a full-grown human huddled under the teacher's desk. His clothes were in tatters, his hair in a mess and his eyes rolled in panic at the scraping sound of the snake catchers' feet. Though unscathed, he faltered so many times in his step that Afzal thought it best to carry him on his shoulders and take him to the nearest house. When the man proved too heavy to be lifted by him alone, the snake catcher sought his cousin Faizal's help. Holding the man's head while his cousin grabbed his legs, Afzal trudged to a well-lit house and knocked on the door.

"Bodhisattva *babu*," gasped the man who opened the door. No matter how much he fanned him and the glasses of water and warm milk he brought, the panchayat leader remained immobile, surveying the bare walls. Eventually his brothers, who had been promptly informed, came to take him home.

In an hour, the snake catchers caught eleven out of the dozen snakes and continued to search for the last one. Even a stick, a branch or a coil of rope compelled the villagers to give it a second glance. Someone claimed to have sighted the snake climbing out of a grilled drain and another swore he had seen it clinging to the bamboo bridge. By the time they spotted it garlanding Bishnu Roy's brand-new television set, Emperor Shah Jahan had been laid to rest beside his beloved wife amidst copious tears and heartfelt prayers.

The morning train chugged out of the station; a group of children ran for a while, waving and calling out to their departing relatives. The Natyamadhura members sat comfortably in their seats, their drowsy faces dappled with happiness. Money from three plays instead of one filled the little steel box lodged under Benoy's right arm.

"Snake, snake!" Kartik pointed towards Kiriti, who had started to doze as soon as the train picked up speed. Jolted out of his reverie, he turned, only to see Champa's long braid dangling over his arm, as she leaned against him unintentionally in her sleep. Their co-actors burst into peals of laughter, which continued like an epic across towns and villages, from the changing room to the stage, stringing each performance to the next.

The Dawning

Savitri held her breath as she chewed the fish to prevent its smell from assailing her nostrils. She hated to throw it down the bin. Her mother had fried it until it got a crunchy golden coat, pitter-pattered it with thinly chopped tomatoes, onions and coriander, and meticulously measured pinches of *jeera*, *dhania* and red chilli powder. Then she sunk it under just enough water to channel through the rolling landscape of fine-grained rice in the other Tupperware box. She recalled her mother's raised eyebrows when she had tried to concoct excuses against carrying lunch from home and mumbled that she would buy a *thali* from the canteen as she did on most of the days. It was not every day that her mother, stricken with various age-related ailments, could rustle up a meal before she dashed out of the house at 7:30 AM to catch the chartered bus.

A bearded man, about a decade older than Savitri, appeared across the table. He pulled back a green plastic chair, thudded his multi-chambered steel Tiffin box on the seat of another chair and called out to the cleaner to wipe off the spilled *dal* from the white table surface. She glanced at her watch. It was 1:10 PM in India, hence 9:40 AM in the UK. She could not afford to spend an entire day pushing down her throat the remaining rice soused with fish gravy. Mr Robert Graves, the programming manager of her client organisation, expected her to start the online demonstration at 10:00 AM sharp. Trashing the contents of the Tiffin box with more than a little sense of guilt, she turned on the tap of the washbasin to rinse her hands. She spread out her fingers under the electronic drier, listening intently to the drone of the machine to interrupt her mishmash of thoughts.

Back in her cubicle, Savitri positioned the land phone right next to her keyboard and dialled Mr Grave's office number. She navigated to the online meeting site while waiting for him to answer. As the webpage loaded into her view, she copied the password from the meeting invite email and clicked on a dark blue button to join the session.

"Hello."

Savitri heard her client's crisp voice at the other end of the line. She also noticed the small diamond shaped icon blink beside his name in the chat window, indicating he had joined the meeting. The session went on for over two hours. Savitri logged into various interlinked applications, typed in fresh sets of data and hit several buttons to show the outcomes of the different operations.

As the presentation ended, Savitri, brimming with satisfaction, clicked the oval green button on her chat window to stop her computer screen from being displayed on her client's PC. She rose from her seat and traipsed to the balcony without stopping at the coffee vending machine. She could hear it growling out bittersweet coffee into her teammate's personalised mug. On other days, when she stood against the railing overlooking the street and the lake beyond, her fingers would be curled around the handle of a porcelain cup imprinted with her company logo. The steam would weave into her breath and the thick liquid ripple at her puckered lips that were hesitant and eager at the same time for the first scorching sip.

Savitri took a deep breath. The leisurely sunlight drew glittering spines along the curved backs of the orderly waves. Squeezed by the swirling grey clouds, the sky had shrunk into snaky passages and muddy blue blots. On finding sudden openings across the murmuring waters, it canopied over the skyscrapers and laced the frilly eucalyptus tops. The strip of reddish sunlight from the horizon to the centre of the lake reminded her of the concluding pink line in the PregaNews kit. She typed the good news to Rohan instead of calling him as he could be in a meeting. Even with her comfort flung on the carousel of nausea and her plans enmeshed by apprehensions, she was swept over by a happiness which knocked at the deepest of her thoughts like one knocks on her friends' doors to invite them for a gambol. An intensifying excitement sprinkled over the slow burning tension and then there was sheer bliss rooting itself unchallenged through the layers of consciousness and subconscious.

Rohan had cooked garlic chicken for her. And served it with warm, round *chapattis*. They had slumped on the floor soon after dinner. The day had been dizzied with activities. They had tripped to an overcrowded, newly restored fortress, visited a museum whose appeal of unending displays lay in the intimidating weight of history, and strolled in a Mughal garden dotted with fountains and decked with tiers of seasonal blooms.

The cooler purred as they sprawled on a floral-patterned mattress, chuckling at the memory of being denied a room in a hotel as they were not married. He had not bothered to buy furniture for his temporary home. His books and CDs remained stacked against the wall. His laptop occupied the pride of place a couple of feet behind his pillow, which was darkened in the centre by its daily eight-hour tussle with his nightmares and dreams. Picking up the knick-knacks strewn across the floor, Savitri had assembled them on top of the cooler, the larger objects behind the smaller ones. These included a sequined notebook from his ex-girlfriend, pocket-sized mementoes from his former office colleagues, a copper amulet from a relative, a matchstick house he had bought at a fair and the tiny stone animals he had carried back from a trip.

"I don't want to have any morning-after pills. It's high time we have a baby," she said, fiddling with the holy chain he wore around his waist.

Rohan opened his eyes and stroked her face, tracing the specs-depressed ridge of her nose and skidding down the slope of her lipstick-smudged upper lip. "Whatever you wish," he responded, "I'll marry you within a month if you conceive."

"If I don't, we can wait a year longer for your parents to come around," she added, flushed with happiness that he had accepted her wish without a fuss. The windows of a neighbouring house thwacked open. An orange glow chasmed the sweaty darkness through a hitherto unnoticed gap between the hurriedly drawn curtains.

Rohan's parents had been delaying their marriage on one pretext or the other. It seemed they wanted Savitri to buckle under the tremendous pressure on a woman to get married within a certain age, and leave him for a man who could wed her sooner. Or they hoped that his interest in her would wane over the years and he would call off the relationship eventually.

Soon after arriving at her office in the morning, Savitri had dropped her bag on her desk and rushed to the washroom. With a little brown paper bag clutched within her trembling fingers. Pimples had erupted the day after returning from Rohan's flat. Her face had felt like Braille paper against her probing palms. Her limbs had been aching since the following week and the nausea started on the fifteenth day. When four days had passed since the expected date of her periods, she got a married friend to buy her a PregaNews kit. An unmarried woman buying one could have caused tremors in the medicine shop.

A single beep in Savitri's mobile phone announced the entry of a new email. The design for the railway ticket booking system had been finalised. Hurrying back to her quadrant, she swiped the electronic card dangling down her chest and swung open the glass door. Struck by a sudden shot of exhaustion, she paused. After settling in front of her PC, she downloaded the design document from the mail, turned open the cap of her bottle and took a few sips of water. The complex specifications and the elaborate block diagram gave rise to questions. Once satisfied with the explanations provided by her project lead, she maximised the window of her development tool and proceeded with the coding. The busy cursor occasionally tapped open the old folders to check on certain programming syntaxes.

The techie lifted her eyes from the screen for a few more sips of water, wondering when Rohan would call. Whom would the baby resemble? Her mind drifted to a video from his childhood. Rohan was propped against the tub wall, his light eyes blinking through the transient waterfall from a tilted bucket, his front teeth clamped on the handle of the bathing mug while the soap-suds on the floor gathered into a foggy island beaded with bubble-domes.

Her eyes trailed the glow on the white table back to the screen, her palm enveloped the mouse and was about to click when the mobile phone, lying next to her handbag, began to ring.

"Can you go to some place where you won't be overheard?" Rohan asked.

"Sure." Savitri almost leapt from her ergonomic chair, but reminded herself that she should not move so fast for the next nine months.

A couple of men were sipping coffee on the balcony. She scampered out of it and took the lift to reach the topmost floor. Another flight of stairs took her to the terrace. She rested her elbow on the upper edge of the parapet and pressed the mobile phone to her ear.

"We can't have the baby," he said softly.

For several seconds, his words remained stuck in the moist air around her like a decree paper on a wet wall.

"What?" she managed to utter.

"I can't marry you now. My mother will turn hysterical and my father may have a heart attack."

"You said you will marry me even if they raise objections and it was oblivious that they would." She was surprised at her ability to argue, even at the peak of her benumbing indignation.

"I'll marry you, but not so soon."

The entire impact of his decision finally seeped in. Her breathing stopped for a moment as if all her orifices were blocked by the scattered parts of an exploded promise.

"I didn't lie to you that I'm popping the pill. It's not exactly a shock for you," Savitri shrilled through the silence of the terrace which was swiftly being sheeted into a box-like enclosure by the lowering clouds.

She heard a deep sigh at the other end.

"The time we had spent in my flat was so beautiful and magical that I had agreed to the impossible," he said after a long pause. A pause which seemed to Savitri like the opening mouth of a prehistoric animal she had assumed to be extinct.

"It was my mistake," he continued, "I'll make you forget about it by being a great husband someday. You will conceive again after our marriage. I'll be a great father too. You will see..."

"Why can't you marry me now?" she asked, steadying her voice. A voice made wooden like the furniture one ducks under to shield from a rain of glass smithereens.

"There are no auspicious dates for marriage in the coming four months," he blurted out.

"Who cares?" Savitri hissed.

"My parents do. They will never accept a marriage solemnised on any random day. Moreover, we have so many relatives. It will take several *lakh* rupees to arrange a wedding reception at such a short notice and invite all, and if I don't, my parents will lose their face. You know my father has to pay off his house loan and I have my education loan to settle." His words tumbled out at breakneck speed, leaving no vent for breathing.

"You mean a feast for your relatives is more important than our child? What will they lose if we don't invite them to our wedding?" Savitri reasoned by groping at the moorings of her wavering composure.

"It will affect my parents' reputation. I don't mean to sound harsh but that is more important to me than a child who is not yet born," Rohan replied, emphasising the last few words.

Savitri slowly climbed down the stairs with her hand on the balustrade. Pressing the button, she slumped against the wall and watched the floor position flash beside the closed doors of the lift. Her gaze shifted to the sacred red thread her mother had made her tie around her left wrist to protect her from all sorts of illnesses and other perils. Inside the elevator, she stared at the grey floor carrying her downwards, backtracking through the ecstasy of wish fulfilment, the nail biting anticipation since the last three weeks, the glimmer of hope when the symptoms started to show and the warm satisfaction of finding her thoughts and Rohan's fitting in each other's grooves in the rented single room flat.

Didn't he notice the rapture in her voice when she was talking about her symptoms? *"The child not yet born."* The phrase rang in her ears. Didn't she tell him about her office party before the nausea began? She had refused her favourite dish. As it was sprinkled with ajinomoto — a spice considered harmful for expectant women. Instead, she had gobbled up the tasteless temple *prasad* on her way home, wondering if prayers were sometimes, at least *sometimes*, answered. His tone had been indulgent too. But now that it was confirmed...

Back on the third floor, she lifted her head, straightened her shoulders and marched down the corridor while imagining her colleagues glimpsing her three months old bulge and nudging each other, then glaring at her five months old bump and whispering loud enough for her to hear. At seven months, they would invent flaws in her work; at eight, they would discuss how girls like her are degrading the county's culture by aping the West. Finally at nine months, when she would meet the HR to get her maternity leave approved, he would survey her from head to toe as if she were an alien.

Savitri halted before the door of her quadrant, but swivelled around and nipped to the balcony. It was packed like the Monday morning trains transporting office-goers from the suburbs to the core city. There was a power-cut. The AC had been turned off to reduce the load on generators that allowed the computers and elevators to function as usual. Employees had poured out of their stifling cubicles to feel the gusty wind rush through their sticky shirts and skim across their tired faces. They looked over the railings as the breeze pounced on the plants thriving along the edge of the lake, tossed the water into alligator shaped creases and rolled the rusted cans out of the makeshift shops. The surge of nausea had abated. Savitri wondered if it would remain lulled for long. Moreover, a sickening sensation still lingered in her throat. She turned to her mobile phone. So fast were her fingers that it seemed an entire cavalry had descended on the device.

"I know you are upset but...." Rohan began.

"I'm having the baby," she said. The lady standing near her swung around, adjusting her golden framed spectacles.

"Now darling, I've already apologised for my mistake and I've explained to you the reasons why we can't..." Rohan proceeded in the manner of a guardian speaking to his ward.

"Mistake?" Savitri cut him short. "Agreeing to have a child and then aborting it is not the same as scribbling wrong information and erasing it."

By now, Savitri could sense not one but several gazes in her direction.

"I don't need to marry you," her voice oozed with the self-assurance she had acquired over the years. It seemed every pat she had given herself for every tiniest of accomplishments had returned as the beat of a dauntless song. Raindrops lashed at her. She stepped back from the wet railing to avert the risk of falling ill.

"You want to be an unwed mother when all your unmarried friends still pretend to be virgins?" he sounded incredulous. "Do you think you are in Europe-America?"

"I'm aware of where I am. The law of our land does not discriminate between married and unmarried women, even if our society does," she responded. The men huddled in the middle of the balcony exchanged glances, fingers frozen on their coffee cups, mouths dropped open like wilting poppies.

"Why is this foetus so important? Who will stop us from having children after our marriage? Why can't you wait till then since you have already waited so long..." The shower of questions rivalled the rain.

"Because it is not an accidental pregnancy. I've wanted this baby. And so it matters that it's from a particular sperm you will never release again and an egg I will never produce again."

Thrown together in the balcony, some people shuffled their feet. Some others even pricked their ear-holes with their little fingers as if to scrape out the objectionable words like "sperm" and "egg."

"Rohan, my decision is final. You can call me later if you want," she spoke loud enough to be heard above the rumble of clouds. The centrally controlled lights in the balcony had been switched on to combat the growing darkness. All glances intersected on her when she paused for a moment before striding out of the balcony, her back to the railing, her five feet tall frame braced against the silvery wall of incessant rain. Since she would face those stares for the rest of her life, she wished to get used to them from this moment itself. Then she walked to her quadrant, her impending isolation challenged by her multiplying images on the glass walls. Her footsteps resounded on the square marble slabs like introspective clicks on folders stowing her individual and cultural past. She imagined tomorrow's dawn, when the little patch of earth just outside her threshold would be matted with newly sprouted grass and threaded with runnels of melting hail.

About the Author

Lahari Mahalanabish

Lahari Mahalanabish (Chatterji)'s short fiction/poems had been short/long listed for the international awards: Grindstone Short Story Prize 2020, Mslexia Poetry Prize 2021, Erbacce Poetry Prize 2009 and 2010, and Eyelands Book Awards 2019 and 2020. Her short stories were published in the anthologies 2020 Grindstone Anthology, Where the Kingfisher Sings (2021) and Moolah (2021); prose pieces in Through the Looking Glass: Reflecting on Madness and Chaos Within and But You Don't Look Sick. Her poems have found places in anthologies such as Yellow Chair Review 2015 Anthology, Freedom Raga (2020), The Kali Project (2021), The Ocean Waves (2021), New Normal (2021), and Van Voice: Forests and Their People (2021). Her collection of poems entitled One Hundred Poems was published by Writers Workshop, India (2007).

A software engineer by profession, she blogs (*http://theserpentacursedrhyme.blogspot.com*) to chronicle her travels and highlight the work carried out by a rural empowerment initiative she is associated with.

www.ingramcontent.com/pod-product-compliance
Lightning Source LLC
LaVergne TN
LVHW041915070526
838199LV00051BA/2625